LYDIA IN THE
HAREM

LYDIA IN THE HAREM

Philippa Masters

This book is a work of fiction.
In real life, make sure you practise safe sex.

First published in 1995 by
Nexus
332 Ladbroke Grove
London W10 5AH

Copyright © Philippa Masters 1995

The right of Philippa Masters to be identified as the
Author of this Work has been asserted by her in
accordance with the Copyright, Designs and Patents Act
1988.

Typeset by TW Typesetting, Plymouth, Devon
Printed and bound by
BPC Paperbacks Ltd, Aylesbury, Bucks

ISBN 0 352 33051 1

Foreword

In the first volume of my great aunt Lydia's memoirs, which I have called *The Awakening of Lydia*, we followed the astonishing events which occurred during her time in southern Africa. For an English girl of only sixteen, brought up in that Victorian social environment in which girls were required to be innocent (though ignorant would be a more realistic term) to find herself on that savage continent in the late eighteen-nineties, would have been of itself an adventure. To find yourself the subject of strange advances by officers of the local garrison, to be kidnapped and carried off by natives, would have shattered the personality of any ordinary girl. Yet Lydia not only survived her many months as the plaything of the tribe's earthy desires, but through her innocent common sense learned to accept the physical delights they brought with them – even earning the titles (much sought after by the women of the tribe) of *mantolla* and *bassawiti*, which signified that she was an enthusiastic and eager partner in sex and was wonderfully skilful with her mouth. When she returned to 'civilised society' her astonishing experiences had turned her into a shrewd, resourceful (and very naughty!) young woman whose powers of observation and sense of humour are sources of inspiration.

This, the second extract from her reminiscences, tells of her sea journey away from Africa, leaving because of the impending war between the British and the Boers, and the adventures that befell her. Though perhaps 'befell' is not the right term, for, as you will see, Lydia herself instigated many of them!

When I first read these pages, sitting in her own armchair, in her own cottage, some time after her funeral, I was both spellbound and staggered. How could these events be part of the life of the sweet, distant, very proper lady I had known and been just a little afraid of since childhood? The thought of my great aunt Lydia, straight-backed and correct, hat square on her grey bun of hair, marching along the lane to church on Sunday mornings, being the same person who, as the voluntary concubine of a Turkish Bey, floating veiled and bejewelled to his bed chamber and dancing at the Prince's banquet, would have been unbelievable except for a few items of objective evidence which confirm at least some peripheral details.

The town of M . . . ., for example, where Lydia learned the ways of the seraglio, actually exists in southern Arabia, and was part of the Turkish Empire at the time. Great aunt Lydia's address book, which I have by me as I write, has the names Alice Prendergast of Portsmouth, Tiliu Sharpe of Southampton, Felicity Nasseri of Cairo, and Farah Suleiman of M . . . ., among dozens and scores of others – inevitably, in view of the woman revealed by this story, nearly all male!

Naturally, after all this time, these ladies have passed away, so I was unable to contact them to seek direct confirmation of my aunt's astonishing tale. Not that such confirmation is really needed, for the personality which shines from these pages, with its honesty, sharpness and sense of humour is evidence enough, at least for me.

I commend to you Lydia, great aunt and one time concubine!

Philippa Masters

One

As I sat down in my little cabin before changing for dinner, I felt a little sadness to be sailing away from my lovely Jonathan. That hurried, loving shag up against those crates on the dockside, from which I was still moist, would surely be our last; for I was off to England, and he was to remain to do his duty if the threatened war with the Boers actually broke out.

So much had happened since I arrived in this savage and beautiful country less than two years ago. So many experiences and revelations. So many delights. How could I leave it behind without pangs of longing and regret? I was not yet eighteen years of age, but I had already seen and experienced what few girls have ever been privileged to know.

I slipped into a reverie. In my mind I was with Jonathan that sweltering day beneath the tree by the stream, when he had kissed me for the first time, and touched my breasts, and I had been too young and naïve to understand the strange sensations he aroused in me. I drifted into the memory of Talesi, my escort and guide after my kidnap, tense with nerves as he smoothed that protecting unguent over my naked body, and then, in a flash, I saw myself kneeling before him – was it really only a few days later? – and taking his beautiful cock into my mouth, greedily sucking what had so recently terrified me. I was with Jonathan, in the stable on my first 'riding lesson'; with Captain Mackay, Felicity's father, on the knoll, when I'd 'got heat stroke' and he'd had to undo my clothes; with my wonderful Motallo, being licked and nuzzled to desperation – all these and more. Even the ridiculous Dr

1

Williams, our prurient vicar, drifted through my mind as the ship sailed away.

Would I ever know such joys again? Why ever not? True, I was leaving the friends and lovers I had known in Africa, but would I not be aboard this ship, with its complement of officers and crew, for several weeks? There would surely be plenty of opportunities for frolics. I got up from my seat and began to change my frock.

Mr Sharpe, the ship's purser, had expressed surprise when I insisted that Tiliu have a cabin next to mine, for she was ostensibly my maidservant, and an African to boot. Had he only known the adventures we had shared, he would not have wondered. Felicity Mackay and our chaperone, Alice Barnet, who were also returning to England because of the threat of war between the British and the Boers, each had a cabin nearby to mine and (happily, as it transpired) quite close to those of the ship's officers.

In the bustle of boarding and sailing out of the harbour, there had been little time to get to know the ship's officers, nor to learn what other passengers were on board with us. Now, having changed for our first shipboard dinner, I looked forward eagerly to making their acquaintances.

The ship's master, Captain Prendergast, a large, sober-looking man, naturally took the head of the table. Mrs Barnet, who had told me to call her Alice since she was now my companion rather than just my dressmaker, was looking very cheerful and, I noticed, was paying the Captain shrewd attention, sat on his right. I was seated close to the head of the long table, opposite Felicity, with Mr Sharpe on my right, and a silent, eastern looking gentleman dressed in civilian clothes on my left.

The officer on Felicity's left was very attentive to her, as well he might be, for she looked as ravishingly lovely as ever; while the one to her right (a very young-looking person) never looked up from his plate. As usual, though, she was behaving in that slightly superior manner she always adopted with male company (except Jonathan's of course),

2

and which I found so annoyingly hypocritical. I wondered how long it would be before she came to confide in me that some officer or other had become 'carried away' and she'd 'had to let him'. She always expressed it thus, for in her rather slow mind she had convinced herself that she was a 'good girl', afflicted with a beauty that made men lose control. In reality, of course, she was just as eager for the delights of shagging as I was, but would never dream of admitting it.

Conversation around the table, apart from the gentleman to my left, was lively, and light-hearted. Mr Sharpe told me about some of the places we would call at, and offered to take me on a tour of the ship on the morrow. I glanced into his eyes as I accepted the offer, but could detect no motives there other than dutiful sociability. Ah, well, the voyage would provide plenty of time for exploring that sort of thing! The purser was quite a handsome man, in his late twenties I would surmise, with short, fair hair and blue eyes. That he had chosen to sit next to me, and had invited me to tour the vessel, might just be social duty rather than a sign that he found me interesting, but time would tell. Besides, the last week or so of goodbyes to my gentlemen friends had been so active that I was not actually 'in need' yet.

However active Tiliu's last few days had been I know not, but that she had wasted no time at all on the ship I discovered when I returned to my cabin after dinner. She was not there nor in her own cabin, and only returned, looking dishevelled and somewhat distracted, an hour or more later, when I had already donned my nightgown and climbed into my bunk. Being a 'servant', she had dined with members of the crew. She soon composed herself enough to tell me all that had transpired.

The mess, as the place the ship's crew took their meals was called, was cramped and crowded, and Tiliu's entry had caused not a little tension. Any wholly masculine company will inevitably react to the sudden presence of a

3

young female, and all the more so when that female has a slender, high-bosomed figure, eyes like an antelope and a heart-shaped face the features of which can go from kitten-ish mischief to demure innocence in the bat of an eyelid.

Just such a figure is my lovely Tiliu, and a silence had fallen over the dozen or so seamen as she entered the crowded room. The men had glanced at each other, and looked Tiliu over surreptitiously as she helped herself to food from the tureens on a counter. At first she had found it rather disquieting to be the object of such tension and so many stares, but soon she had begun to find it amusing.

I well knew, not only from my time with her among her tribe the Tukanna, but from seeing her with Jonathan and several other gentlemen in P . . . . . ., that Tiliu can be a cunning flirt when the mood is upon her. I could easily im-agine her pretending nervousness, fluttering and simpering, looking about her wide eyed, while all the while sizing up which of the assembled men were likely playmates.

At last, it was Tiliu who broke the silence, remarking in a little-girl voice upon how very hot it was, and plucking at her bodice as though the material were sticking to her bosom. At once there had been a babble as the men rushed to engage her attention, agreeing with her, telling her it would get hotter around the equator, offering to take away her emptied plate, get her a drink, anything they could think of to catch her attention.

One of the company, a dark-eyed, broad-shouldered man sitting on one side, remained aloof, watching careful-ly, seeming withdrawn from the other men. He looked, when Tiliu caught his eye, as though he was as amused as she by the fuss, and was in fact entirely aware of her little manipulations. More than that, though, there was a still-ness, a self-assurance about him, and a depth in his black eyes, she said, that caused her skin to prickle, and made her feel that he could actually see into her mind. That he smiled quietly when he looked into her eyes only confirmed her instant superstitions that, in her words, he 'had juju'.

She was not aware that he had left the room, only that,

4

when she managed to disengage herself, he was waiting outside. She almost bumped into him as she turned a corner of the narrow passageway on her way back to our cabins. There was little preamble. As she started with surprise at encountering him, he took her arms as if to steady her. He did not straight away release her, instead held her and looked deep into her eyes. Nothing was said. It was as if, simply by the power of his gaze, he had taken control of her will.

When he turned and walked along the passageway, Tiliu found herself following. He led her round corners, down ladder-like steps, along passages, and she followed as though drawn on a leash. At last, he pushed open a metal door, and stepped aside, still saying nothing. Tiliu knew that if she entered the spartan cabin, she would be surrendering herself, would be giving up any chance of control over what happened to her. Even so, she could not help but step across the threshold.

The man closed the door and leant against it, a cool smile playing over his lips. His eyes moved over Tiliu in frank appraisal, and she felt entirely incapable of movement. He reached forward and began to unbutton her frock. Tiliu stood like a statue, staring at the man's calm face as he untied her sash, eased the material from her shoulders, and let the frock fall to the floor about her ankles. Since living with me, Tiliu had become accustomed to wearing European dress, and now stood as if hypnotised as the man loosened her first petticoat, then her second, and let them fall to join her frock in the puddle about her feet. Next came her chemise, which the man managed to pull over her head without at any time touching her quaking skin with his fingertips. In untying the waist of her drawers he pulled Tiliu a little towards him, and she almost tripped on the huddle of clothing around her ankles, which her drawers now joined.

As Tiliu stood there, naked save for shoes and stockings, the man looked her over slowly and dispassionately. He did not touch her for what seemed an eternity, and it was

5

as though his glance itself was teasing her skin, setting off pins and needles in her breasts and loins. Tiliu knew that he would do with her whatsoever he wished. He reached forward and with a single fingertip, traced the curve of her neck and shoulder. His hand smoothed down to cup and lift her breast. In the silence, Tiliu could hear her own heart thudding.

The man stepped close, and his warm, slightly spicy aroma filled Tiliu's breath. His hands moved over her skin, each touch sending shivers of tense anticipation through her, setting her breasts tingling, and starting a warmth in her loins.

The cabin was tiny. There was no bed and Tiliu found herself wondering how the man would position her for what she knew he would inevitably soon be doing. The man at once solved the puzzle.

Still without a word, he indicated two metal brackets close to the ceiling. Like an automaton, Tiliu found herself moving to stand with her back to the cold metal of the wall, and reaching up to grasp the brackets. She could hardly get to them. The man grasped her about the waist, his hands almost entirely encircling her, and lifted her as though she were a feather. Gripping the brackets, Tiliu hung there, her toes barely reaching the floor, as the man continued to look her over. At last, not undressing, but simply unbuttoning his canvas trousers, he moved towards her.

The sight of the member he revealed sent a chill through Tiliu, for it was as rampant as any she had ever known. He reached down and slid his hands between and beneath her knees, lifting and spreading her so that she was held splayed on the crooks of his elbows. As if guided by some magical force, his cock at once found Tiliu's trembling cunny. Then he was in her with a single thrust that made the helpless girl cry out with shock and awe. Never had she been so stretched, never filled so deeply, never so powerfully penetrated that her very womb seemed choked!

He took a long time, thrusting slowly, overwhelmingly

at her, the canvas of his trousers scratching her splayed thighs, the metal of the wall grinding against her spine. As though the very discomfort of her precarious position were reinforcing the sensations of the shaft moving within her writhing quim, Tiliu swirled towards a come which built and built, and had her sobbing with wild churnings, long before her mysterious ravisher quickened towards his own climax. When at last he did begin his come, pumping furiously at her helplessly jerking body, she lost her grip on the brackets and fell against him, grabbing for his shoulders, her breasts crushed against his rough tunic, her entire weight bearing down on the cock throbbing inside her. The last thing she knew, as she lapsed into a faint, was his grunt of triumph, and his hotness flooding her depths.

When she came to herself, Tiliu was alone, slumped naked on the floor, her discarded garments spread about her. She struggled into her clothes, feeling stiff and sore, her skin still tingling from her overwhelming comes. As she wandered through the vessel trying to find her way back to our cabin, all that was in her mind was that the mysterious stranger had not spoken a word to her, yet had seemed to see inside her head, and that she would surely encounter him again.

You may be sure that my emotions were not unmixed as my dear Tiliu related her tale to me while I bathed the grazes on her spine, and eased the swollen folds of her sated cunny with tepid water. Tiliu had enjoyed many men, of all shapes and sizes, and if this stranger had so overwhelmed her, he must be fearsome. I tried to imagine a man so impressive that he could scare even a lascivious minx like my Tiliu, and make her faint with the power of his comes. I could not. I tried to visualise the kind of man who could dominate such an experienced and strong-minded girl as she was by the force of his personality alone. He must indeed be a hypnotic man!

My interest in this strange man multiplied the next day, for Tiliu was actually nervous of going to eat with the crew

7

in case he was 'there again. To think of Tiliu, ever eager, ever alert for any juicy encounter, as being reluctant for a shag was very strange.

My tour of the ship with Mr Sharpe, accompanied by Tiliu and Alice Barnet, but not Felicity, who for some reason remained in her cabin, was fascinating, not least because the purser turned out to be quite charming. It also provided me with the opportunity to meet some of the other officers, and to see, though not encounter, the silent man who had sat next to me at dinner last night. It excited my curiosity to see that he was accompanied by a slight, heavily veiled figure, obviously female, for he had been alone at dinner last night, and nobody had mentioned the existence of a companion. Over the following days my curiosity grew deeper, for whoever the female was, she never appeared for meals, and I only saw her fleetingly, in the company of her silent escort, and only from a distance.

These two were the only other passengers, so the other people we saw on our tour of the maze-like innards of the ship were members of its complement. There were only five British officers: Captain Prendergast; Mr Sharpe the purser; the mate, or first officer, a charming, dark-haired man, in his middle thirties I guessed, called Donaldson; a very taciturn chief engineer called Grimes and the lad who had sat silent beside Felicity at dinner, a very shy young midshipman called William Forbes. This young man, hardly more than a boy really, for he was only a year or so older than myself, blushed and stammered when any of us addressed him, and clearly found female company acutely uncomfortable.

We saw several groups of seamen working at various tasks, and I watched Tiliu carefully in case one of them happened to be the mysterious stranger who had so thoroughly fucked her last night. Whenever we heard or saw such a group, Tiliu would stiffen and her eyes would dart about nervously. That he was not among the group would be signalled by an audible sigh (of relief I wondered?) and a relaxing of her tense shoulders.

The seamen we did see were a varied lot, mostly Laskars, but with one or two Africans, and some who were clearly Oriental. One group, painting parts of the superstructure in the bright sunshine, were stripped to their waists, and it was pleasant indeed to watch their gleaming bodies as they worked. The way they, in their turn, glanced at we females, and especially at Tiliu, betokened that their thoughts were not entirely on the job in hand.

Tiliu's nervousness when we toured the ship, the reactions to her of the seamen we encountered, and most of all the fact that she had not gone to the mess for either breakfast or luncheon, nagged at me, and I decided to talk with her that afternoon in our cabin. Since she had first elected herself my 'apprentice', as it were, while I was serving the menfolk of her tribe, I knew Tiliu to be irrepressible and enthusiastic with regard to men and all and any licentious activities. To see her thus discomposed at having been shagged by the enigmatic stranger was a surprise to me, for I knew she had accepted and relished all shapes and sizes of men, and more than one at a time. To see her actually reluctant to encounter him again worried me. That she lapsed out of the excellent English she had learned over the last year or so when I tackled her was further evidence of her state.

'No ridja! No, missy!' she blurted when I put the question to her. 'It not the cock I scared of. It pain me, but it all right. It his eyes frighten me. He have powerful juju.'

I remonstrated with her, tried to comfort her, to reassure her, but she was convinced that he was a powerful juju-man. Just as we had convinced Benjamin, our house-servant back at father's station, that I was a powerful witch, so Tiliu was convinced that this man was a powerful witch doctor. There was no way around it. Tiliu was afraid and would not go back to the crew's mess where she had first encountered him. Unless I did something, the silly girl would starve herself to death!

I spoke with Mr Sharpe. He agreed that it was entirely sensible that my 'maidservant' should assist the steward in the officers' mess and, like him, eat in what seemed to be called the 'galley' – the kitchen by any sensible name. What was more intriguing was that when I described the man concerned (though not, of course, telling him the true reason for my enquiry) Sharpe could not place him at all, which seemed odd to me, for the whole ship's company could not have numbered as many as fifty men, and surely a responsible officer should know them all. I soon put the puzzle aside, though, for there were other games afoot.

With Felicity keeping to her cabin, Alice Barnet spending a great deal of time in the whereabouts of Captain Prendergast and Tiliu assisting the officers' steward, I found myself thrown much on my own company. In my wanderings about the vessel, I frequently encountered the midshipman, William. He had been told by the captain to look after the passengers' welfare, a duty he seemed to find excruciatingly difficult, for he blushed and stammered if I so much as glanced at him. He was a pretty lad, and well built, and it became a pleasant game for me to find ways of gently teasing him.

I would oblige him to engage in conversation. I got him to show me various parts of the ship, and explain the functions of the complicated derricks and davits and capstans and such. I found all these things genuinely interesting, but what was much more enjoyable was poor William's constant embarrassment, especially when we were in a place that obliged close proximity, or a roll of the ship allowed me to 'accidentally' lean against him. And the cause of his embarrassment was frequently evident, for the white ducks he wore by way of uniform were quite tight and entirely incapable of hiding signs of excitement in the trouser area.

I took to teasing and flirting quite outrageously. When occasion demanded that we mount the half-ladder, half-stair arrangements they called 'companion ways', I would arrange to climb up first, ensuring that he would have the greatest difficulty in avoiding a glimpse or two of my ankles. In walking about, I would take his arm 'to steady myself' against the movement of the ship, and make sure that I clung tightly to him, pressing my breast against his upper arm. I praised his knowledge of matters nautical, fluttered my eyelashes at him and played all the little tricks of flirtation I had learned over the past year or so to tease a man. That I had my effect was very obvious, and not just from his blushes, but he continued to act more as if terrified than enticed. I decided that he must be entirely inexperienced in negotiations between the sexes, a notion which intrigued and excited me. How could I set about introducing him to such delights?

Naturally, I elicited the help of my Tiliu. Together, we managed to jam the little tap used to draw water to the wash basin in my cabin. Tiliu told William of our difficulty. I concealed myself behind the curtains of my little bunk. Sure enough, there soon came a slight tapping on the door. I ignored it. It was repeated. A pause. The door opened and William walked towards the offending tap. I emerged from behind my curtains, as though just aroused from sleep.

William jumped as though stung, and span around. His eyes boggled, and he backed against the washstand. If he had been flustered by my company on deck or in the officers' mess, when I was fully dressed, now he looked like to die, for we were in my little sleeping cabin, and I wore only a nightgown. (It never did occur to him that it was odd for me to be sleeping in mid-afternoon, but then, circumstances were not such as to allow him coherent thought!)

'Ah, William,' I said, moving towards him with a smile of welcome, ignoring his shocked expression and the way he stared at my nightgown, which was of a heavy organza I had carefully chosen for the fact that it not only clung where it touched, but also had a slight translucence that suggested to the eye the shape within. I bustled close to him. 'I'm so glad you are here! I seem to have broken the tap, and cannot finish my ablutions! Do please come to my rescue!'

11

I had placed my hand upon his arm, and was gazing at him beseechingly. He choked and stammered, and almost fell over the washstand in his anxiety to keep away from me. I stepped back. His starting eyes were running over me rapidly.

'Why, William, what on earth is the matter?' I cried. I feigned surprise, then confusion. 'Oh, William! How awful of me. I did not realise.' I clutched my hands to my bosom, 'accidentally' pressing the thin material to me and outlining my breasts even more clearly. I fluttered and smiled shyly, and moved to place a hand upon his arm. 'But it is all right. We are friends, and you are too much of a gentleman to take advantage of a girl all undressed and alone.'

That he would decidedly have taken advantage had he known how to manage it was amply demonstrated by the perspiration which had broken out upon his forehead, as well as by the distortion at the front of his trousers. William stood frozen, his face as red as the sunset, trembling in every part.

'We *are* friends, aren't we, dear William?' I said, moving close again, and gazing up at him with all the wide-eyed innocence I could muster. 'You will not take advantage of me, will you, even though . . .' I slipped my hand onto his exciting bulge. 'Oh, you poor man! You must be in agony. I am so sorry.'

The duck of his uniform was not thick. The impressive cock I was squeezing with my fingers jerked and throbbed. Suddenly, poor William stiffened and gasped and pulsed. Oh, no! He was having a come. There, under my hand, he jerked and shuddered, and a warm, damp stain spread over the rough material. We were both flustered, he with embarrassment, I with amazed disappointment that he had come so quickly.

'Oh, you poor boy,' I murmured. 'What have I done? Such a mess – you cannot go about like that!' I became businesslike. 'We must wash those. Take off your trousers, William. I will rinse them. You cannot be seen thus.'

William looked as horrified as he was embarrassed. He

shook his head, his mouth working like a beached fish, though no words came out.

'Come along now,' I said, sternly, reaching for his belt-buckle. 'We must remedy this unfortunate accident. Be sensible!'

Looking as if he had been scolded by some strict nanny, William stared at me. I unbuttoned him, and pulled at his trousers. At once he struggled quite wildly, and for a moment I was nonplussed.

'Now don't be silly,' I scolded, as he tried to push my hands away. But as I managed to tug the canvas-like material down over his hips, in the process revealing as pretty a cock as you could wish for, he became suddenly passive. He stood perfectly still as I tugged his trousers down to his ankles, and lifted his feet one at a time so I could pull the material over his footwear. He looked, actually, a little ridiculous in his socks and boots, trying, and failing, to conceal himself behind the tails of his shirt. But what he was trying to hide, despite his painful embarrassment and its softened state, was nicely impressive. I persisted in my nanny-like manner.

Dropping the trousers onto the floor, to be rinsed later, I took up one of my handkerchiefs and began to mop at the stickiness about his thigh. He gave a sort of stifled yelp, and I am sure would have backed away actually through the washstand had that been possible. I mopped him very thoroughly, and lo and behold, his cock began to rear again. I looked up at him mock sternly, and grasped his swelling shaft in my hand.

'What! So soon!' I scolded. 'Why, what a very excitable boy you are, to be sure. We must do something about this.'

His eyes were on stalks as I stood and gave his now quite handsome cock a couple of rubs. He was trembling, and I thought I detected a tear welling in his eye. I became solicitous.

'Oh, William, do not be afraid. It could happen to anybody. Come, let me help you.'

I stood close to him, smiling up into his erudescent face

as I gently rubbed his deliciously thickening member. He gasped, made as if to say something, gasped again and screwed his eyes tight shut, the throbbing in my hand telling me he was about to have another come. And come he did, all over the front of my nightgown. To have two comes in such a short space of time promised well for future pleasures.

'Oh dear me!' I cried, leaping back. 'Now you've got me all damp, too.'

At once, before William could even begin to recover himself, I pulled the nightgown over my head and dropped it, to join his trousers on the deck. He stared at me, mouth agape with shock, unable to tear his eyes away from my nakedness. I stepped close, obliging him to look into my eyes, and incidentally teasing my excited nipples against his tunic. I squeezed his cock again, and was delighted to feel it twitch in my hand.

'Don't be afraid, William. I won't tell anyone.'

I smiled up at him, and rubbed gently. The delicious boy was already stiffening. Leading him by his splendid cock, I backed towards my bunk. He had no choice but to follow, still trembling and wide eyed.

'Come, William, I won't hurt you. Have you not been with a girl before? Have you never . . . ?' I sat on my bunk, giving his cock another little squeeze. He shook his head so briefly, so nervously, it was more like a tremor than a controlled gesture.

Oh, glory! A delicious boy, with a splendid and already swelling prick, who had never experienced the delights of shagging. I unbuttoned his tunic and pushed it from his shoulders. I slid my hands up his body, lifting his undershirt. His tummy was pale, flat and firm; his chest hairless. His cock stood like a baton straining for the ceiling. I lay back, and pulled him towards me.

He was clumsy and over-eager, even hurt me a little in his excitement, so that I had to coax him and coach him. But oh, what a sweet shag he was! That he had come twice

14

in only a few minutes helped to prolong matters now, and he fucked me as though his very life depended upon it, wild and unskilled, but so deliciously excited. His third come, deep inside me, wracked him so violently I thought he would crush me through the bed, and he bucked and gasped as though in agony. It was wonderful.

Afterwards, while he lay recovering on the bunk, I dressed and got him to tell me where his cabin was so that I could go there to rinse out his trousers and get him some dry ones. Luckily, I encountered nobody in my quest for his replacement clothing, for how on earth would I have explained? Even as William stood to pull up the clean trousers, his cock began to stir again. He looked at me, half-shy, half-eager. I gave his pretty red plum a playful tap with my finger.

'Now, now, William,' I scolded. 'You must not be too hard on a poor girl. Besides, we must save something for later.'

Looking as though he had been given the greatest present in the world – which I suppose he had – William tidied himself and sneaked out of the cabin, looking back at me just once, with eyes that betokened great keenness to see me again soon.

At dinner that evening it was rather difficult to feign unconcern, for William, despite his obvious efforts at control, was like a coiled spring of eagerness and barely concealed excitement. That and the fact that whenever I caught Tiliu's glance as she served the various dishes her eyes held that impish gleam I knew so well, made it hard for me not to grin with pleasure at my delightful coup of the afternoon, and the knowledge that it would take a body of armed troops to prevent William from coming to my cabin later. I would, though, need to work hard to cool his excitement in the company of others, for the last thing in the mind of a healthy and inexperienced lad with the prospect of plentiful shagging suddenly before him was the need to be discreet.

Two

You may be sure that I did not have to wait long for William when I retired to my cabin that evening. Hardly had I put my reticule on the shelf and pulled open the curtains of my bunk, when there came a quick knock on the door. William slipped around it almost before I had it properly opened, and at once I was held in a hot embrace, kisses raining over my face and neck. I almost had to fight him off as his hands fumbled at my breasts.

'Sshh! Calm yourself,' I whispered. 'Do not rush so.'

I was able to cool him somewhat, although his eyes and flushed face continued to demonstrate his excited condition. He knew nothing of lovemaking, wanted only to get me on my back and thrust away. When I pushed him off after that first rush to grab me his face fell like that of a slapped puppy. I smiled, kissed him lightly on the cheek, and assured him that all would be well, but he must not be rough with a girl. He looked puzzled, even a little crestfallen. I told him that I would teach him how to please a lady, how to make love so that any woman would become his eager plaything.

Oh, what a glorious prospect lay before me. A pretty, vigorous and well-endowed boy, keen to learn the arts of love, ready to conform to my every whim. Heaven! And learn he did, over the next few nights, so that he soon became nicely skilled, and deliciously sensitive to my wishes. Too many men seem actually oblivious of the fact that a girl, too, has sensations. They seem to think that just grabbing her breasts and pumping their cocks in and out of her cunny until they have a come is all that shagging entails.

17

With William, I had the heaven sent opportunity to teach a man otherwise – and I am sure that in striving to please me, William himself got heightened pleasure.

On this our first night together, I got him to undress me slowly, revelling in the eagerness in his eyes and the trembling of his fingers. When I was down to my chemise, drawers and stockings I let him kiss me and caress my breasts. His hands slipped to my bottom. He groped for my quim. I made him wait, made him concentrate on my breasts, which were tingling and tensing deliciously. He took off my chemise. I stood leaning back against the wall as he fondled and nuzzled me, his hot mouth sucking and lapping at each nipple in turn as I guided his head. His kisses, the rasping of his eager tongue upon my nubs, sent arrows of delight darting to my loins – delight heightened by the knowledge that my wildly excited partner was mine to toy with, seemed ready to do anything I demanded.

I moved to my bunk, let him pull off my drawers. His eyes raced over the delights now revealed to him. He explored my thighs, my flanks, my bottom. He was fondling me tentatively, almost as though seeking permission. I parted my legs. His hand moved between them, cupping my cunny, slipping a fingertip between my folds. At my whispered command – whispered because I was already breathless with pent arousal – he knelt between my knees, bent his head to kiss me. With gentle, trembling fingers, he parted my folds, kissed me, began to lick and nuzzle.

Oh, that most wonderful of sensations! To have a man nuzzle and kiss that most sensitive and responsive of places is such as to drive a girl to heavenly madness. I writhed and gasped. My fingers clawed at his thick hair. I had to force myself not to grab him, not to cram myself upon him, lest I scare him. Oh, the glory! His hot breath sent electric shocks through me. His rough tongue lapped at my folds, at my burning cherry, even dipping into my entrance. I was spiralling to the sun, churning into spasms to drive me

18

mad, my whole inside writhing for his tongue, when suddenly he stopped, jerked back, groaned aloud.

Stunned, I struggled to sit up. What was wrong? Why had he deserted me so? Through the dizzy disappointment of my frustrated come, I saw that William was back on his heels, his face glistening from my effusions, and wet too from tears that were welling from his eyes. What could be the matter? I leaned forward. Suddenly, helplessly, I began to giggle, for there, at the front of his ducks as he knelt, was a spreading mark of damp. The poor boy had had a come. Again! Another pair of breeches to wash.

Only the hurt and embarrassment on his face prevented me from howling with delighted laughter. The poor boy was a-squirm with shame at his mishap. I reached forward, took his face between my hands, and kissed him.

'There, there,' I said, patting his cheek and kissing him again. 'Never mind. We were going to take them off soon anyway.'

I had to coax him a little to cheer him up, but soon he was eagerly stripping off his uniform. William had a lovely body, slim and pale, with smooth thighs, a tight, firm bottom and flat tummy, athletic rather than muscular, promising great strength when he became fully a man. An important part of him, though, was very evidently already manly, for despite having had a come just minutes ago his handsome baton was already thickening and starting to rouse by the time he pulled down his trousers.

I reached forward and took him in my hand, delighting in his sudden gasp, and the twitching of his cock as my fingers encircled him and I pulled back the cowl of skin that half covered his plum. If he were not already fully grown here, he would be a fearsome lover when at last he was, for he was a handspan and more in length and as thick as my wrist. He stood like a marble statue, frozen in stillness, as I caressed his delectable member. It gazed at me from its single eye as I stroked its veined length, the satin of his skin sliding oh, so smoothly over the iron of

19

the muscle within. I could not help myself. I bowed my head, opened my mouth.

I heard him gasp as my lips slid over his plum. He was scrumptious. Hot and smooth and musky, sliding between my lips, across my tongue, like ambrosia made flesh. He could not quite keep still in his excitement, and I had to match the movements of my head to the jerking of his pelvis lest he push too far and choke me. He was a juicy boy indeed, for within only a couple of minutes he groaned and jerked and pumped his essence onto my tongue so suddenly and so copiously that I had to gulp for my life so as not to choke.

Swallowing all, I took his hand and pulled him down onto the bunk beside me. We lay close, neither speaking, our bodies touching from head to toe because of the narrowness of the bunk. There is a heavenly comfort, a warmth beyond description, in lying skin by skin with one's lover while each, sensing only, without conscious thought, sighs into the warmth of the other's body. We had the whole night. There was no hurry. It was an interlude, a period, an age of luxurious sensuality.

Slowly, at some century in my dream of delight, William was above me, between my splayed knees, in me, moving with gentle, breathtaking, wonderful sensitivity, his divine member ploughing my depths. I had a come, in slow, driving, vertiginous spasms of ecstasy. Perhaps many comes. Or maybe just one, unending. I cannot remember. I only know that William shagged me. Shagged me out of my mind, out of my body, out of everything save the glory of his cock driving to my soul. It was a long, slow, sumptuous dream, a dream of absolute opening, of clinging, wrapping, encapsulating, of penetration beyond wonder.

I came to myself in a haze of contentment. William was asleep beside me, crammed between my body and the bunk wall. His hand was upon my breast, his steady breathing a warm caress on my hair. One leg lay bent across mine, and

20

his beautiful prick, slack now, lay upon my hip. I reached down and gently grasped it, delighting in its soft vulnerability, in the way it lolled in my palm.

Carefully, so as not to wake my comely boy, I eased myself off the bunk and knelt beside it. Still sleeping, William sighed a little, and shifted to a more comfortable position. He lay on his back now, one arm up beside his head, the leg nearest to me bent a little. His treasures now lay entirely open to me, to the fingers which softly traced the shape of his thighs, to the lips which could not but kiss his tummy-button and the bush of silky hairs which spread at the delta of his loins. As I took him into my mouth he shifted again, opening himself more to me, but not waking.

I cupped his crinkly, tightening pouch, covered in its silky hairs, and squeezed him gently as my tongue explored the shape of his soft plum. In his softened condition I was able to take the whole of him into my mouth, pressing down so that my lips touched against his root, then pulling back, sucking and squirming my tongue so that I stretched him. To my delight, he began to swell, to grow and thicken in my mouth.

I stretched my hands out on either side, smoothing them over the firm curves of his thighs and up across his smooth chest. He had a handsome body, which now stirred gently in his sleep as his member grew rigid under the ministrations of my lips and tongue. How on earth could he remain asleep yet grow so erect as I fellated him? What kind of dream was wafting through the head that now rolled slowly from side to side as his loins began to stir?

I could no longer resist. Carefully, for there was not much headroom in the bunk and I did not want to waken him, I eased my way above him, knelt astride. I positioned myself over his baton, eased its plum back and forth along my crease, positioned him, and sank onto him with a single motion which stretched my writhing sheath and sent heatbursts from my tummy to my head and back to my loins in such waves as made me gasp aloud. He was still asleep. My head bent from the lack of space, I gazed down at him as he slept almost cherubically while I ground myself slowly upon his glorious cock, circling my loins, crushing my writhing folds against his hardness.

Oh, he was in me to my ribs! I moved carefully, fighting the urge to grind myself to a come, fighting the cramps and spasms that were growing more and more demanding in the centre of my universe, prolonging this astounding, delicious fuck as long as possible. Alas, I was not completely in control, for even though William was asleep, whatever dream he was in must have been replicating the reality of my shagging him, for he began to move, to push, to throb. I groaned, unable any longer to prolong my come as he pulsed and jerked, and suddenly came awake at the moment he began to spurt his glorious heat into my soul.

To feel a man flooding his essence into one's body is delicious beyond description, especially when one is churning through a come of one's own. Where William got it from I cannot imagine. He had already come several times that lovely night, but he pumped and pumped and pumped, his eyes wide with delight. I think I actually cried out as my own come exploded from my sheath to the extremities of my nerve-endings and back to my uncontrollably writhing loins, in spasm after spasm that knocked my breath from me. I wilted down onto him; every inch of my skin grateful for the feel of his hard body against it; my breasts crushing themselves upon his ribs; my sheath pulsing and churning in one last, shattering series of cramps, clinging greedily about the rod that had so overwhelmed me.

William visited my cabin every night his duties (which he called 'watches' for some reason) allowed after that first heavenly occasion. Long nights of lovemaking; sessions of wild passion interspersed with hazy, dreaming recovery followed by slower, fuller shaggings which left us both adrift in seas of golden softness. Periods of sleep in which dreams of gentle fondlings became reality as I drifted into wakefulness to find William's hands and lips moving over me with

22

the lightness of butterflies, soon followed by the delicious penetration of his glorious cock. Oh, those nights were as good as I have ever known!

If by night William was a sensitive and energetic lover, by day he was the sweetest of boys, perfectly polite and controlled, though often looking at me in calf-like manner which made me worry that someone, in this closed, shipboard society, might soon suspect that something was going on. Dear Alice Barnet surely did, and early on, for I often caught her looking from William to me with a twinkle in her eye.

Busy as I was with my delightful William – and what is there more exciting and rewarding than to have a vigorous and gentle lad eager to learn and share the delights of the bed, and grateful for it – I still found time to appraise the comings and goings of my companions. Dear Alice had struck up a close relationship with Captain Prendergast, and it was a delight to see the way that otherwise rather stiff and formal gentleman cast soft glances upon my friend when, as always now, she sat next to him for meals.

She told me, in one of our little chats one evening after supper, that he was unmarried and, though rather strict and narrow in his views, she thought him a decided prospect. He was very decorous in his behaviour towards Alice, calling her 'ma'am' or 'Mrs Barnet', handing her through doorways or into chairs with only the slightest touch on her arm, and never making the least gesture that could be construed as an advance.

'Oh dear. Poor you,' I said in genuine sympathy, for I know Alice to be a healthy and worldly woman who would not look askance at the opportunity for a frolic.

'Don't you worry, my dear,' she said smiling, settling back into her armchair and glancing at me archly. 'There are signs. Definite signs.'

It seemed that she was pretty sure of her ground, for she had caught him in several surreptitious glances at her figure, which he had covered up with throat-clearings and collar-adjustings when detected. He had not, though, been able to cover up his blushings.

'Nothing more?' I asked.

'Nothing yet, my dear, but it is early days. He is a rather shy man under that Captain's exterior, and not used to female company.' She glanced at her hands, and folded them into her lap before smiling again. 'I have to be careful not to scare him off, for he's a very good catch. He has a good income, some shares in the shipping company, and maintains his own establishment in Portsmouth. A woman could do a lot worse, you mark my words.'

With such a handsome and capable a woman as Alice Barnet, I thought, a man too could do a lot worse.

'Has he kissed you?' I enquired.

'Of course not,' she laughed. 'Why, I'm not even sure he knows how.'

'What!' I was astonished. 'You mean he hasn't – he doesn't – he's never . . . ?' The thought that a man could reach the captain's age and station in life without ever knowing feminine companionship amazed me.

'As to that, you saucy girl,' cried Alice, laughing and flapping an admonitory hand towards me. 'As to that, I have yet to learn.' And she sat back with a smile that told me she had every intention of learning as soon as she could safely manage it.

And how she managed it, in the space of less than a couple of weeks, had all the simplicity of genius. Maintaining the greatest propriety, she launched a pincer movement. While taking great care that her appearance, though modest, should emphasise her womanliness, she fed him tales of her loneliness since the death of Mr Barnet so long ago, of the defencelessness of a woman alone in the world, of how fortunate were those women who had the strength of a gentleman to protect them.

I can see her now in my mind's eye – her hair neat and modest; her eyes downcast; the bodice of her frock, cunningly cut to show off the treasures within, heaving as she sighed her loneliness. I can see, too, the soft and brimmingly grateful eyes she turned up to him at any gesture of kindness on his part, the meekness and admiration she wrapped him with in their conversations.

The poor man did not stand a chance. While his solitary state, and Alice's undoubted charms made him yearn for her, his strict sense of morality forbade him from making the normal advances a man makes to a woman he fancies. And so, he proposed matrimony to her. Wonder of wonders and joy of joys! My lovely Alice, true friend and companion since I had got away from Hendrick, had achieved the reward her hard life and constant good humour deserved. To be wed, and to a man in a comfortable position, was everything we could pray for.

The ceremony was simple and quickly arranged, for once the die was cast her fiancé could not wait. Passing temporary command of the ship to Mr Donaldson so that he could perform the office of 'Shipboard Marriage', the couple were united only two days after the proposal. A lively wedding breakfast was taken in the officers' mess, the only flaw in our gaiety being the awkwardness and embarrassment displayed by the groom when it came time for the happy couple to leave us for their real nuptials.

After their departure to his cabin, followed as bride and groom will always be by arch glances and a few *doubles entendres*, those of us remaining settled down to our own little party. The officers' steward had conjured up a delicious fruit punch, and a merry game of cards, well laced with good humour, ensued. Only Mr Grimes, the engineer, and the mysterious Egyptian gentleman remained in a less than light-hearted mood, but they soon departed and left the field to we younger people. Tiliu was assisting the steward in his duties, and as they scurried about pouring refreshments or handing around little plates of sweetmeats, I thought I detected, from the glances and half-smiles they exchanged, and the way they did not quite avoid brushing against each other in their moving about, that my darling

25

Tiliu had struck up a happy arrangement. Perhaps, I thought, she had got over her thrall of the mysterious stranger (who, incidentally, I had still not laid eyes on).

The three officers were excellent company, just nicely flirtatious, for the mood of a wedding breakfast party is conducive to a little flirtatiousness, especially after the departure of the happy couple. Mr Donaldson was 'on watch', and had to pop out occasionally to check the steersman, or some such, but he fitted with easy confidence into the conversation after each of these absences. William was very gay, and I knew from his glances, and the glint in his eye, that I was likely to see a lively time when I retired to my cabin. Mr Sharpe paid equal attention to me and Felicity, and I found myself wondering – since he had not made any advances in my direction – whether he had struck up a liaison with Felicity.

Since our departure from East London, that young lady had rather kept herself to herself. Not that she had ever been exactly outgoing, even since her seduction by Jonathan. Lately she had seemed somewhat subdued, though I confess that since starting my delightful games with William I had hardly paid her any attention. Now, after the little wedding party, I discovered the cause of her quietness.

She had left the party a few minutes before me, and as I tripped happily towards my cabin cheered by the knowledge that young William would soon join me, I made my discovery. Turning a corner, I was stopped short by an amazing sight.

There, up against the wall, stood Felicity. Her skirt was up to her waist, and between her splayed thighs was Donaldson, his hips working energetically. I say Felicity 'stood' but it was more like 'hung', for her body drooped against his, jerking in time to his powerful thrustings, her head lolling on his shoulder, eyes closed, mouth open to emit sighing gasps at each upward thrust, her toes hardly touching the floor. She was being as thoroughly fucked as any girl has ever been and, to judge from her face, and the

26

way her arms clung to him, and the half-gasps, half-grunts she gave as Donaldson pumped into an obvious come, was entirely abandoned to it.

I was astonished. I had not had the slightest clue. I crept back around the corner so as not to disturb the busy couple, but you may be sure that at the first opportunity the very next morning I tackled the naughty girl about her secrecy. At first she denied that anything was happening between her and the good-looking officer, but when I pressed her, and gave exact details of what I had seen in the passageway, she broke down and told me all.

It seemed that it had begun on our very first night at sea. She had been ready for bed and on the point of climbing into her bunk when there had come a gentle knock on her door. Thinking it to be myself or Tiliu, she had opened the door all unsuspecting, only to find Mr Donaldson stepping across her threshold. He had smiled, not saying a word, and it was obvious from the way his eyes ran over her what he wanted. Felicity had behaved exactly as one would suspect such a silly, hypocritical girl to behave. She had flustered and flapped.

She could have slammed the door against him. Instead she fell back against the frame of her bunk. She could have slapped his face when he moved close. Instead, she covered her face with her hands and whimpered. She could have struggled when he grasped her breasts. Instead . . . Ah, despite all her protestations of 'purity', and her airs and graces, I know Felicity's true nature very well. She could never dream of instigating matters as I had with William (and quite a few others), but at the first approach of a man who is a little determined her 'defences' are abandoned and, in her equivocating phrase, she 'has to let him'.

'But he is so strong!' she said, in a tone that sounded strangely like awe. 'He just took me. It was awful. He was kissing me so hard he bruised my lips. And then – and then . . .'

Holding Felicity with one arm tight about her waist,

27

kissing her with passionate fury, his other hand had roamed very freely. Soon, 'though I fought as best I could' she told me, he had got her up against the wall.

'My nightgown was up around my ears,' she said. 'His hands were everywhere. What could I do? He is so strong! He . . .' she blushed deeply and dropped her eyes to her lap. 'He likes doing it up against the wall. He says tha – that having me up against the wall gets it up harder. And he likes it when, well, when it makes me come before he does.'

Ah! I could see it all. All it needed to brush aside Felicity's ladylike façade was a little forcefulness. Had not a spanking from Jonathan just after he first seduced her turned her into an eager wanton, driven away all her airs and graces and made her his eager plaything? Now, being dominated by Donaldson, being 'taken' as it were, had acted as a switch to release her wanton nature.

With Jonathan, though, Felicity had not become withdrawn as she had been lately. Indeed, during that delightful time when Jonathan, Felicity and I had made an intimate trio, Felicity had actually become more relaxed and open. What could be the difference now, I wondered. Slowly, as she described to me Donaldson's nightly visits to her cabin and, with rather more detail than seemed strictly necessary, the activities he engaged her in, the answer dawned upon me.

She had convinced herself that Jonathan loved her. Indeed, I remembered numerous occasions when she had protested her love for him and begged him to say he loved her in return. What she was really doing, I suspected, was camouflaging from herself the eagerness of her bodily desires under a dressing of 'love'. That way, she could still think of herself as a 'good girl' who had been obliged to surrender to a man's overwhelming desires. I remembered, too, the way she always described her numerous other 'lapses' as being the result of the gentlemen in question getting 'carried away'.

With Donaldson, it seemed, she could find no such excuse to cover up the fact that she was being regularly

28

shagged, and responding to it. Donaldson, apparently made no protestations of adoration; did not wax eloquent about her beauty; was never feverish with passion for her. He simply went to her cabin or, it transpired, got her alone in some deserted corner, fucked her very thoroughly and went on his way. And her confession that he liked to have her come first, which she always did when he had her up against a wall, betrayed the fact that her wanton body responded well to a little roughness.

Poor Felicity. She was stuck in a quandary, compelled to acknowledge the physical pleasure Donaldson gave her, while at the same time unable to excuse it to herself under some label such as 'love' or having to 'let' a man who had become carried away.

I have never been patient with such false guiltiness, such self-deception. For me, a good shag is a good shag, a luscious bodily excitement to be enjoyed for itself, and harmless so long as the social proprieties are observed. True, our mealy-mouthed society surrounds it, as so many other pleasurable pursuits, with such a barricade of hypocritical taboos and rituals that to confess openly that one enjoys, or even knows anything about, frolics between male and female is regarded as the deepest of shames.

Sadly, Felicity had not had the advantage of spending time with Talesi and the tribe, as I had. There, the attitude towards sex, the open and happy acceptance that physical pleasure is something to delight in, not hide away, is so much healthier than the two-faced approach of our own society. Among the Tukanna, I went about happily naked, delighting in the breeze on my body and the daily bathing in the river, and in the respect and popularity my tokens of value gave me. The little rear loincloth that had betokened my status as *mantolla*, and the topknot that had signalled to the world that I was *bassawiti* were so much more honest than the fripperies we 'civilised' women have to surround ourselves with.

We 'ladies' give huge amounts of time and attention to

our appearance, to the setting of our hair, to our complexions, to the cut and style of our clothes, and why else but to present an attractive picture to the world? And more than that, to the *men* in the world. We flutter and fuss, and play all sorts of feminine games, and faint at the drop of a hat, and why? Surely for no other reason than to attract the attention of men. And the end aim of attracting the attention of a man is to catch him, to entwine him in our web.

Why, were not this element of our lives so prominent what excuse could there be for the constant and all pervasive attention to 'shocking' things? For a society which places such emphasis on propriety, we seem to pay rather too much heed to covering the legs of pianos and sideboards lest they inflame the senses, and to never being alone with a man who is not one's relative lest he lose all control. If we were really so proper, such things would never enter our heads.

Among the tribe, if a man fancied a girl, or vice versa, they sent and received signals and, if the feeling was mutual, enjoyed themselves and moved on happily. Marriage was a separate contract entered into openly and healthily, with no mysteries. In 'civilised' society, though, anything more than eye-fluttering and the touching of a hand is regarded as loose, at least until betrothal. Even after that contract is entered into the couple must always be chaperoned, and may go no further than a chaste kiss upon the cheek. Thus, when the marriage is actually contracted, they know nothing of each other.

And if, as must surely often be the case, the poor girl in question has indeed remained as chaste and ignorant as society requires of her, what shocks is she in for! I well remember my own fright and confusion when Talesi first slipped his finger into what I then called my 'private place'; how worried I was when I saw Miss Blake being shagged that night on our march; how nervous I was when Talesi lay beside me near the campfire and I felt his member grow hard against my side.

To enter the arrangement of marriage knowing nothing of the physical side of it must be horrid indeed. How scared must an ignorant girl be when, having brushed her hair and donned her pretty wedding nightgown, she gets into bed knowing something is about to befall her, but not knowing what it will be. And how terrified must she become when, instead of lying gently beside her, and being polite and decorous as he has always been so far, her new husband whips up her nightgown, throws her legs apart, and fucks her to a finish. How awful it must be if she has never been caressed before, has been kept unaware of the potency that lies between a man's legs, has never even had her breasts teased. How can a society so condemn a girl that she is required to go from ignorant, untouched virgin to wife in one moment? Good shagging, shagging where both partners get the joy, requires time and development. The girl should at least know what to expect. But how can she if society insists that such matters must never be discussed?

It strikes me, too, that another glaring hypocrisy of our society is that the man is *not* expected to be inexperienced. Where on earth could he gain experience if all women are chaste? Yet to raise such an obvious question would be regarded as horribly shocking. So silly!

Felicity is the perfect example of such hypocrisy. Despite having been shagged by Jonathan and several of the officers from the barracks, and now by Donaldson, and despite always dressing so that her face and figure are shown off to the best advantage, and despite being expert at all the little flutterings with which women tease men, she still manages to convince herself that she is a 'good girl' whose occasional lapses are the fault of men who get carried away. She will wed, I am sure, and will go to her nuptial bed like a blushing virgin – and what delights her husband is in for when he discovers what a wanton she really is.

Three

What with Alice Barnet paired off with Captain Prendergast, Felicity 'having to let' Mr Donaldson shag her whenever he felt like it, and my own delightful frolickings with dear William, I became curious about Mr Sharpe. He was a handsome and healthy man, and you may be sure that I had not failed to flirt a little with him, yet he seemed oddly withdrawn. We often had occasion to be together, sometimes actually alone, yet never once did he betray the usual reactions of a man with a girl. There were no sidelong glances, no flicking-away of the eyes lest one catch him looking at one's bosom, none of the preenings, which are the normal preambles to 'negotiations'. I became curious.

I 'tested the waters', as it were, by becoming just a little softer towards him, glancing just a little more admiringly into his eyes, hanging just a little more raptly on his words, being just a little more flirtatiously welcoming in my attentions. He remained unfailingly polite and attentive, but nothing more.

I made efforts to spend more time in his company (for which I had to placate a rather jealous William, which was not at all unpleasant) and the more I saw of him the more interesting I found him to be. He had, I noticed, a grace and precision of gesture rare in a man, and his manner was never brusque even with members of the crew. As I have said earlier, he was a distinctly handsome man in both face and figure, but most noticeable and attractive of all were his eyes. The rich brown of the irises, and the ray of fine creases which spread from each outer corner (from staring, I supposed, at the sunlit sea so long) were themselves worthy of attention. More, though, much more intriguing, was the odd shadow of reticence, almost of sadness, I fancied I saw in them all too frequently.

Whatever lay behind that soft expression, its effect upon me was to increase my growing fancy for the purser, and also to puzzle me greatly. Of all the men I have had dealings with, none has failed to react at least a little to the fact that I am a girl – and, if I flirted even only a little, to try for his advantage with me. I tried with Mr Sharpe all the little ploys I could think of. I know that he was aware of my attentions, for he did indeed react, but not in the normal face-reddening, quick-breathing fashion I was used to. It was indeed most odd. His fingers did sometimes tremble, but more, it seemed, with nervousness than lust. And once or twice he actually seemed more frightened than simply nervous. It was most puzzling.

I made up my mind to take drastic measures. Promenading alone with him on the deck one afternoon, I feigned to trip. I fell against him and tumbled to the boards, making sure my skirts flew up. I yelped and clutched at my knee, my skirts nicely raised. He had a full view of my stockings and drawers. I improved it by raising my knee high, then pretended shock and embarrassment by hastily throwing my skirts down to cover myself (I have learned that few things excite a man more than a girl's fluster at being caught exposed). Whether Mr Sharpe was excited was impossible to tell. He was frozen, his mouth agape, his starting eyes fixed on the place my skirts had just concealed.

I wailed, called to him to help me, cried that I had hurt my leg. He gathered himself, bent, scooped me up in strong arms, carried me to my cabin. I lolled as if half-fainting in his arms. Any other man, I am sure, would have taken the opportunity my 'helplessness' presented by cupping my breast as he carried me. Mr Sharpe did not. Though he was a little breathless by the time he got me to my cabin, I suspected it was more from exertion than excitement.

34

He lay me on my little bunk. He would have left me had I not grabbed his hand and detained him.

'Oh, please do not leave me,' I pleaded. 'My knee hurts most awfully. Please look at it for me. I think I have twisted it.' I hoicked my skirts high again, dragging his hand (and his eyes) to my raised knee. He snatched his hand away as though my stocking had burned his fingers. He stared into my eyes, his own burning with many questions.

He took a deep, sighing breath. His eyes clouded over and his shoulders drooped as if in resignation as he dropped to his knees before me and touched my own knee with gentle fingers. It was as though he was reluctantly surrendering to a duty any other man would have leapt at.

My skirts were at my hips. Everything from my drawers to my button boots was displayed to his gaze. He massaged my knee with both hands, remarking in thick tones that he could not detect any swelling, and that perhaps I was not badly hurt. I protested that I was, begged him to massage me further, told him he was easing me. I slid a little forward on the bunk, which conveniently parted my thighs rather more.

There was a long moment of stillness. I had placed myself at his mercy. I was half lying on the bunk with my skirts up and my legs parted. Any man I had ever met would have been on me like a wolf. Suddenly, Mr Sharpe gave a groan and sank back on his heels, his shoulders slumped and his head hanging, the very picture of misery. I was absolutely nonplussed. What on earth could be wrong?

I sat up, reached out and lifted his chin, my eyes anxiously searching his face. That lost sadness I had noticed so often in his beautiful eyes was back, doubled and redoubled. He looked actually miserable.

'What is the matter?' I asked breathlessly, puzzled and even a little moved by his strange condition. 'Have I done something wrong? I didn't mean to upset you. Don't you like me?'

35

He knelt unmoving for long minutes, his eyes avoiding mine. Then, as if having made a hard decision, he drew in a deep breath and raised his eyes. There was no sadness in them now, for they were searching, almost desperate.

'You have done nothing wrong,' he said, almost whispering and as though his collar were suddenly too tight. 'It is my own fault. You are a very beautiful young woman. Sweet and soft, and I do not want to hurt you.'

'Hurt me? How could you hurt me? You are a dear man and I want ... I desire ...' I was strangely flustered and could not think what to say. 'I am not, um, ignorant.'

My voice tailed off. Mr Sharpe, his face becoming quite mask-like, got to his feet. He stared down at me.

'Please stop,' he said. 'I have guessed that you are not – that you are experienced. You are lovely, and make my blood race, but I cannot – must not ...'

By now I too was on my feet. I stared up at him, clutching his arm. 'But please,' I found myself whispering. 'You can. I want you to.'

He took a pace backwards. His face and voice were suddenly calm, resolute. 'I cannot. I have a difficulty.' I pressed; I cajoled. He blushed, sighed, relented, began fumbling with the buttons at his trousers. In a moment I learned what the 'difficulty' was – and such a difficulty!

As he pulled aside his fly there lolled into my amazed vision a cock of such proportions, even soft as it was now, as to stop a girl's heart. As thick as my wrist, it hung half way to his knee. He did not speak nor move. I stared in fascinated awe. I reached forward and touched it with tentative fingertips. It was beautiful. I am not, in respect of a man's manhood, a shy person, yet now I did indeed feel shy. Mr Sharpe stood like a statue, his whole being tense as if in some turmoil. I glanced up at his face. I almost asked him for permission to encircle his wonderful organ with my fingers.

He told me – though not all at once, for there were 'interruptions' you may be sure – that he had long ago been convinced that his member was too big. He had tried; had succeeded only in scaring potential partners; had even been turned down by what he called 'ladies of the night' (it seemed that there are women who entertain for money, a new and startling idea for me) on account of his dimensions. He had learned to control his urges, convinced himself that no woman would take him. Hence his apparent lack of reaction to my flirtings. Oh, he had been aware of them. Had indeed fancied me very much, but had confined himself to what he called 'wanking' (apparently, men can give themselves some kind of satisfaction by rubbing their cocks vigorously while imagining some girl or other) rather than try, and inevitably fail because of his size, to engage with me.

At that moment, though, at the moment my fingers first encircled him, I was conscious of nothing save wonder. He was warm and soft in my hand. I could veritably feel the tension emanating from his body as he actually fought *not* to react to my touches. So deep had been his torment over the years about his 'difficulty' that his instinctive response to temptation was to shrink rather than grow.

Several days later, when (as shall be related) he had become more relaxed with me, he told me a tale about his youth. He lived then in a town to the east of London called W . . . . – a thriving dockyard area apparently. He was only just fifteen but was, as I could well guess, a striking lad, and had been tempted aside by the wife of the landlord of a local public house. They had gone into the nearby railway shunting yard. He had been a virgin. In his excitement, as the woman leaned back against a sooty pillar, her skirts up and her hips forward, he had thrust with all the impetuosity of a lad whose first time it was, only to be greeted by a squeal which scared him witless and roused the constables. He was an innocent lad, had not known he was too big, had never compared himself with other lads. Suddenly, torn by the fright of her scream and his own irresistible need to come off, he had been lit up by

37

a constable's lantern, shouted at and struck as a villain because his cock was part-way up an obviously scared woman, and arrested. The fact that he had spurted into the air as he was dragged back, even splashing the constable's uniform, only deepened the humiliation. Naturally, hypocrisy being what it is, the publican's wife did not confess that the whole escapade was at her behest, though she did – to her eternal credit – refuse to press charges against the lad.

The next time he had attempted congress with a female had been with the daughter of a neighbour, Betty by name. She was known to be 'easy': there is at least one such girl in any village or neighbourhood. Betty had canoodled with him in an alley, had got all the way to having her frock undone so that her breasts were free and her skirt hoicked up so that her lack of drawers was obvious, and had kissed him passionately as he thrust his fingers up her plump cunny. Only when he had put her hand on his rampant member, begging her to put it in had she frozen, pushed him away, cried out that he was a monster and run off.

He *was* a monster, but a glorious one. In fascination, I sank to my knees as he stood there in my cabin that first time. I held him with both my hands. His 'difficulty' was such as to make him reverse the normal instant reactions when a man's cock is in a girl's warm hands, but slowly he began to thicken and rouse. Oh, he was magnificent! A monster indeed. I could not close the fingers of one hand around his shaft. He was so tense that I could almost feel the rigidity of his spine, the shallowness of his breathing. But I was too enthralled at that moment to think of anything except the glorious, pale member that was warming and thickening between my palms.

I glanced up for a moment. His face was a mask, his eyes screwed shut as if in fear or dread. A surge of understanding swept through me. He had not wanted to hurt me. The organ that was even now rousing in my hands, twitching and stirring to raise its head, could indeed have hurt an unwary girl. Yet it was a wondrous thing, fully the size of my forearm as it reared higher.

There came a sudden change in my emotions. I felt a pity for him, for to be endowed with such a fearsome cock must have been a burden rather than a blessing. I knew instinctively, and sorrowed for him, that the poor man must have been rejected by many a woman scared of being split asunder by his proportions. Even I was nervous as, with both hands together encircling him, I stroked his length. As he became engorged and stiff, the cowl of skin covering his plum parting to expose his single pink eyelet, I could not help but bow my head to kiss it. At that moment, nothing in the universe existed except the wonderful object in my hands, before my fascinated gaze.

It would not fit into my mouth. I could do no more than kiss and lick around his pink-purple bulb, suck no more than the very tip, flicking my tongue across his eyelet before raining licks and kisses along his astounding length. I was enthralled, spellbound. Through my daze I felt his hand upon my brow. He was pushing me off. Forcing me back, preventing me from adoring the most bounteous cock I could ever have imagined.

It was then that he first tried to tell me the story of his 'difficulty', to explain his reluctance to engage with a woman. As I listened to his halting words, kneeling before him, his member, now looking directly into my eyes, became an object of necessity for me. I confess that my motives were at least as much to assuage my own urgent desires as to show charity towards him, but whatever the case I determined to shag him, and thoroughly.

He was reluctant. Nervous. I insisted. I got him onto his back on my little bunk. There was not enough headroom. I made him lie on the floor. I dragged his trousers to his knees. His cock reared like some tree stump. I rubbed it, kissed it, tore at my clothes. I got astride him.

He lay rigid, both hands covering his face, as I rubbed my oozing cunny-lips across his plum. I reached down with both hands. Grasped him. Wriggled my entrance onto his tip.

He was right. He was too big. I gathered myself. Drew in a long breath. Relaxed myself. A swirl of glory engulfed me as I managed to move down upon him, so filled, so stretched even in those first moments that my heart was like to burst. How much I took I cannot say even now. The joy was that he did not move, allowed me entire control, kept still except for his hands which moved to lie one on each of my thighs, not pressing but holding, as I moved upon him. Only when he began to come, a century at least after I had begun mine, did he move, and then, with hands pressing and loins rearing, to push just so much deeper and harder as to explode my brain and burst my womb into a million greedy tongues as he pumped me full with his heat.

Oh! I cannot even now describe the wonder of it. Not Jonathan, not Talesi, not even Motallo with his wonderful tongue, had ever driven me to such a come. From my toes to my scalp I was a burning, writhing mass of sensation. My nipples, where they ground against his tunic, were aflame. My legs registered every fold and crease of the trousers they pressed against. Even my toes curled in delight at the feel of the grain of the wooden planks and the roughness of his duck breeches between which they were squeezed. Oh, I could have died then.

As though my shagging of him had torn aside a veil, Mr Sharpe changed, relaxed and became less reserved. I eased myself gingerly off him and lay down. He was gazing at me with shining eyes. I kissed him, moved my hand down to caress his softening cock, now slick with my juices. In everything he was gentle, tentative, as though having a girl who was not scared were some precious revelation. He kissed me again and again, on my lips, my eyes, my neck, my breasts. He caressed my cunny with a gentle hand, slipped fingers into me, rolled my cherry with his thumb, stirring in me those slow, delicious cramps which can suf-

fuse a girl after she has had a come and her nerve-ends are
still electrified.

For myself, I could not stop feeling his wonderful member, cupping his balls in my palm, sliding my hand along
his stiffening length. I moved, rested my head on his
tummy so that his cock reared close before my eyes. The
cowl of skin had rolled back from his glossy, red plum as
it reached towards the ceiling. I licked a fingertip and
traced it over the great dome and down around the curve
where it met his pale shaft. He twitched under my touch,
moving like the graceful neck of some wondrous antelope.
Encircling as much of him as my small hand could manage,
I caressed him, moving my head to kiss his base, his tight
balls, his firm thighs and belly. I licked and kissed the
length of his shaft, feeling the blood throb under my
tongue.

He gasped, twitched. I licked around the curving fold
where his shaft joined his plum, over and around its hel-
met-like shape. I kissed his little eyelet, licked up the drop
of clear saltiness that had seeped from it. Oh, he was like
hot iron, and I was lost in the wonder of it! He gasped as
my tongue moved over him. His hips tensed. I felt him
twitch and throb. I clamped my gaping mouth atop him,
taking and swallowing all as he burst into a delicious,
spurting come which made him groan with effort and me
churn into a come of my own.

He had to leave me soon after that. Neither of us wanted
him to, me least of all, but he saw by my little travelling
clock that it would soon be time for his watch. After he
had gone I lay on my bunk daydreaming about the treasure which had been revealed to me. My breasts were still
aching from my transports. I could still taste him in my
throat, still feel the way he had stretched my sheath. I mar-
velled that I had been able to accommodate him at all, and
my folds were still swollen from him. Somehow, in my
dream-state, my hand found its way to my cunny. My
mind's eye drifted to a vision of him doing what he had

called 'wanking', rubbing the length of his alabaster shaft with both hands, his visage ruddy, his eyes screwed shut as he visualised some girl or other.

My fingertips, all unconsciously, had found my cherry, there near the apex of my crease, and were circling and teasing it. I felt waves of delight burning through my folds. I had never touched myself thus – never considered it necessary. Now, as my fingertips rolled and circled more and more rapidly about my pulsing nub, visions of Mr Sharpe's glorious member filled my head, and surges of sensation, each tenser, tighter, than the one before, filled my loins with heat and blood. Was I, like he, 'wanking'? I knew not: knew only that my body was building towards such a come as to drive me mad. And from my own touchings.

I could bear no more. I mauled at my swollen folds, thrust fingers into myself, bucked and churned and groaned aloud. At that instant, at the very moment when my soul was about to burst in that glorious surrender to the shattering cramps and pulsations of a helpless come, Tiliu's face swam into my sight. Stopped short, shocked, for I had not been aware of her entry, I froze. Her face was alight with what seemed, in my dizzy state, to be delight. She snatched my hands away from my cunny. She dipped her head. Suddenly her tongue was lapping at me like a cat's. Lightning burst in my head and my loins. Whether I screamed or not I cannot be sure. I think I did. I know that my hands fell upon her head, gripped her as she tongued me: that my thighs clamped upon her: that my cunny pumped itself against her tormenting mouth until I collapsed in a near faint.

When I came to myself again, my beloved Tiliu was lying beside me, her arm around my shoulders, on her sweet face such a gentle smile as to pluck the heart. I snuggled against her, warm and secure and sated. I slept, snug and comforted, as I had not slept since I was a tiny child, to be awakened at last by my huge-eyed, softly smiling Tiliu with the news that it would soon be time to go in to dinner.

42

I washed myself and dressed to ethereal music. I drifted along the corridor towards the officers' dining room (I refuse to use the term 'mess'). The floor, the painted metal walls, even the mesh-covered lamps, seemed beautiful. Only William's lowering features as I floated into the dining room dragged me back to earth. Oh heavens, William! I would have some explaining to do, some slighted ardour to assuage. It was obvious that he guessed from my manner that something significant had transpired. What should I do? Should I confess and risk upsetting him? Or should I prevaricate and keep him sweet?

I have never been one for prevarication. To judiciously conceal one's frolics from a mealy-mouthed society is one thing. To pretend to a lad bent on getting his shags and has perhaps become possessive is another. It is a sad flaw in men's characters that, whereas they themselves feel free to fuck any female who shows at all willing, the very idea that their partner, their fuckee as it were, might also enjoy a variety of partners, is anathema to them. It is as if they are in competition with one another. As though the very act of stuffing their cocks up a girl gave them rights of possession. They boast (I have heard them through cracks in doors, and other places) of their 'conquests'. Yet it never enters their conceited heads that if *they* get to shag a girl so might others, or even that it might be the *girl* shagging *them* – and I well know that one healthy girl can out-shag any number of men.

'You have been with Sharpe,' he said the moment he entered my cabin. His tone was accusing, his face dark and sullen.

I affected lightness. 'Why, William, what on earth is the matter?' I smiled, placing a hand lightly on his forearm. He snatched it away.

'You have – Sharpe has – Don't lie to me. You have . . .' He was actually spluttering.

'Don't be silly,' I snapped, becoming very dignified. 'I am not a person to tell lies. Say what you mean.'

He started at the sharpness of my tone, stared at me a

moment, took a deep breath, his face working as he tried to frame his words. 'You – Sharpe – You have let Sharpe . . .'

'Have let Sharpe what?' I was becoming impatient at his presumption and his clumsiness. 'Have let Sharpe enjoy what you want all the time? Have taken him to my bed, just like I take you. And what if I . . .' I broke off in astonishment, for suddenly William turned, threw himself into my chair, covered his face with both hands, and began to weep. I was flabbergasted. I had been ready for a quarrel, ready to face his wounded pride and talk him round to a sensible acceptance. I had not been at all ready for this sudden change.

Suddenly, I felt like some nanny calming a little boy who has hurt himself in a tumble. I knelt by his side, patted and sshh'd him. He protested that he loved me, thought I loved him, could not imagine loving another, hated the idea of me loving another. Through his babble I slowly calmed him, got him to blow his nose and wipe his eyes, talked to him about the reality rather than the illusion of men and girls. He gathered himself and nodded as if in acceptance, though I could tell that inwardly he did not accept. And on one point he was obdurate.

Never, ever, could he love, make love, with another girl. Any other woman would leave him cold; none could ever stir him after me. Oh, the poor boy was so gripped by the propaganda of our society that he could not conceive that love and sex are not at all the same thing. He truly believed that because we shagged so deliciously together we must be 'in love'. I could not talk him round. The more I tried, the more stubborn he became. At last, I challenged him. Let us put it to the test. He looked puzzled for a moment then, proud in his stubbornness, he took me up. Anything! He could not be moved. Telling him to stay still, I went and knocked on Tiliu's door.

What ensued was as amusing as it was delicious. As I ushered Tiliu ahead of me into my cabin, William stiffened

44

and set his face stubbornly. He was clearly determined to hold himself aloof from her, to demonstrate his love for me by remaining cold to Tiliu. As if he ever stood a chance.

I had seen Tiliu smile and bob and turn when we were together with her tribe, and provoke even the proudest, most distant of men to engage with her. I had seen the subtle glances, the turnings of the hips, the little smiles with which she stimulated such delightful distortions in the breeches of young officers from the barracks in P . . . . . I well knew that if she wanted a man, my sweet Tiliu always got him.

Now, there were no little flirtations, no sidelong glances. She simply stood in front of him, still and silent for long moments. He had turned his face away. She reached forward, took his chin in her delicate hand, and moved him to face her. She leaned down and kissed him softly upon his lips, lingering as he took in a sharp breath and hardened his mouth. Releasing him, she took a step back, unbuttoned her frock and shucked it from her shoulders. William turned his face away again as Tiliu moved to fold the garment and lay it upon the washstand, though I noticed, from my discreet vantage point in the corner, that his eyes did flick momentarily in her direction.

Tiliu returned and stood before him again. He faced her, his visage stony. She gave a little smile, untied the waist-strings of her petticoats, and bent forward from the hips to get them from around her feet. William's eyes were pulled to where the top of her chemise sagged out as she bent, and he was hard put to drag them away from the pert breasts thus revealed. She did not fold the petticoats, but simply tossed them aside. Standing there in her pretty chemise and drawers which, like her stockings, were white, she was the very image of loveliness.

William was sitting rigid in the chair. I noticed a tiny speckle of perspiration on his upper lip. Slowly, Tiliu untied the bow at the neck of her chemise. She slipped it from her shoulders, wriggled a little to help it slide down to her waist. William was breathing quickly, and rather noisily, through his nose, his face still set. Tiliu paused. Then, in a seemingly unconscious gesture, she reached up with both hands to smooth her hair. Oh, she well knew that such a gesture would lift and emphasise her small, firm breasts, on which William's eyes were now locked as though he were mesmerised. Well he might be, for Tiliu had the loveliest of figures, lithe and slender, her tip-tilted breasts, the nipples now perking prettily, positively crying out for the hand and the mouth.

She posed thus for long moments then, with the quickness of a cat, she whipped off her drawers and chemise, threw them aside, and stood before William naked save for her white stockings. The lad was gripping the arms of the chair so hard he was like to crush the wood. I could not help but admire his determination, even though it was so foolish, as he struggled to avoid open reaction to the delicious sight before his starting eyes.

Gracefully, Tiliu sank to her knees. Looking up into his burning face with a gentle smile, she slid her hands along his thighs. He was trembling now, and perspiration dewed his brow. Tiliu's cunning hands smoothed over his crotch and he gave a tiny gasp, almost like a whimper. Slowly, smiling up at him all the while, she undid his buttons. William turned his head towards where I stood in the corner. His eyes were staring in appeal. Then they rolled and closed and he groaned as Tiliu's hand darted into the opening in his ducks and tugged forth his straining cock. So much for his assertions that no other woman could excite him.

His face showed how torn he was, torn between the excitement of Tiliu's delicate fingers teasing his cock and shame that his defeat had been so easy. Tiliu's head bobbed down. Her full lips slipped over William's glowing plum. He groaned aloud as she began to suck him slowly, knowingly. I well knew what skill her mouth possessed, with what loving cunning her tongue could draw out a man's very soul. William was now slumped in the chair, his

46

knees wide, his head lolling back, as Tiliu worked upon his straining manhood. I stepped close, smoothed his burning brow with my hand, smiled as for a moment his eyes flicked up to mine before closing again as he gasped and his hips jerked into a come which wracked him as though he were in torment.

Tiliu took him all, swallowed with little grunting noises of pleasure and sank back onto her heels – a smile of delight on her impish face as she wiped her lips with the back of a hand.

Strangely enough, despite having just had a most emphatic come in Tiliu's welcoming mouth, William looked more hangdog than happy. Men are such odd, unreasonable creatures. True, he had lost the challenge, as anybody of sense would know was inevitable. But in doing so he had been treated to the sight of a most beautiful girl stripping off her clothes for him, and kneeling and sucking him with a mouth so skilful as to drive much more experienced men from their senses. Yet he looked crestfallen. Looked as though somehow he had lost rather than gained. What *could* one do with such a blinkered boy! I decided to shock him further, to force him to accept that girls were not the delicate, passive creatures his upbringing had led him to believe.

Still behind his chair where he could not see me, I rapidly shucked off my clothes. Swiftly, I moved to join Tiliu where she now stood in front of him. I stood close to her, put my arm around her waist. William was now confronted by two naked girls, the one African-dark with white stockings, the other European-pale with black stockings. I am a little taller than Tiliu, and with fuller breasts. Apart from that, and the contrast between my light-coloured hair and Tiliu's curly black mane, we must have presented to William's frozen gaze something like the negative and positive versions of some illicit and voluptuous photographic plate.

His eyes were almost bursting from their sockets. His mouth gaped and jerked as though he were trying to speak through a soup of confusion. Tiliu glanced at me and winked her eye. We dropped to our knees. As one, we tugged at his trousers, hauling them down over his unresisting legs. As one, we dived our hands and heads to his loins, each eagerly licking what we could get to. To have two tongues, two pairs of lips, two pairs of hands darting, licking, fondling, must have been hard indeed to bear.

I managed to beat Tiliu in the race to engulf his soft plum. She, never at a loss, dipped her head and licked upwards beneath his ball-sack, then flicked at his shaft with her near-prehensile tongue, her hand burrowing beneath his buttocks. He gave a yelp of surprise, and in an instant his cock leapt alive in my mouth. I did not need to see it to know that she had slipped a finger into his bottom-hole and was squeezing his balls with her other hand. He actually shouted 'No, no' aloud, his hips bucking uncontrollably under our joint depredations, as he burst into a come so copious that I was hard put to it to keep it from flooding out between my lips, so filled was my mouth.

William, sweet innocent young William, was utterly defeated. I cannot say he took an especially active part in what ensued – but then, with two experienced and eager young women enjoying themselves on him he did not need to be active, merely to respond and co-operate. Between us, we quickly got him naked. He protested a little, for he was still trying to maintain his pretence that he 'loved only me'. In reality, I think he was rather frightened of his situation, and shocked at the wanton manner of our seducing him. Tiliu, her knees on either side of his head as he lay on his back on the floor, began to smooth and caress his brow and temples. We both knew without saying that, after two such forced and reluctant comes in such a short space of time, we would need to gentle him if we were to get any value from the night.

While Tiliu soothed his head I knelt back on my haunches watching. William's firm, pale body lay sprawled and limp before me, a faint red mark about his waist showing where his belt had been pulled rather too tight. The slender muscles of his long legs were covered with fine hairs which invited the hand to smooth over them. At his fork, the delta of thicker, dark brown curls spread a little way up his flat tummy. Slowly, the panting of his recent tense activity eased, and his chest rose and fell to a gentler rhythm. His eyes, which had closed under Tiliu's gentle ministrations, flicked open when I ran my hand lightly along his thigh, but I smiled to show that he should not be afraid.

They closed again as my fingers moved softly through the hair on his loins. I did not want to arouse him yet, simply wished to delight in the sensation of his body under my fingers. The insides of his thighs were warm, increasingly so as my fingers neared his fork. His pretty cock was lying limply towards his left side, and his balls weighed down their crinkly bag between his parted legs. As Tiliu bent her head to kiss his lips, I slipped my hand beneath his balls and gently weighed and hefted them. He took a sharp little breath, but I did not want to force him, so went no further.

Tiliu's head had moved down and she was now kissing his chest, her lips and teeth teasing his nipples as her hands caressed his sides and waist. In moving thus, her breasts now brushed his face. I knelt back again, not touching him for I was fascinated by the gentle movements of Tiliu's hands, and the way her nipples turn by turn moved across his face. I knew her purpose was her own pleasure, for the sensation of another's skin tickling across an erect nipple is a joy to be savoured. Even so, the effect upon William was visible, for his cock thickened and moved upon his belly, though it did not yet stiffen.

I moved back a little way. Tiliu's head moved down William's body, her kisses tracing his ribs and belly to circle his tummy-button, into which her tongue flicked like a greedy kitten's. Her hands were now caressing his flanks and the outsides of his thighs, and with sinuous wrigglings she was rolling her breasts upon William's chest. I felt myself becoming hot at the wonderful vision of my friend moving upon William, and was amazed that he should lie passive under such sensuous ministrations.

She moved further down, kissing and licking his belly and the tops of his thighs, her own sweet cunny hovering oh, so close above his face. How could he not reach up and kiss her, taste the ambrosia that was so close. I was hard put to resist doing so myself.

That William was not impervious was amply demonstrated as his cock thickened and lay straight upon his belly. Her tongue darting pinkly, Tiliu flicked and lapped at his stiffening member like a cat with milk. It twitched and stirred and lifted. She circled his shaft with a small hand and, her head bobbing, lapped rapidly at the eyelet of his bulb. He gave a groan and came fully erect. With a swift, sinuous movement, and not letting go of his cock, Tiliu was up, and around, and astride him, parting her plump cunny-folds with one hand and guiding his cock with the other. Her face was the very picture of joy as she sank upon him, slowly lowering herself onto his thickness until the tufts decking her own loins were tangled with his.

Tiliu stayed pressed down on William's pale body for long moments, as though pausing to ensure complete control. Then she moved up so that some inches of his glistening shaft was visible between their bodies, and sank down again to grind and circle upon him, her eyes closed with the joy of shagging him slowly and deliciously.

William's hands slid along Tiliu's shapely thighs, rose to caress her firm breasts, uptilted now as her slender body arched with pleasure, then descended to grasp her hips as his own body began to move. Like all men, I suppose, William's one thought seemed to be to pump as deep and fast as he could, to reach his climax without delay. Tiliu did not let him. Gently, but brooking no denial, she pulled his hands from her hips, told him to be still, to let her do it. She pressed herself firmly onto him to stop his bucking, moved his hands when he tried once again to grasp her thighs, placed her hands on his belly to keep him still, and began oh, so slowly to ride him.

Moving up so that only his plum was within her folds, her pelvis circling in tiny movements, she began a series of insidious movements which held me spellbound. Sinking down to take in just an inch of his straining shaft, she would at once rise again, though not quite so far, then pause before sinking to engulf another inch of him. In this way, sinuously, with fiendish control – for whenever she felt the poor boy twitch she would freeze until he was calm again – she slowly sank further and further onto him until once again her cunny-lips were crushed against his pelvis. There she remained for a long time, fully impaled upon his helpless cock, controlling his every sensation and reaction by moving or freezing as she willed, the subtle, rhythmic clenching of her tummy and thighs showing that she was controlling her very sheath to squeeze and release him.

Still pressing her hands on his belly, she rose up again until he was almost out of her, and repeated her spellbinding, maddening performance. Poor William was gasping. Perspiration stood out on his brow and chest. His teeth were gritted as if he were under torture. I myself was in no little torment, for the sight of my lovely Tiliu so sensuously shagging William had got me pretty hot. I moved to the boy's side and mopped the sweat from his forehead. I kissed him and whispered in his ear.

'Be still, my darling boy. Hold yourself back as long as you can.' His eyes flicked open and stared into mine, filled with appeal and a suggestion of despair. He was being driven mad. I kissed him again, and stroked his cheek. 'Sshh, Sshh!' I whispered. 'Let Tiliu do it to you. She will let you have your come soon, I promise.'

I looked up at Tiliu. Her face was suffused with that admixture of ecstasy and tension that told me she was close to her own climax. Her slender body was quivering like a bowstring, her nipples straining like fingertips as she sank the last inch onto him. For a long, breathless time she was as still as a statue, only her face working to show her excitement. Then it was as if a light had burst in her face as, with a gasp of joy, she suddenly began to writhe and grind as her come exploded. Instantly, William too began to buck, grunting as though he were being punched hard in the stomach, his hips jerking and pumping uncontrollably.

With a gasping groan, as if her very breath were being dragged from her, Tiliu wilted and fell upon his chest, her round bottom jerking and circling as she milked everything from the still twitching loins of the exhausted William. It was only when my own come suddenly exploded in my womb that I realised, all unconscious in my excitement, I had been mauling at my own cunny, and in fact had shoved several fingers inside myself.

One of the great disadvantages of our ship's cabins was that the bunks, though very comfortable, were narrow – hardly three feet wide. Had we been elsewhere, back in Tiliu's village for example, we three could have snuggled down together and made a delightful night of it. As it was, William alone took up nearly all the space in my bunk. With a grimace of mock despair, belied instantly by an impish grin, Tiliu kissed me goodnight, drew on her frock and crept out of the cabin, the rest of her clothes bundled under her arm. Nudging William to move over and make some space, I slipped beside him beneath the blankets.

He was, as you may imagine, in a state of no little confusion. Hardly an hour ago he had been denying the possibility of desiring any other woman than me, then straight away Tiliu had shattered his self-delusion (albeit in the most delightful way imaginable) and sucked and fucked him to exhaustion. The poor boy felt guilt and confusion, and tried to apologise to me, and tell me he was worthless, and that he loved me, all in a jumble of words slurred by my kisses. I hushed him, told him not to be so silly, told him I was delighted he loved my friend too, put my arm about his shoulders and rocked him until he dropped asleep, his head nestled on my bosom.

He looked so sweet and innocent in his sleep, his face even more youthful than usual, and I did not wish to disturb so gentle a picture. Leaving the lamp burning, I drew the bunk's curtains with my free arm, and settled down to sleep myself.

At some stage during the night I was half-awakened. As

if in a dream, I felt William's hands moving over me, cupping my breasts, teasing my nipples. Slowly, as light as a butterfly, his fingers roved over my inner thighs, circling and moving up until his hand brushed against the down above my quim. He cupped me with the flat of his palm, slid a fingertip along, between, my moistening folds, circled my cherry, slipped into my entrance a little before moving back to where my cherry strained for attention. Then he was above me, between my parted thighs, pressing his hot bulb against me.

Dreamily, I reached down and guided him to my seeping entrance. He slid into me oh, so smoothly, snatching my breath away as he pressed to the hilt before beginning that rocking, thrusting motion which so sets my nerve-ends a-writhing. He fucked me gently, powerfully, building me to my come, keeping me there as his silk-and-steel shaft moved deep within me. For such a beautifully long time I felt I had died and gone to heaven. His own come jerked my body and flooded my heart with his warmth. He did not pull out, but lay still on me, his soft breath warming my neck, his adorable cock slowly shrinking inside me as I drifted back to sleep.

I was awakened by a yelp and a bouncing which almost threw me out of the bunk. It was William, tearing at the curtains and struggling to climb over me, in a state of considerable alarm. As soon as I gathered my senses I realised why. With the curtains parted, I saw brilliant sunshine pouring through the round window which they call a porthole. It was broad daylight. We had overslept after our strenuous pleasures of the night.

Muttering, almost whimpering in his panic, William dragged clumsily at his clothes, nearly toppling over when he caught his foot in his trouser leg in his rush. Without even pausing, only casting me a scared look over his shoulder, he rushed out. I lay back on the bunk, butterflies in my tummy at the enormity of our mistake. In the closed shipboard community everybody would soon know that

William had been late up, and probably that he had not slept in his own cabin. Oh dear! There would be such a scandal.

For some while, I confess, I dithered and worried. Even though I do not agree with the petty hypocrisy which bedevils our society, I know its destructive power. I would be labelled a scarlet woman and, such is the insidious influence of gossip – for gossip there would surely be – an exaggerated reputation would go before me wherever I went. Gathering myself at last, I rose, washed, dressed with care, and went out to 'face the music', as the phrase has it.

Four

Breakfast was long over by the time I entered the officers' mess, and nobody was about. I could hear the steward in his little kitchen, and called to him to request some coffee. When he brought it I knew the news was abroad, for he avoided my eyes with studied significance as he placed the pot, cup and paraphernalia on the table. Ah well, I thought, I might as well enjoy the excellent coffee before the storm breaks.

I had hardly begun when one of the Laskar seamen, panting, burst through the door. Seeing me he came to a halt, his face working as he gathered himself.

'Missy, please missy,' he stammered. 'Captain, he say come please. Come his cabin quick. Very serious!'

So, that stern personage was aware of the disaster, was summoning me for retribution. A devil was in me. I would *not* hurry to face him like some naughty child. I told the seaman, gently for he seemed in something of a state, to kindly wait while I finished my coffee, and that I would attend upon the captain when I was ready. He seemed amazed that I should not hurry instantly at his master's command, but he went and stood outside the door to wait for me nevertheless. I was myself rather surprised at my coolness and I made myself savour my coffee slowly, as if by doing so I was in some way establishing my defiance. Even so, as I rose and followed the seaman towards the captain's cabin (I think they call it a stateroom) the butterflies invaded my tummy with a vengeance.

Captain Prendergast was sitting at a narrow desk by the cabin wall when I entered his stateroom. I was surprised to find that it more resembled an office than a cabin such as my own. Then I noticed an open door, and realised that the captain had two adjoining cabins, presumably one for sleeping, the other, this one, for working, like a study or office. Mr Donaldson was standing by a wall, his face a mask, while the captain's visage was stern and erudescent with what I assumed was outrage. I drew a deep breath, and faced him.

'Miss Masters,' he intoned in a harsh voice. 'Miss Masters, there has come a scandal aboard my ship. One of my officers has disgraced himself, and thereby disgraced this whole vessel.'

I steeled myself.

'Midshipman William Forbes was tardy at watch this morning. It was discovered that he was not in his cabin. I have interviewed the young man, and you may be sure he will be disciplined. I am deeply offended that an incident such as this should occur aboard any vessel of mine. I have to tell you, Miss Masters, that this disgraceful young reprobate was not in his cabin because he was in the cabin of another. A female. And that he was there for the entire night.'

Oh, why did he not get on with it? Was he getting some kind of perverse satisfaction from dragging the thing out? Why could he not just say he knew that William had slept with me and be done with it?

'I am sorry to say, Miss Masters, that the young man admitted to whose cabin he was in.'

Get on with it man.

'I have to tell you, regretfully for I am aware of the sensibilities of well raised young ladies, that Midshipman William Forbes has seduced your maidservant. He has . . .'

I did not hear what the captain said next for my mind was an explosion of shock. Everything was revealed to me in an instant. William had been caught out, hauled before the captain, charged and convicted. And in all that, even though his career must be in danger of ruin, he had shown the wit to defend *my* reputation. What a wonderful boy!

I confess with some shame that, in my relief at learning

56

that my own reputation was safe, I did not at first consider Tiliu's nor William's. It was wrong of me, and had I really had the courage of my convictions I would at once have corrected the accusation. I did not. I am ashamed to say it, but I was as weak and hypocritical as all the rest. At the time, though, my euphoria that I had not been found out was such that I was hard put to respond coherently to Captain Prendergast, let alone consider the connotations of what he was saying.

Then one statement the captain made jerked me back from my silly state of joy, and made me very angry indeed. So angry that I was forced to defy him.

What he said was 'Forbes will be confined to his cabin except when on watch, and will be dismissed the ship at the next port of call. As for your servant, I would otherwise have obliged the young man to wed her, but she is only a native and so . . .'

I almost exploded. This 'only a native' business infuriates me.

'Sir,' I spat, cutting him off so abruptly that he actually started back in shock. Perhaps ship's captains are so lordly upon their own vessels that being interrupted is beyond conception? I went on. 'Sir, my maid is my own business. She may be "only a native" to you, but she is a friend and helper to me. I will deal with her. If, and I say if, you have any foundation other than the words of a young man I know to be in thrall to your rank that this thing occured, I will deign to review it. In the meantime you will leave Tiliu to me.'

The captain's face was a picture, a war between outraged dignity and doubt about what to do in the face of my unexpected attack. From the corner of my eye I noticed Mr Donaldson stiffen and cast a keen glance at me.

'Will that be all, sir?' I continued, my tone cold and angry. The captain merely gaped, entirely lost for words, so I turned and marched out with all the dignity my outrage could muster.

* * *

57

The results of this peculiar and, so far as I at least am concerned, productive interview were interesting to say the least. The captain consulted with Alice Barnet (they were not yet affianced) and she used the opportunity to wax wise in his estimation. Mr Donaldson, following up his appraising look when I told off the captain, suddenly became very friendly towards me, as though he hoped he might find some advantage with me.

I spurned him, for I dislike the kind of man who thinks all he has to do is to hint and a girl's drawers will fall off. Felicity's might (always did, in fact) but mine were going to stay firmly on, at least with respect to that arrogant gentleman.

Our main concern, Tiliu's and mine, was poor William. It was my fault he was in such trouble. Had I not chosen to enlighten him, chosen to prove his illusions mere illusions by asking Tiliu to seduce him, none of this would have happened.

Captain Prendergast's puritanical streak came to the fore concerning what I heard him call William's 'debauchery'. William's cabin, when he was not on watch, was under guard. When he stood his watches he was never left alone for a moment, and indeed was kept in parts of the ship not easily accessible to passengers. He took his meals in his cabin, for Tiliu served in the officers' dining room and they had to be kept apart. And indeed the atmosphere in that place when the captain was present was very cold indeed in so far as Tiliu was concerned.

I was desperately anxious to speak to William, both to thank him for his gallant defence of my reputation, and to assure him I would do anything I could to mitigate his fate.

I could not think of any way to approach the captain myself. He was of much too stern and puritanical a nature to allow of any attempt to seduce him and, besides, any such thing would spoil Alice's courtship with him. Then again, any attempt to persuade him towards leniency might cast doubt upon my own propriety, for I would necessarily have to propose an easier view of William's 'sin' than a proper young lady should hold. What could I do?

One tack was to beg Alice to intercede with the captain on William's behalf. Although this all happened before her engagement was announced, she was already on very close terms with that adamantine man, and if anyone could soften him it was she. Knowing her as I did, I felt that there was every chance for success, since she is a wise and persuasive woman when needs must.

The fact that William's cabin was to be under guard promised to be a major difficulty. How could I, or Tiliu for that matter, get to speak with the lad if there was a sentry to bar the way? Suddenly a thought lifted my heart. I remembered from my tour of the vessel and Sharpe's description of the various officers' duties, that it fell to the purser to organise the work of the crew. Sharpe was the purser. If it fell to him to arrange William's guards, perhaps I could have some influence upon him?

After our first encounter you may be sure that gentleman gave every sign of wanting to be alone with me again. He was a sweet man, and later, despite the proportions of his extraordinary member – which I always found difficult to accommodate – became a sensitive and gentle lover. Perhaps it was his sad sexual history which made him so sensitive, or simply his awareness of the perils of his excessive size, but he never pressed himself upon me like so many men do.

He did not come to me until the night after William was incarcerated. While it was very clear what his purpose in coming to my cabin was, he was so sweetly nervous and tentative that my heart went out to him, and I would have done my best for him even had I not had an ulterior motive. His fingers were actually trembling, and his eyes held a nervous appeal as he moved to sit in my chair rather than, as was William's wont for example, throwing his arms about me and raining hot kisses on my face.

It was thus I who kissed him, making the first move as

59

I so often seem to do. Kissing led to fondling, and soon Sharpe was tugging at my buttons and ribbons. Just as Tiliu had done for William, I stood before him and slowly removed my clothes. It is a delicious thing to watch a man's growing excitement as one strips off one's garments, and a delight to find ways of delaying the process, turning one's undressing into a kind of teasing dance.

Sharpe's eyes fixed greedily on me as I unbuttoned my frock, stepped out of it, folded it carefully, and placed it on the wooden chest in the corner. It is amusing how men get so excited at seeing a girl in her chemise and petticoats. It is not as if they can see any more of her, apart from her arms and shoulders perhaps, for she is still covered from neck to floor.

I untied the ribbons of my petticoats, and stepped out of them too. Sharpe was begun to breathe quickly, and his face was growing red. I had on a very pretty chemise of pale green silk (Alice had made me some lovely under-things) over loose drawers of the same material. On a sudden inspiration, I pulled my drawers off first. My chemise was quite long, reaching down almost to the tops of my stockings. As I moved to place my drawers with my other clothes, Sharpe's eyes were riveted on the little segment of my naked thighs that could be glimpsed between the hem of my chemise and my garters. His eyes were standing out, and he was so red I feared he might have an apoplexy.

His trousers, too, were under obvious strain. Loosening the ribbons at my neck as though I were about to take off my chemise, I suddenly changed tack. I dropped to my knees before him and began tugging at his belt and buttons. Every part of him was a-tremble with tension. He gave a gasp as I ran my hand quickly over his bulge before pulling open his breeches.

The object which leapt out before my eyes was just as breathtaking as the first time I saw it. A veritable truncheon of pale muscle rearing for the ceiling, a tracery of pulsing veins standing out beneath the soft skin which slid so easily upon the steel within as I circled its base with tentative fingers. Like a pillar of hot marble, it rose in glory from its bush of hairs to the thickening curve of its plum – though I confess it was more like a small apple than a plum.

Dragging my fascinated eyes from the glorious member, I concentrated on getting Sharpe's clothes off. When he moved to assist me I stopped him, begging him to let me perform the task alone. I knew that doing so would not only prolong our encounter deliciously, but that the delay would make us both even more aroused than we already were.

As I worked on his clothes, getting him to lean forward so that I could remove his tunic and to raise his hips so that I could tug off his breeches, Sharpe sat as stiff as his cock; the only movement that of his eyes staring down the loosened front of my chemise when I bent, and at the flash of my thighs when I moved around him.

By the time I got him naked I was breathing pretty near as quickly as he. His body, though pale as pale, was smoothly muscled and handsome, with a dusting of fine hairs upon his shapely legs and the middle of his chest. As he sat with his hips forward in the chair, his knees apart and his hands gripping the arms, the prick which reared from the fork of his thighs seemed even more disproportionately large, so engorged now that the cowl of skin was rolled right back from the ruddy, purplish bulb at its end, and the shaft was almost flat against his belly.

I did not yet remove my chemise, nor let him caress me. Between my legs already felt so moist and sensitive that I knew one touch would send me shuddering into a come. At my request, he stood and moved to my bunk, his pole standing out so strong you could have swung from it. I needed a delay, both to calm my own urgings and to work out a manner in which I might accommodate this mighty weapon without over-stretching myself.

Perhaps because of his unfortunate experiences with women in the past, Sharpe had given himself over to me completely, obeying and responding rather than trying to take a lead. He lay on his back, his legs a little apart, his eyes expressing both his arousal and an element of doubt. I touched my hand to his cock and kissed him gently on the lips.

'Sshh,' I whispered. 'All will be well.'

I kissed his brow and neck. My hand discovered his stiff nipple, and I caressed it before moving to take it between my lips. He was breathing slowly and deeply in his efforts to remain passive. As I moved my lips and tongue from one nipple to the other, my hand slid down over his ridged tummy. He tensed as my fingers neared the root of his cock, but I avoided it, moving on instead to caress his thigh, sliding my palm from his knee almost to the fork, scratching lightly with my fingernails along the inner side. He was trembling, and his breathing had quickened again.

My hair was loose, and trailed over his chest as I kissed along his tense torso, stopping to flick my tongue into his tummy button, which made him gasp a little. My hand slipped up between his thighs and I cupped his balls, which firmed and tightened under my touch. My face slid down until I was kissing the musky base of his magnificent cock. Oh, how much I wanted it inside me, no matter how stretched I would be. He kept very still, only his cock twitching as I began to kiss and lick it, circling around, tracing its immense girth and length.

At last, my face was poised above his glossy bulb. I licked around the circle of skin, explored the curve from its ridge to its eyelet, lapped at the clear little droplet of his essence which bedewed it. Even opening my mouth as wide as ever I could, I could hardly accommodate more than his mighty plum. Perhaps, I thought, if I gave him a good come this organ would be less fearsome when I got it into my cunny? With one hand still cupping his balls, and the other circling and caressing as much of his shaft as I could, I sucked and rasped my tongue over the hot satin that filled my mouth.

He groaned aloud. I felt him throb. I rubbed and sucked

harder. With an agonised gasp and jerking hips, he suddenly burst into a come so copious I could not take it all. I pulled back lest I drown, and felt gouts of his essence spurt over my face and hair as he jerked and gasped on and on. Suddenly, as if emptied, he groaned. With a final spasm, his body went limp; his head rolled to one side and his cock began slowly to subside in my hand.

Dragging myself up, for I felt trembling weak, I went to the washstand. I washed my face, then took the flannel and mopped off the pearly splashes that bedewed Sharpe's torso. Even soft as it now was, his cock was of impressive proportions as it lolled on his belly. I felt my nipples perk as I looked down at him. His soft eyes, still hopeful and tentative, engaged mine. I was as hopeful as he. I wanted the fulfilment of that beautiful organ inside me. Fully inside me.

My tummy lurched and melted at the very thought. I realised that I still wore my chemise. I grabbed the hem and pulled it off over my head. Even as the soft silk cleared my eyes I saw his cock twitch and thicken. I stood before him, naked save for my stockings and garters. He moved to climb off the bunk. He stood before me, took my shoulders in warm hands, kissed me so gently and lingeringly that my legs weakened. He cupped my breasts. I could feel the tension and eagerness emanating from his every pore, yet he was careful and gentle and sensitive. So many men, especially when, as his did now, their cocks bump up against a girl's tummy, would have leapt to push her back, throw her legs apart, thrust deep.

He did not. He kissed me, and fondled me, and waited. A hand descended to my quim. Gently, so tenderly my heart melted, he caressed my folds, his other hand moving down to fondle the cleft of my bottom. He cupped me with both hands, front and rear.

I could not have stopped my knees parting if my life had depended upon it. A finger found my entrance and slid in as his hard palm kneaded my folds. His plum pressed

63

against my tummy. I gripped it as the hands between my thighs bestirred me. My breasts were crushed against his chest. My legs were jelly. I could not breathe.

Wordlessly, but as though we knew each other's innermost desires, we sank to our knees on the wooden floor. His hands slipped hotly over the skin of my bottom and waist as, without thought, I turned and knelt, knees splayed, and presented my rear aspect to him. He moved forward. I felt his plum sliding along my folds, parting them, seeking his haven. He found it.

I gasped and shuddered as he began to press home, and strove to expand myself as much as I possibly could. He entered me, clasping me by my hips. I was so stretched. I gasped relief as his plum passed the muscles of my entrance.

He paused, letting me relax a little, then pressed again. My head burst and I was panting uncontrollably as slowly, inexorably, his huge member slid into me, seeming to press my internal organs into my chest. I tried desperately to control myself, for I was already building up a come before he was halfway in me, and I had to remind myself that this was supposed to be for his benefit.

I felt his hips press against my buttocks. Felt the touch of his balls against my stretched and puffed folds. He began to move, not so much the in-and-out thrustings of a normal fuck, more a pressing and relaxing which drove me to rapture. His fingers dug into my hips as he moved. I was so filled I did not know what to do.

I was on all fours, but my arms got too weak to support me. I sagged – the only thing in the world the cock stretching and owning me. My thighs were one great spasm. My breasts were bursting for a comforting hand. My stomach cramped and churned. My sheath, so stretched, so ravenous, was a million greedy tongues.

Oh, I wish every girl should know at least one such fuck in her life. I had been in a come since he had hardly begun. When he himself reached his come I knew I would die. Nothing in the whole universe existed save the wonderful organ filling me, driving me, pulsing me to my nerve-ends. Then, he jerked and spasmed and thrashed, and grunted and the heat that flooded me made me scream with the wish to die now, at this moment of ultimate glory and surrender.

I collapsed in a twitching, gasping heap on the floor. Sharpe sagged with me, his breath hot and rapid on my shoulder. I sobbed afresh as he slowly pulled out of me, for even shrunken after his come he filled my sheath and it clung to him greedily.

We lay there together exhausted. He, despite our first, partial attempt, had never shagged properly before. I had never been so hugely, so thoroughly, so overwhelmingly fucked even while I was with the tribe. We both took a long time to recover. And as I lay slowly gathering myself I knew that had he laid even a single finger on me, whispered even a word, I would have burst into tears of contentment and exhaustion.

Five

Afterwards, both of us were a little shy: me because I was still awe-struck by his filling of me and, I confess, a little concerned that I might be so stretched as to be unsuitable afterwards for a normal cock; he, I learned later, because he had long ago reconciled himself to the fact that no woman could take him. And I had.

He showed his appreciation. Perhaps being deprived so long of a real shag, being reduced to this thing he called 'wanking', had deepened his sensibilities, strengthened his imagination. However it was, he set to it to please my senses with his hands and his mouth.

Soon, oblivious of the hard wooden floor on which I lay, I was sighing and writhing beneath his caresses. His hands and lips and tongue found every part of me. Found that spot at the join of my neck and shoulder which so makes me melt and shiver. Made my breasts want to burst with his sucking and the rasping of his rough tongue across my tingling nipples. Kissed me from my toes to my brow. I was in a trance of sensation. Had he been an army of lovers I could not have been more transported. And then his tongue crept to my swollen cherry, and I went to heaven.

He was kneeling beside me as I writhed under his caresses. His arms came around my raised legs and he parted my thighs to give his mouth access. His gentle fingers spread my cunny lips, and his tongue went to my soul. Ever since Motallo first introduced me to this way of pleasure, I have known that nothing can so drive a girl to nirvana as a tongue and mouth lapping lovingly at the centre of her being. As though he were worshipping at

67

some shrine, Sharpe licked and sucked and nibbled at me, tormenting every nerve-end of my bursting cunny, lapping even into the entrance of my sheath.

I was in an agony of pleasure, if such is possible. My lungs were afire, my breasts bursting, my thighs and tummy cramping uncontrollably. Somehow, for I was not conscious of any change in our positions, he was kneeling astride me, his cock moving against my cheek. I looked down between the valley of our two naked bodies to where his face was buried between my trembling thighs. I looked up. His pale thighs were columns bridging my face, joining above me at the beautiful fuzz of hair which decked his loins, and from which his awesome member stood out. Without thought, my mouth sought him. I grasped his shaft with both hands, pulled him towards my lips, and licked at the great bulb which throbbed beside my cheek.

I could not take more than a fraction of him, but what fraction I could take I licked and sucked as though my very life depended upon it. The scent and the taste and the heat of his manhood filling my mouth only multiplied the sensations he was causing between my legs.

Whether by skill or instinct I cannot ever know, but at the same moment as his wonderful tongue flicked with appalling, glorious rapidity across my bursting cherry he slid a finger into my rose-hole, and I was lost. I know I became a wild thing, for the next morning I rued the grazes on my lower spine from where I had ground my back upon the wooden floor. Tiliu, too, let me know by minxish smiles that I had screamed out.

At that moment, though, I was delirious, oblivious of anything save the wonderful tongue which flicked from my cherry to my opening and back, and the fingers which now ploughed both my bottom and my sheath. He did not pull back when I thrashed and spasmed into my come. Indeed, he seemed to become more fired, to lap and suck at me more greedily, until I could come no more. And then I did come more, for he too exploded into a come, and all that existed in the universe was the glory he was spurting onto

68

my tongue, into my throat, over my chin, such ambrosia as my heart could burst for.

I think I fainted. I have a vague memory of sagging limp with exhaustion, of being gathered up in caring arms, of being lifted and placed upon the bunk, of blankets being tucked snugly around me. I know that the next thing of which I was conscious was Tiliu gently shaking my shoulder, a cup of morning tea in her hand.

She was all eagerness to know how I had got on. Only as I was in mid-description did I realise that she did not yet know about Sharpe's 'difficulty'. When I told her, her mouth gaped and her eyes near fell out. Then she collapsed into such a storm of giggles I could not help but join in. Amid all our laughter about Sharpe being a 'poor hard done by man' and how soon Tiliu could get a chance to see this astounding weapon, I suddenly realised that I had completely forgotten to ask Sharpe about William's guards.

The realisation sobered us both. We considered what to do. To go directly to Sharpe and apprise him of my concern would surely have been too blatant. On the other hand, he did owe me a considerable debt – after all, had I not given him what he thought no woman could? Was not my quim still tender from his stretching of me? We determined to face him, but I insisted that Tiliu accompany me for courage's sake.

We eventually found Sharpe in the little cubby-hole he called his office, which was filled with shelves a-drip with papers, fearsome looking forms and ledgers piled on the desk. Sharpe himself looked up from a tome, his face registering delight at seeing me, then puzzlement at seeing my companion. There was no chair except the one Sharpe sat on. He leapt to his feet, knocking a snowstorm of papers off a shelf with his shoulders. I sat. Sharpe had perforce to crowd close to Tiliu because of the smallness of the office. I came straight to the point.

'Did you enjoy yourself last night, Mr Sharpe? Did I please you?'

His face registered stupefaction. He looked wildly from me to Tiliu and back, his mouth agape with shock.

'Come now, sir,' I continued remorselessly, despite the butterflies in my tummy, lest our attack went wrong. Who knows how deep the puritanical propaganda of our society may stretch? 'Was not being with me better than whatever this thing you call "wanking" is?'

He was not a stupid man. In seconds his shock was nearly controlled, and a narrowing of his eyes told that he was weighing up the situation. I smiled, lest my attack should seem too severe. He drew in an audible breath and straightened his shoulders, glancing again from Tiliu to me.

'Miss Masters,' he said at last, his voice tight with dignified censure. 'I am not sure – I do not think – in front of . . .'

At that second, as though she had been rehearsing the moment in her mind, Tiliu slipped her hand slowly down across his bottom. He started as though shot. Span round despite the constricted space. Turned a face of outraged dignity on her.

After a second of frozen silence, Tiliu began to laugh. With one gesture, one sweeping, impertinent, brilliant touch, she had cut through what might have been ages of negotiation. Sharpe would have gone on to trot out all the trite clichés with which our society hides its embarrassing occurrences – 'it did not happen'; 'not in front of the servants'; 'these things must not be talked about' and such. In response, I would have had to upset his dignity, actually say aloud what we had done last night, even, if you will, have used it as blackmail.

By touching up his bottom in such a lascivious manner, Tiliu had cut through all that. At the sight of we girls giggling uncontrollably, Sharpe's outrage puffed out of him in a great gasp of astonished resignation. He sat down on the desk like a marionette with its strings cut, looking distinctly nonplussed. When at last I was able to control my giggles, I set to it to reassure poor Sharpe and lay our position before him.

'We have come', I told him, 'on a mission of relief for young William.'

Sharpe's features registered surprise at the mention of the midshipman. He had clearly not expected such a tack, possibly thinking I had come to embarrass him in some other way.

'You came to my cabin last night,' I continued. 'We had a splendid time, did we not?' Sharpe blushed to his roots, and cast a scared glance at Tiliu. I placed my hand upon his thigh.

'Do not be concerned, my dear. Tiliu and I have no secrets from one another. None at all.' I moved my hand higher up his leg, stroking him lightly, making sure he fully took my meaning. His blush told me he did. 'We think it is unfair that poor William should suffer punishment for doing what you yourself so enjoyed last night. We have not come to cause you trouble, simply to plead with you to find a way to make the poor lad's fate easier.'

To make my intentions even more clear, I slipped my hand actually onto the member contained within his trousers. At the same time, Tiliu moved close to him and began to stroke his cheek with a gentle finger, her thighs touching against his arm.

The poor man was in a tizzy. His was a world in which sex was a secret thing – in which the man made the approaches, and the girl remained shy and compliant. Now here he was, faced with two girls ready to talk openly about that forbidden subject, who shared each other's secrets, who were far from shy, and were clearly ready to be active rather than simply receptive. His features showed that he was hard put to it to grasp a situation he could never have expected to face.

We worked on him, petting and cooing, and avoided shocking him by too open a mention of matters carnal, but getting him to understand our simple point. We were healthy and enthusiastic girls. He, like any other man,

71

enjoyed romps with such as us. Had indeed thoroughly enjoyed such romping only last night. William was no different. It was not fair that William should suffer for enjoying exactly the same pleasures as Sharpe had.

For a moment, Sharpe's face registered amazement that it was I with whom William had spent the night, and not Tiliu. I used the point to reinforce the unfairness of William's fate, stressing how honourably he had behaved in protecting my reputation.

Sharpe was won over by our arguments (and possibly by the tender caresses he was receiving). Our battle was not won, though. Captain Prendergast was an unforgiving man. His word was law on the ship, and he rarely, if ever, changed his mind on a matter of discipline. What with this rigidity and his rather puritanical views, it would be difficult indeed to alleviate William's fate. Sharpe would try, but held out small hope.

What he could manage, however, as the officer who organised the crew's duties, was to do something about the guards outside William's cabin when he was not on duty. He looked a little askance at my suggestion that, if there were only one guard instead of two, a distraction could be arranged so that someone could slip in to speak to William. He obviously guessed what form any distraction would take, and, although he did not really approve, he reconciled himself to the suggestion and agreed to reduce the number of guards at night.

In saying this, though, he let slip that his agreement was based on the assumption that Tiliu would do the distracting and I the slipping in to see William. Such assumptions always irritate me. Tiliu was 'a native', and a servant to boot. Any distracting of a Laskar seaman would naturally fall to her, while the English girl would go to the English man. Huh! I at once determined that the roles would be reversed, as much out of my natural naughtiness as out of pique at Sharpe's snobbery. That, however, was yet to come: other games were afoot now.

* * *

72

When I had described to Tiliu my adventure with Sharpe, she had expressed disbelief at my description of his immense cock – a disbelief quickly overlaid by a desire to see for herself. In the crowded little office, as we worked to persuade Sharpe to our way of thinking, the little minx had been subtly teasing him. She had been getting close behind him, touching his neck with soft fingers, pressing herself against him so that he could not help but be aware of the warmth of her body, whispering so that her soft lips almost brushed his cheek. At the same time, my own hand had been fondling his thigh.

Even a man whose sad history made his reactions far from the usual ones when teased by a girl, and who had just been shocked out of the attitudes of a lifetime, could not forever fail to respond. And respond he did, at least in his person, for at the same time as his cock grew in his breeches, he became more and more nervous.

We were in his office; someone might come looking for him. We were two girls with one man. We were taking the lead in what was happening, making advances upon him – rather than the other way around. He would, I am sure, have found a means to shoo us away if we had let him.

We did not. He jumped like a startled rabbit when my hands went to his buttons. He would have wrested them away had not Tiliu pulled his head back and kissed him on the mouth, her clever tongue darting between his lips. I had to get his breeches fully open to drag out his swelling cock. Tiliu gave a mew of delight at the sight of it, and instantly fell to stroking and licking it. Sharpe groaned and surrendered, leaning back against the wall and giving up any effort at resistance.

Tiliu moved around to kneel between his feet, her hands and mouth busy upon the rod which now stood rampant. She darted a hand into his trousers and cupped his tight balls. Her hands flew knowingly about his bag and shaft. The glance she gave me before taking his straining bulb into her gaping mouth was an admixture of delight and awe. I held my breath in admiration at the amount she was

73

able to take into her little mouth. Her cheeks bulged and caved as she sucked greedily, her fingers encircling him as she stroked the full length of his shaft. Sharpe began to move just a little, obviously rising towards his climax. Tiliu was making little mewing, snorting noises as she worked, the whole of his bulb now inside her mouth.

Sharpe gave a sobbing gasp. His hips jerked as he burst into his come. Tiliu's cheeks and throat worked frantically as she strove to suck and swallow all. At last, Sharpe groaned and sagged, drained by my wicked friend. When she released him and stood up, her eyes were shining with excitement as she wiped her lips with the back of her hand. The delighted gaze she turned upon me said very clearly that she was determined to see more of this superb prick.

As for Sharpe, he was shattered. Only a few days before he had been entirely convinced that his 'difficulty' would forever place women out of his reach. Now, he had not one but two eager girls demanding his services. He must have thought he had died and gone to heaven.

We left him without actually agreeing on any arrangements to follow up, as it were, what had just transpired. Sharpe would, no doubt, find the first opportunity to engage with one or other of us. How would he choose, I wondered idly. Seeing the hungry, wondering looks he cast upon both of us as we left the tiny office, I knew that he would have been happy if either of us had remained behind for a little more fun. For a moment I was tempted. Watching Tiliu suck that splendid cock had made me not a little warm. But there would be time enough for future frolics.

We decided to leave our attempt upon William's cabin until as late as we could. Luncheon, walking about the deck in the afternoon sun, preparing for dinner, dining, all seemed to drag endlessly. After dinner, Tiliu came to my cabin, and we exchanged memories about her tribe and afterwards at father's station to while away the time.

At one point, after a long silence, when I had professed myself bored with the waiting, Tiliu rather undid me by

74

smiling softly, nodding towards my bunk, and raising her eyebrows enquiringly. I shook my head, as much to hide my surprise as to negate her implied suggestion.

Such an idea had actually not entered my head. That she had put it there rather nagged at me because, I confess, it was tempting. Tiliu is a beautiful and lascivious girl, and I was not averse to the idea of lying with her again and feeling her hands on me, and caressing her slender, firm body. It would not have been too difficult, either, because we were both clad in only nightgowns and robes as part of our plan. But now was certainly not the time.

At last, my little travelling clock showed almost midnight, the time we had agreed upon. We crept together out of my cabin and along the passageway that led to the corner around which William's sentry would be on guard. I peeped around the corner. Excellent! There was but one man on duty. Turning to Tiliu I mimed to show her our good fortune, and to check that she carried the key to William's door which Sharpe had given me. I took off my robe and handed it to her.

Our plan was for me to pretend to be sleepwalking. The sentry would certainly find my rather fine cotton nightgown distracting. Taking a breath, I moved quietly around the corner.

At first, the seaman leaning against the wall beside our target door did not notice me, and so I was able to get a good look at him. He was a Laskar, as we had expected, tall, and rather slim in build. He had his arms folded and his head was bent. He might, at first glance, have been asleep had not an eye opened in my direction as I moved along the passageway. This was the truly testing moment.

In thinking about it earlier, I had puzzled over how to make my approach. When one sleepwalked, did one really hold one's hands out in front? Should one's eyes be open or shut? Did one walk normally, or with a slow tread? I decided slow, hands out, eyes shut but allowing me to peep through my lashes.

The guard straightened and stared, his eyes moving over me. I knew my nightgown gave him a good notion of the shape within. I moved slowly, keeping my face expressionless. The guard's face most certainly had expression. Surprise, doubt, appraisal, cunning, desire, all took turns across his dark, moustachioed features.

As I got closer, he stepped away from the wall, staring hard all the while. I suddenly realised that there was something we had not considered. At what point, if any should I 'wake up'? The decision became urgent now. I had planned simply to walk past the guard, to have him follow me a little way, enjoying the shadow show of my nightgown.

He did not let me walk past. Instead, as I approached he reached out and held my arm. I stopped. Unable to think of anything else, I maintained my pose of being asleep. I stood still, concentrating on breathing slowly – which was not easy I can assure you. The man stepped close in front of me. He scrutinised me closely. He glanced about him quickly as if nervous and undecided. He reached out a hand, and very softly touched my left breast. I remained still. His hand became less tentative, cupped me, squeezed a little.

When I did not 'awaken', he stepped to my side, and placed a hand on my back. Taking my arm in his other hand he pressed me forward. Like an automaton, I obeyed, wondering what on earth was to befall me. Through my slitted eyelids I saw that he was urging me towards a door.

The seaman had obviously decided that this sleepwalking girl was ripe for shagging. He was just opening the door towards which he had pressed me, the hand on my back having slipped down so that it was now fondling my bottom, when another sailor marched around the corner. He had me halfway through the door, which opened into a small storeroom, when his crewmate appeared. I must have inadvertently chosen the very time the guard was changed for my ploy. There was a whispered exchange in their own language, beginning angrily, but soon changing

76

to suppressed laughter. Together, they urged me forward until I was inside the storeroom. They followed me in.

Perhaps because I was pretending to be asleep and they did not yet wish to wake me, they were tentative. They did not leap upon me. Whispering together, they lit a lamp and looked me over. I stood like a statue, drooping my head so they would not see the expression on my face, struggling to control my breathing.

A hand reached out. A single finger traced the shape of my breasts. The hand opened and cupped me, but very softly. My mind was racing. When should I 'wake up'?

They began to unbutton the neck of my nightgown. So far, the men were being very quiet and careful, had done nothing to 'shock me awake'. I kept still. They undid all my buttons to my waist. A hand slipped in and cupped my naked breast.

Very gently, as though the slightest touch might 'wake' me, my nightgown was edged over my shoulders. The material slipped down my arms, would have simply fallen off me had the sailors not lowered it slowly.

Was now the time to 'wake up'?

I kept still. The two men moved around me. I could almost feel their eyes moving over my exposed body. They began to touch me. With my head bowed, I was not able to see their faces. It was excruciatingly difficult to maintain my act as, with increasingly excited whispers, the two sailors began to run their hands over me, so softly as to hardly touch me.

My situation was strange and suddenly exciting. To stand thus, naked and apparently unconscious, as four eager hands ran over me, feeling but hardly touching my breasts, and my back, and my bottom, and my thighs, was very stirring.

A hand slipped along the cleft of my bottom, parting my cheeks a little, teasing down to the join of my thighs. Another, fingertips only, traced a line between my breasts, down over my tummy, to my bush, to the curve of my cunny.

77

When it probed a little, slipping between my folds, I 'came awake'. Instantly, a hand was clapped over my mouth. I had jerked 'awake' very suddenly. I acted fright and shock. I had no idea what should happen when I 'woke up'. I knew only that I had to pretend confusion, panic even. The sailors gave me little chance even to act.

The one behind me, the one who had his hand over my mouth, pulled me to him. I could feel his breath hot on my neck. The hand feeling my cleft delved actively, pushing between my legs, reaching even to my quim. The sailor I was facing expressed a momentary shock, then grinned wolfishly. He stepped close. Very close.

They were no longer gentle. How they would have proceeded had I remained 'asleep' I cannot guess. Now, they proceeded very purposefully. They had a naked girl in their clutches. It was the depths of night, locked away in a tiny storeroom. My struggles were only half pretended as they set about me.

I was spun, twisted. My breasts were mauled. The hands between my legs probed and roved. A cock was bounced forth. I was raised up, my thighs were thrown apart, I was impaled.

The room was too small to lie me down. The sailor whose cock was thrusting into me leaned back against the wall. He was tall. I could only hang on, my breasts crushed against his rough tunic, my toes hardly reaching the floor. His hands gripped my buttocks harshly as he hauled me onto his rampant cock.

Suddenly, between the cheeks parted by the hands pulling me onto the man fucking me, I felt a second cock probing. He found my rose-hole, pressed, pushed, entered me. I was crushed between two hard, straining bodies. My insides were crammed with two urgent, thrusting, unstoppable cocks. That little bridge of flesh between my cunny and my bottom-hole felt like to tear apart as my two ravishers had their way with me.

I will not prevaricate. To have a man wild with lust, to feel his hot breath, his hard hands on one's flesh, to have

78

his rampant cock pushing for one's ribs, is glorious. To have two such, to be tossed upon the storm of two thrusting pricks, crushed between two straining bodies, to have two mouths, two pairs of eager hands, devouring one, is overwhelming.

I churned into a helpless come. They sensed it. They slowed their movements, timed them so that they thrust at the same moment, relaxed together, thrust again. I was gasping, my helpless body writhing and churning at this double filling, this two-fold cramming of my depths. They speeded up together, tossed me about like a twig in a torrent, burst into their comes at the same instant, flooding me front and back with their hot effusions.

If I did not faint, I did lose all awareness of anything save my throbbing body, of the heat within my organs, the echo of hard hands upon my skin. Suddenly, the men were gone. I leant against the wall on jellied legs, panting, my legs parted to relieve the hot throbbing in my quim and rosehole. When I managed to compose myself, I grabbed up my nightgown from the floor and pulled it on. It had somehow been torn, probably by the sailors' feet as they ravished me. I crept away.

I stepped as bravely from the cupboard as I could. The man outside William's door grinned wolfishly as I came into view. I suddenly found myself desperately embarrassed, especially when he placed his hand upon his groin and made a very obvious thrusting motion. I rushed away, burning with blushes, the more so when the man's low chuckle assailed my ears.

When I was back in my cabin, trembling with reaction, I poured myself a small amount of the brandy I kept for medicinal purposes, and collapsed onto my chair. Well Lydia, I thought, that was all rather more intense than you bargained for. I let my nightgown fall open and examined my breasts. Luckily, I do not bruise easily, else I knew the very visible thumb-prints that were glowing redly on them would have turned dark and difficult to explain away by the morning.

I pressed a tentative hand to my lap. I have entertained two men at a time before. Talesi and Buthelo sometimes had me that way while I was with the Tukanna. They, though, were gentle and supportive, always working me up first, and timing their penetration so that there was but little strain from their double filling of me. The seamen, by contrast, had been frantic and rough, had cared about nought save fucking me very thoroughly, and I was sore in both my rose-hole and the little bridge between it and my cunny.

I rose and stripped off my nightgown, examining it ruefully. I hoped Alice would have some matching cotton, and would not tease me too much about the rip. It struck me that when I described to her how the damage had occurred, she would find it amusing. Indeed it was, if you looked at it aright.

I found myself chuckling at how my impertinence in thinking to manipulate the guard had led to my undoing, at the image of the haughty daughter of a civil servant being tossed about like a rag as two eager seamen shagged her. I ran some water, and washed between my legs, wincing from the touch of the chilly flannel on my cleft. It made me feel much better.

Only as I was pulling my nightgown on over my head did it strike me. I had forgotten Tiliu. The Laskars had only been at me for what, a quarter of an hour? Tiliu would not have had time to leave William's cabin. She must be still trapped there.

I hurried to her cabin. She was not there. What could I do? All would be lost if she were found in William's cabin. The captain's opinion of William would be confirmed and his punishment increased if the very girl he was supposed to have spent the night with had sneaked in to him. I dithered and fussed. I could not go back and tempt the guard again. He would suspect.

I would go to Sharpe. He knew of our scheme, and must

be able to find a way out of our impasse. Luckily, though his cabin was on the same corridor as William's, it was around a corner, and thus out of sight of the sentry. Wrapping myself in a blanket, for Tiliu still had my robe, and donning my bedroom-slippers, I crept off. I did not dare knock on Sharpe's door in case the guard heard me, and so I simply opened it and slipped in.

All was in darkness, and since I did not dare leave the door ajar I had to grope my way about, hoping the cabin was laid out in a similar way to mine. It was not. I fumbled about blindly, almost bursting into giggles at the ridiculousness of what I was upon, then jumping with shock as my hand touched upon Sharpe's face.

He leapt and grabbed me by my throat. He must have thought I was a sneak-thief, he grabbed me so roughly. Only when, after a moment's struggle, I was able to gasp out who I was, did he let me go. There came some scrabbling noises, a lucifer was struck, and Sharpe lit his lamp.

His face was puffy with sleep, and he looked rather silly with his bare feet sticking out beneath a striped nightshirt, and once again the ludicrousness of the situation swept over me. I could not help myself. I burst into a storm of giggles – and when Sharpe actually became irritated with me, they grew worse. The thought of Tiliu trapped with William, doing who knew what; the sight of Sharpe's puffy, angry, bemused face; my being here in my night attire; the sentry; all combined to make my ribs ache and the tears course down my cheeks.

At last, and then only because I forced myself, I regained enough control to apologise to Sharpe, and explain our problem. He at once brought me back to reality by becoming brisk and businesslike. He swiftly threw on his uniform ducks, told me his plan, scolded me to be sensible. I was still a little giggly, perhaps, it occurred to me, because I was actually rather scared.

Sharpe was brilliant. He marched around the corner, all duty and efficiency, called to the sentry, took him off to attend to some entirely irrelevant task. As instructed, as soon as Sharpe and the guard had disappeared, I scurried to William's cabin and without knocking rushed in. Inevitably, as if some higher plan had determined to make this night as farcical as possible, Tiliu was on her back with her feet towards the ceiling, being very enthusiastically fucked by dear, oblivious William.

I have long thought that one of the subtle differences between males and females is that, except at the very height of a come, a woman is easily distracted during a shag, whereas it would take a blow from a sledgehammer to distract a man once his cock is up a girl. Such was now the case. Tiliu knew of my arrival, turned her face to me, registered my presence. William was oblivious. Even though Tiliu unwrapped her legs from around his hips, stopped pumping her pelvis in time to his thrusts, pulled her face away from his hot kisses, he kept going. To be fair, my interruption seemed to have coincided with the moment he was reaching his come, and so one could not expect him to notice anything of lesser moment than a cannon shot.

Registering my concern, Tiliu rolled her eyes in a manner that signified wait a moment, he'll be finished soon. William's 'Oh, gosh!' when, having enjoyed his come, he became capable of realising someone other than Tiliu was around, would have set me giggling again had our situation not been so urgent.

Tiliu heaved William off as I grabbed up her scattered garments. Together we fled for Sharpe's cabin, only just in time to judge from the sound of footsteps that echoed towards us along the corridor.

We were still clutching each other in helpless, barely suppressed laughter when Sharpe entered. He was in a foul temper and began, in as loud a whisper as he dared, to berate us roundly. Such was his fury that he instantly quelled any laughter left in us, and it was two very chastened girls who, Tiliu having put her nightgown and robe on, crept back to my cabin.

82

Six

The only immediate results of our night's fiasco were that Sharpe forbade either Tiliu or I to go anywhere near William's cabin, and for me to detect a change in the way the officers' steward and the other seamen I came upon that day looked at me.

Sharpe was calmer in the morning than he had been last night, but still very annoyed with us. He was especially irritated that it was I, rather than Tiliu, who had distracted the sentries. For a moment I thought he was about to launch into one of those insufferable speeches about my being English and Tiliu a 'native', but he did not. Instead he pointed out that even had Tiliu been the decoy there would have been gossip. How much worse would the gossip be since it had been an Englishwoman who lured aside the sailors? It would be all around the crew by now. They would be aflame. There might even be discipline problems.

He had a telling point, and I had not thought about that aspect of the matter. Nevertheless, I am not one to be browbeaten by any man. He found my response as shocking as anything he had ever known.

'You may be a ship's officer of vast experience,' I said, smiling and patting his knee as his face puffed redly with amazement. 'You may know your men, but you do not know them from a woman's point of view.'

He spluttered and made to speak, but I cut him off.

'Oh, it is certain the two men last night will brag of their conquest. What men would not? To be standing on sentry duty in the middle of the night and out of the blue to get a quick shag is something to boast of. And true, the rest

83

of the crew will join in the gossip. But I can assure you, dear Mr Sharpe, that it will go no further.'

'How can you possibly say that?' he almost shouted, his chest heaving with outrage. 'You are only a child. You cannot . . .'

'A child indeed! I am seventeen-and-a-half years of age but even so, I might tell you, rather more experienced in certain areas than you are.' I sat straighter and looked him firmly in the eye. 'I know men rather better than you do, sir. The reason your crew will keep their secret is very simple. They will all fancy a chance for themselves.'

My arrow struck home. He deflated. I could see from his confused expression that he was re-assessing his opinion of me. Despite our delightful frolics of the last couple of days, he had still not cast off that silly view men have of women as shrinking little creatures, fluttering and fainting at the very thought of anything physical. I smiled at him and patted his knee again, this time sliding my hand quickly up his thigh.

'You have kept our little secret, now haven't you?' I gave a little chuckle, my hand lighting on his crotch. He jumped as though stung, went very red, made to leap out of his chair. I gave him a little shove, and he fell back, his mouth agape. 'Oh come now,' I continued. 'Don't be silly! You like it as much as I do, if you are honest. And neither of us is any the worse for it, now are we? What happened with your sailors is just water under the bridge. Nothing will come of it, I assure you.'

Poor Sharpe was in a tizzy. His image of womankind was quite turned upside down. He was shocked at my boldness. Flabbergasted at my simple acceptance of what silly men surround with such hypocrisy. But men are simple creatures, easily manipulated when a cunning girl pays attention to the Great God Prick.

All his protestations and blusterings were accompanied by my fingers flicking open his buttons, and were silenced when I took his cock into my mouth – or at least, as much of it as I could.

And in the end I was proved correct, for nothing of the

incident with the sentries ever leaked out to the captain or anybody else.

Mind you, apart from getting him a voluptuous shag with Tiliu, the episode had done nothing to help poor William. That problem was solved by the combination of a delight and a disaster.

The delight was Alice's persuasion of her new husband after their nuptials a couple of days later. Their wedding night, she told me archly, had been very active. To be honest I had guessed as much from the captain's jovial, almost smug, manner at luncheon the day after. However, it transpired that Alice had begun almost at once to gently chide him about his stern treatment of William. During their second, equally active, night as spouses, she had actually whispered in his ear that it seemed rather harsh to punish a young lad for doing what he was at that very moment so enthusiastically enjoying.

The disaster was that something important in the vessel's boiler-room went wrong. I was told that a vital pressure pipe had fractured, though the detail meant nothing to me. Suffice it to say that the engine had lost most of its power to propel us, the damage could not be repaired at sea, and we were obliged to make for the nearest port so that the problem could be remedied.

For me, at the time, it meant little apart from an irksome delay in our progress towards England. But at least it promised some diversion from the daily vistas of an empty sea, which may be entrancing for a time but soon pall. The single visit we had made to a port, to take on coal overnight, had been fleeting and we had not even been able to leave the ship. I looked forward to a break from the constant background thudding of the engine, and some new sights. Had I only known what lay ahead, I might have felt a little differently.

Without the power of the engine, our vessel limped along under a ragbag of canvases and tarpaulins rigged as sails.

William was released from his punishment because of all the extra work that was required, and did so well that his sentence was revoked (though perhaps some thanks were also due to dear Alice's soft words in bed).

It took us a full two days and a night to reach a harbour, a little ragtaggle of a port called M . . . . in southern Arabia. It was too small for our ship to actually go alongside the quay, so we anchored a little way off. It also did not have any engineering facility, which meant, Donaldson told us at dinner, that we would be stuck here until a message could be got to somewhere called Aden, and a replacement part secured. Our spirits fell to our boots when he said it might take upwards of a month.

In the morning, standing on the deck with Alice and Tiliu, we witnessed a bustle of activity. A boat was lowered over the side. Donaldson, resplendent in his dress uniform, climbed down to it, and to my surprise was joined by the mysterious Egyptian gentleman. Rowed by four seamen, the little boat scudded off for the quayside, and did not return until after luncheon.

The news was that the Bey, which was the title of the local Turkish overlord, would extend every facility for getting the ship repaired. In the meantime he offered us his hospitality for the duration of our stay, and said that we passengers were welcome to lodge in his residence. You may be sure there was a happy bustle as we packed bags and chests, delighted that we would not be stuck in our cramped quarters for a whole extra month.

It was an adventure to climb into a lifeboat and be swung out over the ship's side, and be lowered to the water below – although Felicity made a great show of being terrified. In stark contrast to Felicity's silly squeals, the veiled woman, whom I had not seen this close until now, but whose clothing made her actually indecipherable even close to, sat absolutely still and silent.

When Tiliu hissed and clutched my arm, her face registering fear, I was puzzled. She pointed to the group of figures awaiting us on the quay, her fingers digging quite painfully into my arm. I could see Mr Donaldson and the Egyptian gentleman, plus several uniformed men. Tiliu hissed in my ear and indicated another figure, standing a little back from the others, taller, and wearing tight white breeches that stopped below his knees and an oddly shaped red cap I later learned is called a fez. His arms were folded across his chest, and a large sword hung at his side. It was him! It was the stranger who had so ravished and frightened Tiliu on our first night at sea, but whom neither of us had seen since.

Tiliu positively cringed down into the boat. I stared at the figure that so unnerved her. He was certainly tall, broad and well muscled. He held himself aloof from the other waiting men, and stood very proudly. Only when we came close to the quay and I was able to discern his face did I get an inkling of what Tiliu meant by his 'having juju'.

Whereas Mr Donaldson and the other men were all eagerness to greet us, to assure us we were now safe, to help us from the boat and get up our luggage, the stranger simply turned his head a little, cast a single glance over our bustling party, and returned to his contemplation of the horizon.

But that glance pierced me. His face was an impassive mask. Two deep lines rose from his straight eyebrows to bisect his otherwise unlined brow. His nose was straight and proud, and his nostrils flared like a stallion's. His mouth was slightly down curved, with full, sensuous lips. His jaw was square and strong, with a deep cleft at the chin which somewhat softened it.

But his eyes!

That single glance had been enough. Deep set, fringed by black lashes, with whites that only served to emphasise the black depths of his pupils. They were eyes that knew, eyes to drown in, eyes that – even in the single glance they had vouchsafed me – had an astonishing power to loosen one's sinews.

87

When our party climbed the wet stone steps that led up to the quayside, Felicity, Tiliu and I gathered around Mr Donaldson (Alice had naturally chosen to remain aboard ship with her new husband). The fourth figure, the mysterious veiled woman, though, glided silently to stand behind the Egyptian, a little off from us, and Tiliu's stranger moved to stand near them, as though he were a bodyguard.

He actually proved to be far more significant, as I discovered when we were in the Bey's residence – though palace might have been a better description. It was a low, white, rambling structure, sprawling over a hilltop above the town. Our party was obliged to walk the mile or so from the harbour, and I noticed that, although it was very hot, hotter than I had known it while in Africa, it was such a dry heat that one did not perspire at all. One did, though, quickly become very thirsty, and the tinkling of a fountain that kissed my ears as we entered through a low, arched gateway was like the song of angels.

As we were ushered through a door on the far side of the courtyard, I noticed the veiled woman going in through another, smaller door, the Egyptian and the mysterious stranger leaving her there and going out through the gate.

Felicity, Tiliu and I found ourselves in another, smaller courtyard, deliciously cool after the heat outside. We were greeted by several veiled and voluminously robed women, and led to the suite of rooms that was to be our abode until the ship was repaired. There, bowls of fruit and flasks of a cool, sweet drink called sherbet waited to refresh us, and you may be sure we fell upon them eagerly.

Our rooms were beautiful and luxurious, with delicate lattices admitting soft daylight from yet another courtyard. The hangings, furnishings and decorations were remarkably different from anything I had been used to. There were huge cushions instead of chairs, small tables, delicately inlaid and no more than knee height, low divans and richly brocaded hangings covering several doorways. A frieze of patterned tiles ran around the top and bottom of the walls, and I noticed that there were no pictures or portraits.

I noticed, too, that there were no men about. Women there were in plenty, carrying our bags and boxes to our various rooms, moving silently about on whatever was their business. One, a middle-aged woman who bore herself proudly, seemed to be in authority, and to have appointed herself our warden.

There was a difficulty with language, for she spoke neither English nor the rather clumsy French I tried, and none of us could fathom her tongue. After some minutes of fruitless talking and attempted sign language, she turned, clapped her hands, and called something in a strong, musical voice. After hardly a pause, there came a flurry and several younger women hurried in, glancing nervously at us, before standing with bowed heads before the older woman.

There was a rapid exchange, during which heads were shaken and curtseys bobbed. Then one of the young women turned to face us. She was plump and her round, pretty face was made all the prettier by the huge, nervous eyes she turned on us. Haltingly, taking a deep breath as though she were about to leap into a race, she spoke, and in English. Her face lit up with joy when I replied, and hands were clapped and little dances jigged by the other women as they shared her pleasure.

Her name, we learned, was Samara, and she became our interpreter and almost constant companion. Though her English was rather limited, such was her boundless goodwill and ability to invent sign language that we got along very well. She showed us around our quarters, which comprised a small chamber each to sleep in, and the luxurious room we had first entered, which was to be our common parlour. She then led us out and showed us two places that took my breath away with surprise and delight.

The first was a wide, cloistered garden courtyard, with tinkling fountains, winding paths among shrubs and beds

89

of flowers, fruit trees of half a dozen kinds, and the cheeping of many birds. To find a place of such Elysian beauty actually inside the walls of this place was a joy we could never have anticipated.

The second place Samara led us to did indeed have people, half a dozen or more young women, all naked, who squealed and scampered away at the sound of our arrival. In the centre of the room was a huge, oval pool, and on the tiled floor surrounding it were more divans like those in our parlour. It was clearly a communal bathing place, and our arrival had disturbed some women at their ablutions.

This room, the fact that there seemed to be many rooms leading off it with no doors, except to the outside, and the absence of men all struck me as more and more curious. When I questioned Samara, she seemed amazed that I did not already know what kind of place this was. How could I not know that we were in the Bey's harem or seraglio, his women's place, where we could be safe from the eyes of men?

Not only did I not know it, I could never have dreamed that such places existed. And the more I pressed, the more surprised I became. It seemed that a ruler such as the Bey always gathered about himself a number of women, some of whom he married according to Islamic law, but all of whom served as his wives. They resided together here in these women's quarters known as the harem or seraglio, kept private from the eyes of men, their lives dedicated to serving their lord's pleasure.

I found the whole idea amazing and, I confess, intriguing. The women, I learned, were actually rather proud to be regarded as the property of their lord, at his beck and call, and secluded from any company other than that of his choosing, doing nothing save while away their time, keep themselves beautiful, and await the summons to his bed.

While Felicity, as usual in any unfamiliar situation, put on her pampered flower performance, and refused to do else but recline in our parlour or sulk in her sleeping chamber, Tiliu and I felt free to explore this fascinating place. No let or hindrance was placed upon us. Indeed, Samara was our eager guide and informant.

Physically, the harem centred around the bath-house and the luscious garden-court, with shady cloisters running off it, from which sleeping chambers, parlours, kitchens and other offices led. It seemed to be entirely self-contained, except that supplies came from outside and, of course, there were no men about.

Of women, there seemed to be three kinds. There were those, like Samara, who carried out the roles of servants and helpers, although this seemed to be more or less by consent, for they were still 'women of the Bey'. The second kind included the women who were fairly new here, or had received favour by being frequently called upon. These ladies, who treated Tiliu and I far more timidly than did the first group, seemed to spend most of their time in the bath-house, being pampered and beautified.

The third class was the actual wives of the Bey. There were, apparently, four of these ladies, though the only one I had any early contact with was the woman who had first greeted us, and given us Samara. By virtue of their status as wives, these women held sway over the other occupants of the harem, and alone, I learned, had the right of access to the Bey's bedchamber. All the rest had to await selection.

I learned how this selection was conducted a few days after moving into the harem, but more of that later. In the meantime, Tiliu and I agreed that while we were here we should relax and get what benefit we could.

The first of these was clothing. Since living among Tiliu's tribe I have found our European clothing, designed for different climes, a stifling burden, as did Tiliu. We had done our best to make them less stifling, choosing lighter materials, wearing loose-legged drawers (and often none at all, especially in Tiliu's case), avoiding corsets except on formal occasions, and keeping things as loose and light as social propriety allowed.

The women of the seraglio were much more sensibly clad. Though voluminous and many-layered, their clothing consisted only of loose draperies of fine muslins, which floated when they moved and lay softly upon them when they were still. And although each layer was so fine as to be amost entirely translucent, the many layers combined to conceal them almost as well as the strictest decency required, while allowing a coolness and freshness our European garb forbade.

When I asked Samara whether Tiliu and I might be lent such clothes, she was astonished, for she thought our garments exotic and beautiful. Nevertheless, she hurried off to find the Bey's wife. News of our strange request caused some excitement, for not only did that lady soon appear, but with her came a gaggle of other women, all staring and giggling like schoolgirls. Clothing was brought, and great excitement ensued.

At first it was rather disconcerting, for the women obviously expected us to undress then and there. Then I caught Tiliu's impish grin, and our undressing became an actual performance. As each garment was undone and taken off, a murmur swelled among our audience, and it was snatched away for close examination.

Our frocks and petticoats were held up, tried against figures, passed from hand to hand. Our chemises and drawers caused especial excitement, as did my body when I had removed them. Apparently they had never seen a European woman before, and seemed delighted and curious that my body was like their own, but was so pale all over.

With such an innocent eagerness that no offence could possibly be taken, many hands reached out to touch me, pressing and rubbing as if to see that my flesh was warm like theirs and whether my colour might rub off. I had loosened my hair while undressing, and much excitement was generated by the fact that it and the down on my cunny were light in shade, though that down below is naturally darker in hue than my tresses.

At last their interest in my nakedness changed (they were not so concerned with Tiliu's, for several of them were also Africans) and they began to deck us with their kind of clothing, tussling and haggling to have the honour of draping us. The veils were indeed light and cool, even though there were many of them, and the little slippers, which were the last things we were offered, were comfort itself. We felt so much freer and cooler in our new clothes, Tiliu and I, that we immediately decided to recommence our exploration of the harem.

The second blessing we determined to take advantage of as soon as may be was the bathhouse. Among the tribe, we had bathed at least once every day in the river, and bathing was the thing I missed most of all when back in 'civilisation'. I am sorry to say that European society is not among the most fastidious in terms of bodily cleanliness. A bath in hot water in a tub, with nothing to rinse off the soapy residues, was no more than a weekly event, and the daily strip wash I gave myself, with a flannel at my washstand, was no substitute for the lovely, fresh river water. The thought of that beautiful bath awaiting us was heaven.

Dressed in our harem clothes, we were more easily accepted by the women, who seemed much less nervous of us. We made straight for the bathhouse after the women had dressed us and, circumspectly so as not to scare the other women, set out to explore it.

It was in itself something of a palace, comprising of several tiled and airy rooms and lots of little alcoves, each furnished with divans and mirrors and little tables holding flasks and bottles. Apart from the main room with its large pool, there was another housing a series of hot tubs, and a third containing a sort of artificial waterfall beneath which one could stand for a refreshing shower. In each of these rooms sat two or three elderly women ready, I gathered, to assist any bathers who might call on them.

At first, we just looked around, then sat on a divan in the main room. Soon, delicious coffee and sweetmeats were placed beside us, and the women's tense scrutiny eased. Judging the time ripe, Tiliu finished her coffee and strolled towards the hot tub room. I followed.

One of the elderly attendants was already helping Tiliu to undress, and another hurried over to assist me in the same way. She clucked and smiled, and bustled about me for all the world like my old nanny had when I was small. Her eyes twinkled in her plump face, and I felt an instant friendliness towards her. She smiled and chatted, though I could not understand a word, and I became enchanted by the many wrinkles around her eyes betokening a readiness for laughter, and the way she ooh'd and chuckled as she pulled off my veils.

It was glorious to sink into the hot water, to breathe in the aromas of the oils she poured into the steaming tub, to relax back to be soaped and massaged. There is no more luxurious sensation in the whole world, and my mind drifted empty as the dear woman soothed and cleansed me all over.

After the hot tub, glowing pink and still steaming, I floated into the shower chamber amid a cloud of relaxation. The shock of the icy waterfall made me yelp and drove the breath from my body. Only a laugh from my attendant gave me the courage to stay under, and I became so glad that I did. After the heat of the tub and the first breathtaking sting of the shower, I felt such a glow spreading from my insides outwards, and such a tightening of my skin under the spray, each drop of which I seemed to feel individually, that a surge of joy and energy swept across me and I felt as alive as it is possible to feel.

I stood tingling all over as the woman dried me vigorously, delighting in the scrub of the thick towels as they set my skin glowing. I drifted joyfully to the main pool, only a little puzzled as to why the woman had bothered to dry me so thoroughly when I was going to get wet again straight away.

The water was a little above body heat, sparkling clear and azure from the tiles that lined the bath. There was a broad shelf around the edge of the pool upon which one could sit and lean back, the scent from the oils and flower petals in the water seeming to ease the mind and body onto soft clouds of luxuriance. Oh, it was heavenly! If this was the life of a woman of the seraglio, I could do with more of it.

And as a final touch of luxury, when at last I dragged myself back to some kind of reality and rose to climb out of the bath, the woman was already waiting to swathe me in warm towels, and rub me dry, and lead me to a divan, where she smoothed perfumed oils over every inch of my body. I gave myself over to her entirely, lying on my front so that she could massage me from the soles of my feet to the nape of my neck, rolling over so that she could do the same to my front.

So deeply relaxed was I, so lost in warm sensation, that when I became aware she had parted my legs, and seemed to be paying especial attention to the area between them, I accepted it as just another part of this delicious massage. It slowly drifted into my consciousness that the touches had changed from gentle kneading and smoothing of my muscles and sinews, to equally gentle but more pointed caresses around the tops of my thighs, the delta between them, even the cleft of my bottom.

I looked up at the woman with as much curiosity as my dreamy state allowed. Her head was bent towards my loins, on her face an expression of dispassionate enquiry. With delicate fingers, she parted my folds, peered at me, slipped an exploratory fingertip along my crease. Although this was a most intimate and personal investigation, it was very strange, for her detachment seemed to communicate itself to me. I lay with my legs parted, watching this stranger explore my most intimate parts, almost as though I were a spectator rather than the object of her delicate touches.

She turned her head and said something in a soft, low-pitched voice. At once, a number of other women were around me, a circle of faces looking down at me, turning to each other, whispering and smiling. The older woman, who had begun this strange examination, said something and parted my folds again. There came a murmur as of a class at school interested by a curious exhibit. Other hands touched me, tentatively at first, but then with increasing confidence as the 'exhibit' simply lay and accepted their examinations.

It was, I realised in my detachment, the same curiosity the other women had shown when I first removed my clothes back in the parlour. They had never seen a European woman, and thus were curious as to my paleness, the colour of my hair, whether I was flesh like their flesh.

My hair was lifted, cooed over, allowed to run through gentle fingers, spread out on the divan, smoothed, fanned again. Hands slid over my skin, exploring my brow, my ears, my neck. Their curiosity took in every part of me. Whispering to each other, they ran their fingers along my arms and shoulders, down my ribs to my waist and the swell of my hips. My breasts were cupped and fondled.

My eyes, which had drifted shut during this strange, almost impersonal, exploration of my offered body, opened again. Hovering above me were gentle eyes set deep in a smooth, oval face, gazing into mine. The full lips curved into a tender smile, and a hand smoothed over my cheek to touch lightly on my lips. I had drifted into a pliant mood. Of all the hands that were caressing me at that moment, this one seemed the nicest. The smile communicated itself to the huge eyes, and the woman leaned down to kiss me, a lingering, tender kiss which melted me.

As if it were a switch, that kiss turned off my dreamy detachment and turned on awareness of the myriad voluptuous sensations that were washing over my body. Hands were smoothing my breasts. I heard a little cry, as of delight, as my nipples perked and stood stiff. Fingers teased them, and my breasts tightened and tingled. The touches along my thighs were like moths of lambent flame, sending hot shivers in waves to the depths of my tummy. The brush of hair across my skin as lips and tongues explored me from my ribs to my navel was a wave of electric shocks.

I felt my arms lifted and placed above my head. Hands and mouths traced every part of me, from my toes to my fingertips, driving each single nerve-end into a quiver of excitation. I was entirely lost upon waves of greedy surrender. I was kissed on my mouth again and again, searching, lingering kisses that drowned my soul, seeking tongues that drew mine to them and held me. Between my legs, from my knees to my quim, was a slowly burning, glowing, surging swell of yearning.

It did not matter how many women were caressing me, how many hands and lips and tongues were tormenting me. All that mattered was the overwhelming, agonisingly denied aching for release. As though they could sense my own sensations, the hands and mouths brought me to an awesome plateau of longing and held me there, pulsing and swirling and dying to be allowed a come. And then I felt myself groan with tortured rapture as teeth nipped my throbbing cherry and fingers slowly penetrated my cunny and my bottom at the same appalling, wonderful, shattering instant. I churned into such cramps and spasms and explosions of coming that my heart burst, my head flew apart with light, and my hips writhed with greedy bliss.

Ages later, aeons of slowly receding rainbows and cramps and soothings later, my eyes drifted open to see my darling Tiliu smiling down at me, her eyes part comfort, part minxish gleam. I looked vaguely about me. There were women in the pool, others lying on divans or walking about. None paid me any particular attention. Whomever's were the hands and mouths that had so seduced me I could not have told in a million years.

Offering me a glass of tart sherbet, Tiliu grinned.

97

'I think you need another bath now, little Miss Ridja,' she said, using my tribal name and slapping me lightly on my thigh in mock admonishment. 'And then maybe some sleep. Too much excitement wear out a girl.'

I confess that, even after another soak in the soothing pool, I was too languorous to bother with donning the veils that were the women's dress here, and walked back to our parlour as naked as the day of my birth. Felicity's reaction as Tiliu and I entered arm in arm was so extreme and so shocked that, after a moment of amazement I burst into giggles.

Felicity sat there on the divan, primped and encased in heavy clothing, her lovely copper hair scraped and pinned, the shiny points of her button boots peeping from beneath the folds of her skirts and petticoats, her shocked brow beaded with perspiration. She was the very epitome of the ridiculous. Here, in such a temperature as would melt cheese, she was dressed for a Surrey garden party. Here, in a world entirely female, she was outraged at an undressed female.

She sat rigid, her knees and shoulders so clamped one could have sharpened knives upon them. Superiority and scorn distorted her features – and this from the girl I had watched being seduced by Jonathan Andrews, had seen suck off virtual strangers, had witnessed being shoved up against a wall and shagged by Mr Donaldson, had even listened to while she described her 'surrenders' in such detail as betrayed that she relished every instant of them.

If she only knew how ridiculous it all was. How could even such a dull mind as hers fail to realise that what *I* was, *she* was? She scorned me as a wanton, held herself to be 'a good girl taken advantage of', yet at a hint of a 'demand' her drawers dropped off and she 'had to let' whomsoever demanded to fuck her. Witness her submission to Donaldson. And yet she clung to the excuse that she 'could not help it'. At least I held to honesty.

How mealy mouthed she was. My laughter must have had something of hysteria in it, for suddenly I was blazingly angry – so furious that I could not speak. Felicity saw the change in my expression, and actually started back nervously. Tiliu saw it too, and pulled me away to my sleeping chamber, hugging and calming me like a mother hen.

As I settled down to sleep on that, my first night in this strange place, a desire grew in me to prove to Felicity once and for all what she was, to find a way of obliging her to own up that she was as eager and grateful for the delights of the body as I or any other healthy woman.

Seven

The next day began as did most of those we spent in the harem. One of the women woke me at dawn. I bathed, and rinsed myself under that magical indoor waterfall, and lounged in the main pool before being patted dry, and massaged with oils. Breakfast was of fruit and bowls of tangy, delicious pastes (the names of which I never discovered) into which one dipped pieces of thin, unleavened bread, and the most delicious dark, sweet coffee in tiny cups.

We then dressed in our European clothes – or most of them, for Tiliu and I both habitually left off our drawers and confined ourselves to a single petticoat – whereupon one of the women ushered the three of us to a small chamber with an outer door. There she would leave us, for she must not be seen by anyone 'outside', and soon the outer door would be opened. A male functionary would be there to lead us off to a large parlour, where waited one or more of our ship's officers – nearly always Mr Sharpe, often Mr Donaldson as well, and occasionally William: never Captain Prendergast or the engineer Grimes who were, I supposed, busy about the ship.

On that first morning both Donaldson and Sharpe awaited us, and greeted us with cheerful concern to know how our quarters were, and whether we had been treated well. Of course, on that first morning we knew nothing of the real nature of our quarters, nothing of its function as a sort of holding pen for the Bey's bed-partners. Even so, something urged me to conceal details such as the bathing and the veils, so we left the two officers thinking of it simply as 'the women's quarters'.

Later, when we knew its real purpose and Felicity let the secret slip out, the knowledge excited rather than scandalised at least Mr Donaldson, for he became (to quote her words) 'ever so carried away' and from then on shagged her even more enthusiastically than hitherto.

But to return to my narrative.

That first of our morning strolls was most pleasant, and served to reveal even more clearly, had that been necessary, the strange and exotic world we had entered. If inside the harem there were no men, here there seemed to be no women.

As our little party wandered about in the palace grounds, Tiliu, Sharpe and I forming one group, Felicity and Donaldson coming along behind, we saw soldiers on sentry duty at various doors and gates, others coming and going through the main gate, a few gardeners, and what looked to be tradesmen, but no females. Indeed, the presence of we three women seemed to cause shock and sensation, for although the sentries we passed would snap to attention, their eyes would boggle and follow us until they nearly popped out their corners.

It was not until we had been a week or more in the palace, and our morning walk led us out of the grounds and into the town that we actually saw males and females together – and even then, the womenfolk and girls seemed always to be just a little behind the man they were with, or if not accompanied by a male they kept close to walls and hurried along with bowed heads.

It was as though in this society females were of entirely secondary status, appendages of their men, or scurrying creatures hiding themselves away. It was most disturbing. Almost as disturbing, in fact, though less dramatic, as the way men would stop and stare at us, and even call out, sometimes with apparent anger.

It was all in huge contrast to the world of the harem, where all was peace and the womenfolk were relaxed and free in their femaleness.

* * *

102

We would return from these walks around midday. On the occasions when Donaldson had been present, Felicity would always drift off to her chamber in her 'retiring flower' pose, for the officer always found an opportunity to get her out of our sight for a while, and when they returned she would be flushed and wilting from the shagging he had certainly given her.

Mind you, neither Tiliu nor I were shy in that department. There was a place we always headed to in our strolls, a sort of rocky glen with many shrubs, quite concealed. There, much pleasant frolicking occurred.

On the mornings Donaldson was with us it was a little awkward, for we would have to arrange for him to take Felicity off before we could set to. If our companion were just Sharpe, Tiliu would go off with him behind some bushes while Felicity and I waited. I did not mind that Tiliu hogged Sharpe, for to be honest although he was a sweet and sensitive lover, he *was* rather too large for me to find him comfortable.

Felicity always expressed mute disapproval of these escapades, but was in no position to be awkward. How could she, when we knew what *she* was up to. I suspected even then that she was in fact a little jealous, for when both Sharpe and William were present, and Tiliu and I would pair off with them and leave Felicity to wait and stew, she was always in more of a pet than the other times.

On returning to the harem, unlike silly Felicity, Tiliu and I would hurry to strip off our European clothes, and bathe away the heat and dust we had inevitably gathered on our walk. The serenity and luxury of the bathhouse made it the centre of our seraglio world. There was no pretence here, no tensions or formalities – such things are hardly possible when one is lolling in a bath, or sitting naked eating sweetmeats and drinking sherbet.

With Samara as our interpreter, we quickly got on friendly terms with the other women. They were of all types and ages, from the proud (though never haughty)

Farah, the Bey's senior wife, who had greeted us that first day, and who was perhaps in her fifties, to our plump and smiling Samara, who was hardly older than myself.

Perhaps the most noticeable feature of these women was their entire lack of self-consciousness. Clothed or naked, they were easy and relaxed with one another and, as my European strangeness wore off a little, with me, freely hugging in greeting, kissing often and without any apparent motive save friendship.

I had never been in an all female society before, let alone one as strange and exotic as this. And as the days passed I learned that, here at least, there existed few of the little rivalries and pettinesses we women so often demonstrate in mixed society. Perhaps it was because all these women were in the same case, all 'wives' of the mysterious Bey.

Another thing which struck me very forcefully, as I learned more and had time to think about it all, was the way these women adapted to meet their circumstances. It was an all female establishment with a single purpose – to satisfy the physical requirements of their lord and master. The whole point and ethos of the place was sexual. Yet there were in excess of thirty women here. Even if the Bey played entirely fair and kept a strict rotation among his women, it meant a month or more between nights with their 'husband'. And these were all healthy women.

I could not imagine the awfulness of once-a-month-if-they-were-lucky gratification. I soon learned that there are ways around such a daunting prospect.

The bathhouse was the centre of the harem world. They all congregated there. Tiliu and I too as time went on, though Felicity for a long while held herself aloof. They combed one another's hair, ate fruit and drank coffee or sherbet, basked, bathed and relaxed. It was a very haven of peace. But it was something more.

I noticed quite early that the women often seemed to go into particular pairs. The same girl would comb the same partner's hair each day. The same two would sit whispering, would walk off together hand in hand. As I watched, it dawned on me that most of these pairings seemed to display a greater closeness, or perhaps I mean a softer intimacy, than simple friendships. I watched more closely.

Tiliu, being African like a number of the other women, slipped more easily into this society than I, for my paleness of skin and my light-coloured hair seemed to give my companions pause. And as has so often been the case, it was Tiliu who gave me the answer to my little puzzle.

Often times I would sit by the pool and watch Tiliu smile and begin to converse with one of the women, using I supposed links between their native tongues, and wander off with her to one of the alcoves. I followed once, and was struck spellbound by the sight of them lying together on a divan, entwined together between each other's parted thighs, heads bobbing as they licked and nuzzled one another towards rapture.

What struck me, however, entranced even though I was, was that Tiliu's companion seemed to have something in her hand, something she was pressing rhythmically into Tiliu's wriggling cunny. Tiliu's legs were high, and her partner's head was bobbing, and one arm was up around Tiliu, fondling her breast. The other arm, though, was curled around Tiliu's raised thigh, the hand which clutched whatever she was using close beside her face as she nuzzled and pressed the thing into my friend. It was most odd.

Only later did Tiliu explain in response to my questioning. She showed me a device, a strange device of polished ivory. It was carved exactly like a rampant cock, with a ridged plum at the top, and a large bulb at the bottom so it could be held comfortably.

I knew instantly the reason for the peculiar motions of the girl's arm as she made love with Tiliu. She *had* been pumping at something, and the something she had been pumping at was this strange device. Not only had Tiliu been transported by her friend's mouth and hands, but she had been ploughed by this ivory imitation of a cock. Just think! A tongue on her cherry and a smooth, albeit

105

artificial, cock in her quim, all at the same time. No wonder she looked rapturous!

That first time, though, as I watched Tiliu with her new love-partner, I was spellbound. There are few more moving sights than that of two women exciting each other to rapture. With men it is mostly grope, shove, gasp, and come. With women, though, it is all cunning, and delay, and build and tease. As I watched my beloved Tiliu lying back, her heels resting on her lover's back, her lithe and slender body arching in tension and surrender as a clever tongue lapped in long strokes at her swollen folds, I melted, she looked so lovely. I wanted nothing more than to rush in, to clasp my mouth to those trembling breasts, to suck and bite and worship. How I did not I cannot imagine.

Fortuitously, my attention was distracted when Samara tugged at my arm and told me that Farah had to see me, and at once. The Bey's senior wife was in something of a state when I went to her chamber. She greeted me with a wringing of her hands and a flood of words, which Samara was hard put to keep up with. Amid a welter of apologies and side-trackings, it slowly became clear what was her concern. I had been chosen. She was desolate. I was a guest, and a European, but she was helpless in the matter.

It seemed, when I was able to clarify it through Samara, that the Bey was in the habit of looking over his women, and selecting from among them. The decorative lattices high in the walls of the bathhouse were, I learned, actually observation points through which the women could be inspected at leisure. I confess that I felt an odd tightening in my tummy at the thought of the unseen man who held sway over this place watching me as I bathed and moved naked about the baths all unawares.

When the Bey selected a woman after such an inspection of his harem, it was Farah's duty to prepare her and convey her to his chamber for the night. This was her dilemma, for I was neither wife nor concubine, though it seemed the Bey did not know it. Apparently, women were

106

sometimes delivered to the harem sight unseen, often as gifts from people seeking favours or preferment. I would of course refuse to go, Farah said, and rightly, and she would take the consequences – but at least she had carried out her duty in telling me.

The consequences, Samara told me in a frightened voice, were that Farah would be beaten and reduced to the status of fourth wife – an awful disgrace. There was a piquancy about the situation which part-angered, part-amused me. That her husband should so casually select his bed-mates, and hold such power to punish Farah if she failed to fulfil his whim, irritated me. At the same time, to go as his concubine held the promise of sweet adventure. Were Turkish men the same as Europeans and Africans? And what would this all-powerful ruler actually be like?

Farah's astonishment when I said I would go became such joy and gratitude I knew she would have died for me at that moment. As news does, flying on the breeze as it were, the women of the seraglio seemed to know in an instant what was happening, and I was soon the focus of a giggling, whispering audience. Even Farah's sternest words could not suppress their excitement.

When the preparations for my night began, the audience fell silent and withdrew, to sit in huge-eyed groups on the divans around the walls. With Farah supervising, Samara and another girl about her own age stripped me of my clothing, and led me to the hot tub room. I was allowed to do nothing for myself.

Tenderly, for this seemed almost to be a ritual, they bathed me, using their hands rather than sponges or flannels, smoothing creamy, softly scented lather over my body and rinsing me by pouring the deliciously hot water over me from brass bowls. When every inch, from my hair to my toes, and even inside my cunny and my rose-hole, had been gently and thoroughly cleansed, they led me to the waterfall to shower me, then patted me dry with thick, soft towels.

107

This gentle, almost loving pampering felt so luscious that I was already drifting into a languid mood when they led me, pink and tingling, out of the bathhouse to Farah's chamber.

It was larger and much more richly furnished than any of the others. In the centre was a low, satin-covered bench, on which I was told to sit while my two attendants brushed and dressed my hair, trying a number of different styles. Farah was at last satisfied when they piled it high at the sides, fixing it with many pins and clips, leaving the rest to flow in a long tail down my back.

Carefully, the tip of her tongue between her teeth as she concentrated, Samara shaded and outlined my eyes with kohl. Delicately scented powder was brushed upon my face and neck, and down over my shoulders and breasts. Creamy rouge was applied to my lips and my nipples. I was lain back, and the fuzz upon my vee was combed and carefully trimmed with tiny scissors. My fingernails and toenails were filed and polished and painted. No perfume was put on me, except some oil, applied with a glass rod, between my cunny-lips, along the cleft of my bottom, and between my breasts. What it was I never discovered, but as the warmth of my body affected it, I became aware of a deep, elusive, musky odour surrounding me.

My decorating, as it were, being finished, I was made to stand up. Bracelets of gold coins were placed around my wrists and upper arms and ankles. A chain of similar coins, from which hung many smaller chains, was fixed about my waist, and a circlet of yet more coins was put about my brow. An opulent, and surprisingly heavy, necklace of gold and jewels was put on me, so large that it fell from close around my throat, like a jewelled curtain, to lie on the upper curves of my breasts, a huge ruby in gold basketwork lying actually between them.

Veils of such fine muslin as to be all but invisible, save for their gilded fringes, were draped around me as skirts and a voluminous cape. A thicker, though still translucent, veil was hung from the circlet about my head, covering but not concealing my face from my eyes downwards. Finally, after what had seemed like hours of preparation, another garment, this one black and of thick cotton, was put on me, covering me from head to feet except for an opening at my eyes so that I could see where I was going.

At last I was allowed to move, and shown myself in a huge looking glass. I was staggered at the mysterious figure which stood before me. The effect of the black outer garment was to turn her into an entirely shapeless object, only the kohled eyes revealing that a living woman was within. Had I not known her to be me, I would have thought her a phantasm from some gothic novella.

My two attendants placed their hands, palms together, at their foreheads, and bowed low to both Farah and me. One left us, and Samara remained to act as translator. Farah motioned me to sit at her feet – which her age and dignity made seem wholly appropriate – and through Samara instructed me on what I was to expect and how I was to behave to best please the Bey. She went into very intimate detail, and I found myself glancing at Samara. Had she experienced this? Had she been sent for by her lord and master?

She blushed and shook her head at my whispered enquiry. No, she had not been so honoured yet, but was constantly hopeful.

Farah at last led me out of her room and into a small ante-chamber in which was a heavy wooden door. With a low bow, she left me to wait alone. Soon there came the rattling of a key in the lock, and the door swung outwards. A slight, richly clad man stepped forward, nodded curtly in my direction. He eyed me from top to toe, then signalled me to follow him. Flanked by two huge guards, each bearing an enormous curved sword, I followed along corridors, up flights of steps, through doors, as the silent functionary led me to my tryst with the unknown Turk.

* * *

At last, we came to a heavily curtained portal. My guide halted, pulled aside the drapes, and ushered me to enter.

To say that the room I found myself in was sumptuous would be too weak a description. A thick, gorgeously patterned carpet lay upon the tiled floor. Drapes of deep crimson satin, intricately embroidered with gold thread and fringed with long silken tassels, hung from the walls and ceiling. Fat silken cushions lay about as if thrown casually down. On small tables stood bowls of fruits and ewers of various liquids, together with goblets of silver inlaid with gold. An enormous, deeply cushioned divan, surrounded with a mist of silken curtains, stood to one side. An elusive fragrance drifted in the air.

As Farah had instructed me, I stood waiting just inside the portal. The wait gave time for my imagination to work on me. What would he look like? Would I be able to remember all Farah had told me? How old would he be? Would he be slender or fat, handsome or ugly? To be strictly honest, I felt terribly nervous, like a virgin bride might on her wedding night. At last, just when I was beginning to feel like running away, I was no longer alone.

The Bey was very tall, well over six feet, I judged. His face was dark and clean shaven, with keen, black eyes gleaming from beneath heavy eyebrows. His lips were full and suggestive of a sensuous nature, and his jaw was square and sharply chiselled.

He wore a sort of waistcoat, open to reveal his bare chest and belly, which stood out roundly though he did not give the appearance of being corpulent. His loose, embroidered pantaloons were held up by a broad sash, from which hung a dagger, and on his feet he wore pointed brocade slippers.

Hardly more than glancing at me, he sat down on one of the cushions and selected a piece of fruit from a bowl. Farah's instructions in mind, I waited until the Bey was settled, then drew off my outer covering (which I later learned was called a *chadoor*) letting it slide from me to lie in a huddle by my feet. Now, the Bey did look, his eyes

110

moving slowly over me from head to feet and back again, in silent and apparently indifferent appraisal.

When he glanced meaningfully towards the table near him, I hurried over to pour wine, ridiculously nervous of spilling it. Kneeling at his feet as I had been instructed, I bowed my head and offered him the goblet with both hands, holding it actually higher than my head, which is quite awkward. As he drank he clicked his fingers. It was the signal Farah had told me about. I rose and went back to where my *chadoor* lay. The Bey sipped his wine and watched as, one by one, I drew off my veils and dropped them to join the first garment on the floor.

I do not know if I am alone in this, but for me the act of stripping off my clothes for the pleasure of a watching man is very stirring. I thought back to how I had elaborately taken off those dowdy Dutch clothes to tease the secretly watching Hendrick all those months ago, and how excited it had made me.

This undressing, this slow drifting off of countless veils for such an exotic stranger, in such an exotic place, was all the more arousing, and by the time the last veil floated to the floor, my breasts were tingling, my nipples were hard, and my tummy was warm.

Naked save for all my jewellery and the veil across my face, I returned to kneel at the Bey's feet. He reached forward and cupped my breast, lifting it a little as if to weigh it, rolling my nipple with his hard thumb almost speculatively. I was glad my head was bowed, for I was sure my face flushed at the unruly sensations which instantly darted to my loins.

He toyed with my breasts for quite a long while as he sipped at his wine, and I confess that the situation and his hand conspired to make me very tense and hot. Suddenly, the empty goblet was before my face. I hurried to take and refill it, offering it up to him with both hands as before. To my utter astonishment, he thanked me in English.

My head shot up and I stared at him in amazement, and

111

he began to laugh, a deep, rumbling bass laugh which shook his body and echoed from the walls.

'Ah, yes,' he gasped at last, wiping his eyes and panting for breath. 'I speak quite adequate English. I was an attaché in our London embassy for several years.'

I knelt open-mouthed with shock as he continued. He told me that he knew who I was. He apologised for his ungentlemanly ruse in tricking me into his boudoir. I was dumbfounded. For a while I was outraged, beside myself with fury that this man, that *anyone*, could be so arrogant as to play such a cruel trick. Here I was, decked out as a naked harem-girl, only here to save Farah from disgrace, convinced that this man thought me one of his concubines, when all the while he had known exactly who I was.

Seeing the expression on my face, he began to laugh again. There was no mockery or triumph in his laughter, only genuine delight at the success of his ruse. Suddenly, the ridiculousness of it all struck me and I, too, became convulsed with helpless giggles.

Nothing clarifies like laughter, and soon the Bey and I were chatting animatedly. Had I been a 'good girl', such as our society requires and expects, I would have got out of there, got some clothes on, died of shame. I did not. There is in me an imp which seems to seek out naughty situations such as this.

It was, I have to confess, exciting to be kneeling there smiling as we talked of how he had plotted my seduction, and confessing to him my motives in agreeing to come to him had not been entirely to defend Farah, my jewellery clinking whenever I moved, the Bey's eyes and hands moving over me.

He was a skilful seducer, gentle and insidious. After William and Mr Sharpe who, eager though they both were to please me, were quick and clumsy and thought of fondling me only as a preamble to a fuck, it was very heaven to be caressed and coaxed and roused by a knowing lover. My body became an ocean, slow swells of sensation flowing through me. My senses became a harp upon which he played, now sending a low chord throbbing in my womb, now plucking an echoing high note which rippled through my breasts and the soles of my feet.

He played upon every part of me, finding and awakening places I never dreamed could stir me. He kissed my eyes, my neck, my collarbone, the small of my back, the under-curves of my bottom, the soles of my feet, the backs of my knees. His tongue and fingers, fleeting as butterflies, ran from my brow to my toes. His breath wafted over my skin as he kissed and nibbled at my breasts and around and be-tween them.

I was a sea-swell of desire. I longed to feel him inside me, to have my seeping, pulsing sheath beautified by his thrusts. My hands found their way inside his pantaloons, cupped him, caressed him, drew him forth.

That moment when one takes a breath, and licks one's lips, and parts them to greet the hot, silky bulb of a proud cock, is among the loveliest in the whole world. Now, as the Bey leaned back and parted his knees a little, I felt such a wave of contentment as almost made me gasp with gratitude. His scent was of exotic woods, and musk, and blossoms. He reared, coffee coloured against my pale hands. I moved my head forward. Oh, he tasted of heaven!

I kissed him, lapped at him as must a *naiad* have at a woodland stream. I licked and kissed the length of his veined baton, cupping his balls in one hand and circling the base of his shaft with the fingers of the other. The eyelet at the tip of his plum exuded a clear droplet. I licked it with the tip of my tongue, then parted my lips and slowly sank my mouth upon him.

He allowed me to minister to his beautiful cock without moving, not touching me, not holding my head as some men do. Not even moving his loins to push into me. I was in a passion. I wanted to absorb all of him. To drink him dry.

When eventually he reached down with his hands to

raise my head off him I resisted. I wanted more. Longed to suck him to a finish.

He turned me. Lay me down on the rich carpet. Lay with me. His cock was still before my face. I reached for it, sucked at it for my very life. I felt my leg lifted, my thighs parted wide. A warmth, a heat engulfed my quim. With delicate fingers he parted the lips of my cunny. His mouth descended onto my swollen, oh so sensitive folds. His tongue traced the length of my crease once, twice, then again and again. A finger pressed deep into my bottom. His lips found my cherry. He sucked, rasped it with his tongue.

I could not breathe. My swirling mind screamed, 'Now! Please. Do it now! Fuck me now, now, now!' He did not. For a hundred years he kept me on the verge, torturing my helpless body with his teasings as I sucked and caressed his exquisite cock and his knowing mouth drove me mad.

Suns exploded in my belly and behind my eyes. I was one overmastering convulsion of ecstatic pulsings as my legs clamped themselves about his head, my breasts felt like to burst, and I churned into such a come as made me want to die right then and there. I am sure I almost bit him in my ecstasy.

When, after a lifetime, my eyes swam open, his face was above me, his deep eyes alive with pleasure. He scooped me up in his powerful arms and carried me to the divan. I pressed my face to his chest, kissed him, as he lowered me onto the thick, soft cushions. I was his slave. He could do with me whatever he willed. I wanted him, ached for him to possess me, to make me his victim.

He looked down at me as I lay there, helpless and yearning to be used. His eyes were calm, confident. It was I who was used to being the confident one, to being the one who drove my lovers on. Now the roles were reversed. I gazed up at him, every nerve in my throbbing body yearning for him to fall upon me, to fill me, to cram into my helplessly throbbing quim. Slowly, as slowly as I had teased William, and Sharpe, and Hendrick and any number of others, he pulled off his waistcoat, untied his sash, stepped out of his pantaloons.

He was in his fifties at least, and his torso was no longer young and lithe. I did not care. All I saw was his beautiful cock, bouncing a little as it stood proud from the black mat of curls at his loins. I knew he was going to fuck me now. I rejoiced in the knowledge. Held out my arms to him. Spread my thighs even further, raised my knees. He came to me, leaned gently down, his hands on either side of my torso. He paused. I reached down, held him, guided him. He entered me with a slow, awesome, overpowering thrust such as minstrels should be compelled to sing of.

I was lost. All that existed in the universe was the wonderful organ probing to my heart, and the throbbing in my breast, and the swirling of my sheath about the glory that filled me, moved in me, declared rights of possession over me. The come his tongue had started in me burst out anew. Never since Talesi first opened me, or Motallo drove me to raptures with his mouth, had I been so undone.

The Bey did not have a come, or if he did his recovery was instantaneous, for my swirling memory of that night and morning is of his hands and mouth and steely member, and being touched and turned, and filled in my cunny and my mouth and my bottom, and of the exhaustion of constant comes wracking my deliciously tormented body again and again and again until I was like to faint from bliss.

The one clear remembrance came with the dawn, when he awakened me and, smiling, told me that he might well call on my services again. It was as though my mind became imprinted with the vision of him smiling down at me, his dark eyes both tender and triumphant as he turned and walked calmly out of the chamber.

When Farah and Samara came for me, and covered me from crown to toe with a thick *chadoor* lest any male eye fall on me, and led me back to the seraglio, I was dazed. This was the first man to have reduced me so far, to have made me beg. And, I confess, to have made me long for him to 'call upon my services' again. Not Talesi, my guide into the world of physical delight, nor Motallo with his wonderful tongue, nor any of my other lovers had so conquered me.

Eight

Farah herself bathed and cosseted me, her eyes soft and aglow with approval. Later, when I awoke from the deepest of slumbers, she was still with me, sitting on a cushion beside my divan. She smiled and kissed me. Through Samara, she told me that her husband was well pleased with me, and that therefore so was the whole establishment. With a gesture, she indicated a bowl on the floor nearby her. In it lay the bangles and chains and jewels I had worn. They were mine, a gift from his Excellency to the beautiful English lady, offered together with a request.

In ten days time the Bey, Farah's lord, was to be visited by his own lord, a prince from the palace in Istanbul, come on his yearly inspection. A banquet was to be given in his honour. The Bey would be honoured if I would attend, together with others of his concubines, and in the guise of one myself. Without hesitation I agreed. After such a night as he had given me I would have crawled over desert sands to be with him again. Farah clapped her hands and hugged me, the suspicion of a joyful tear in her eye.

When Farah left, all a-bustle with things to do, Tiliu came to me, her cat-like eyes alight with eagerness to hear what had befallen me. Those eyes grew huge with wonder and joy when, unable to find words, I could only gaze up at her and slowly shake my head. She threw her arms about me and hugged me, fairly bouncing with delight.

Then, as only my Tiliu could, she brought us both back to *terra firma* by grasping my shoulders and holding me away from her, putting on a stern, schoolmistress face, and saying 'Now this will not spoil you for other men, will it?'

in a voice of doom. Even as I was swamped with helpless giggles, tears of laughter streaming down my cheeks, I felt a pang of dread that it might.

Felicity, too, lent me perspective. The other women of the harem almost fawned upon me, bringing me sweets and goblets of cool sherbet, brushing my hair, plumping my cushions. Felicity, though, would not look at me. I was not worried. I knew her nature. She might well pretend contempt for me, indeed I heard her whisper the word 'harlot' as I passed her once on Farah's arm, but I knew that her pique was really born of jealousy. Ever since we met she had regarded me as a rival – a thing that amazed me for she was so much more beautiful than I could ever hope to be. But there was something in her nature, some carping thing which made her small, gave her a meanness.

I knew from her many surrenders that her nature was like mine, that she thrived on the attentions of men. I knew too, though, that unlike me she lacked the honesty to admit it, even to herself. Somehow, even though she did not have our language, Farah also knew – or at least knew there was some pique between us. Through Samara, she raised the subject during one of my dancing lessons (I was to dance at the prince's banquet).

She did it through questions to which I only had to give a yes or a no. I was surprised and impressed by her wisdom and perceptiveness. Yes, Felicity was beautiful. Yes, she did have experience of men. No, she would never admit to enjoying the pleasures of the flesh. Yes, I was sure her pretended disapproval was more envy than anything else. No, she would never agree to go to the Bey – unless compelled, when she would wiltingly 'submit'.

Farah nodded, taking in my monosyllabic responses and storing them away, her face expressionless. Three evenings later, Samara came to me, her manner all suppressed excitement. Taking me by the hand, she almost dragged me to a little side room that gave onto the bathroom. Gesturing me to silence, she motioned me to join her in peeping through the portal.

At first there was nothing. Then came a sudden noise as of scolding. Farah entered, her face fierce, her arms waving, her voice harsh. Behind her, half dragged by two of the women, came Felicity, her face a mask of protest. The women bundled her into the room, began to tear off her clothes. I made to rush to her rescue, but Samara held me back, whispering for me to wait, to watch. I did watch, and suddenly I understood.

Felicity's protests, her pushing away of the women's hands, her clasping at the clothes they were pulling off her, were just the same as her repelling of Jonathan that night we had arranged for him to seduce her. This was just the same resistance she put up whenever demands were placed upon her – the kind of resistance which expects, perhaps even hopes, to be surmounted, the kind of protest which begs to be swept aside.

The more of her clothes that came off, the weaker became her protests. By the time she was naked and being pulled towards the hot tubs, she was a drooping victim.

I could not see from where we were the bathing and showering, and I took the chance to question Samara. All she would tell me, through barely suppressed glee, was that Felicity had been told the Chamberlain, the most important man in the province, required her. Then I understood Felicity's half-hearted resistance, and any qualms for her dissolved. Though part of her would be incensed that a strange man should summon her, a stronger part would be flattered that it was an important man – and that part would win.

Samara was as struck as I when Felicity was led out from the waterfall-cum-shower, gripping my hand in awe of her womanly glory. If only I could have been blessed with such fairness of complexion, such a beautiful mane of waving copper hair, such smooth ripeness of body.

She was beauty itself as the women sat her on a bench, combed her hair, painted her face, lay her back and combed and trimmed her bush and rouged her nipples. She was no longer resisting. No protest passed her lips as she was moved, and trimmed, and perfumed, and made to stand to be dressed.

She was not decked with the same jewellery as I had been. Indeed, the bracelets and anklets which were put upon her seemed quite plain in comparison, as did the collar placed about her pale throat, and the looped belt fixed about her narrow waist. Even so, as Farah tied the veil over her face, her beauty was such as to take the breath away, and the eyes which looked up at Farah were so deep, so submissive, that one could have drowned in them.

For a moment all her attendants stepped back, and Felicity was isolated, a breathing statue, glorious in her womanly beauty. That small, cruel part of me I have never been able to entirely suppress noticed that Felicity's nipples were standing hard and uptilted, and she was breathing quick and shallow. By the time she reached the Chamberlain, I thought, she will have already melted.

She did not reach the Chamberlain. Such was Farah's deviousness that Felicity, all unknowing, went to a far different tryst. The moment Felicity was led out of the bathroom, a vision of misty veils, Samara grabbed my wrist and rushed me pell-mell through a maze of doors and passages, finally stopping me, breathless, in an unlit corridor, facing an intricately carved lattice through which light gleamed in myriad shafts. I peeped through the lattice. The room was not the one to which I had been taken, but simpler, though still very obviously dominated by a large divan.

Cushions were scattered about, and a large table stood to one side. An iron stove glowed heat from a corner, a huge coffee pot simmering atop it. The door swung open, and Felicity entered. She stood motionless inside the portal, just as I had done when sent to the Bey. There was a wait of some minutes and then, from behind a curtain which obviously concealed another doorway, stepped a man. A little, round man, wearing what looked like a vast

120

nightshirt, with an enormous black moustache sprouting from his upper lip.

I looked to Samara, astonished. She whispered elucidation in my ear. The man was a gardener – and not even the head gardener, but one of the underlings. Later, I learned that he was a poor man without a wife, who had done Farah some service. Her deliciously wicked scheme was to reward him, while at the same time bringing Felicity down a peg or two.

When Felicity pulled off her *chadoor* and stood before the man, her remaining veils only emphasising the glory of her nakedness, I held my breath. What service had the little man performed to deserve such a wonderful reward. A breath by my ear made me turn my head. Farah had joined us, and was nodding and smiling comfortably at the scene. I turned my eyes back to the lattice.

The gardener was obviously prepared for the sight of a woman, but not such a one as stood before him now. It took him a minute or two of staring before he could gather himself. Then, with exaggerated dignity, he sat on the edge of the divan and clapped his hands. Just as I had done when with the Bey, Felicity hurried to serve him by pouring steaming coffee from the huge pot, her eyes downcast as mine had been. As she knelt and proffered the cup with both hands, even I could not contain the thrill of the sight she made, so lovely, so ripe, so submissive to the ritual she had embarked on.

There was little preamble. As the gardener sipped his coffee, he gestured. Felicity rose from her knees and returned to where her *chadoor* lay on the floor. It occurred to me that by thus moving a little off from the man she (and thus myself when I had performed this ceremony) was in fact giving him a clearer view as she stripped herself.

Slowly, her head still bowed, she pulled off her remaining veils, letting them drift one by one to the floor about her feet. At last she stood motionless, her voluptuous breasts trembling, her ribs betraying her panting breathlessness, as he regarded her.

The chains and jewels which were all she now had on set off the paleness of her perfect skin with their metallic gleam. The burnished glint of her hair, which had been left loose; the veil covering all her face save her lustrous eyes; the long curves of her white thighs; the redness of her rouged nipples; all conspired to present an image of glorious womanhood. So glorious, indeed, that I wondered the little round gardener did not throw himself upon her.

Instead, the gardener took his time sipping the scalding coffee, his eyes all the while moving over every inch of Felicity's waiting body. After what must have seemed to Felicity an eternity of tension, the little man put down his cup and beckoned. I could almost feel Felicity's nervousness as she approached the seated man.

He reached out, and slid his hand slowly up between her thighs, from her knee to her neatly trimmed bush. She trembled and her breathing quickened. Even entranced as I was by this mouth-watering tableau, part of my mind was still curious to have my judgement of Felicity's true nature confirmed. That confirmation came as her knees almost imperceptibly parted to allow his hand to delve.

A flush spread over her chest, and her nipples stiffened. Ah, yes! Her wanton nature was stirring within her. The man gestured her to her knees. He stood, unbuttoned his nightshirt, and pulled it off over his head. He was naked underneath, and the sight of his roly-poly body so close to Felicity's glorious figure gave the scene a bizarre comedy, though the gnarled member which stood out below his round belly was far from comical.

He sat down again, his plump buttocks spreading on the upholstery. He made another gesture with his hand, leaned back, supporting himself on straight arms, and parted his knees. For a moment, Felicity glanced up at him as though in doubt (though the meaning of the gesture could not have been more obvious) then she reached forward, took him in her hands, bent her head, opened her mouth.

I could no longer watch. I was almost in a come from the sight of that beautiful mouth moving towards his rampant manhood, those delicate hands cupping and stroking him. I clung to Samara, my face buried in her soft bosom, her hand smoothing my hair.

When I gathered the strength to look again, the gardener was lying on his back across the divan. Felicity was kneeling astride him. Like some ineffable expression of heavenly lust, she moved on him with a deep and speeding rhythm. Her knees were clamped against his sides. The white moons of her buttocks writhed and flexed against his darker thighs. Rocking, circling, writhing, she rode him like some wild horse, her head back, her body in an arc of passion, her breasts rolling in his hands as she ground her loins against his, and shuddered into a very obvious come.

I was so stirred up myself I could only droop on Samara's shoulder. She knew the state I was in, and put her arms about me and kissed me, and kept kissing me as she helped me back to the women's quarters, and took me into her bed.

The next morning, when she emerged from the bath (what a change a night of passion makes, for she had never allowed herself the indignity of a 'public' bath before) Felicity was coyness itself, all shy twitterings and sighs, inviting questions she naturally refused to answer; all hinted satisfaction. All she would say was that she had been sent for by the Chamberlain; that he had hardly given her a moment of peace all night, and had commanded her to return again this evening.

I could have burst with suppressed glee. Oh my proud Felicity, so prudish in her professions of morality, yet now so blithe at having been thoroughly fucked, smug at being required to return for more – and all because her 'Chamberlain' was such an important man. If only she knew. And the joke grew and grew, for she went to 'the Chamberlain' night after night, and even boasted that he was besotted

123

with her, could not leave her alone, nor keep his hands off her. Oh, lucky gardener! Oh, silly, self-deceiving Felicity!

Nobody dreamed of telling her the truth, of course. That would have been too cruel, would have destroyed her fragile self-confidence. And besides, it was a constant delight to watch her queening it as 'the Chamberlain's favourite', knowing all the while she was striving to give the best shaggings she could to an under-gardener. Why, she even wondered aloud whether 'the Chamberlain' would be able to let her go when our ship was repaired, he was so in thrall to her beauty.

As for the Bey, when I managed to describe to Tiliu the night I had spent with him, she was agog with excitement and delight. She told me that she, too, wanted to experience such a lover, and for days she spent almost her whole time in the bathhouse, wandering about or lying naked in languid poses, hoping the Bey would see her and select her for his bed.

She had been desolate when she heard that Felicity had been 'chosen', and as relieved as she was tickled when she learned the truth. Why she was not selected for the Bey's bed even before me was a mystery, for she is the loveliest of girls. As if her full-lipped, mischievous-eyed face, pert, uptilted breasts, and curvaceous thighs and bottom were not enough to entrance the eye of any man peeping through the bathhouse lattices, the erect grace with which she moved could not fail to catch the eye. Even to see Tiliu walk, with the smoothness and suggested strength of a cat was to see what the essence of woman is.

After nearly a week, I decided to take the bull by the horns. I was on excellent terms with Farah, as much for my agreeing to dance at the Prince's banquet as for anything else, though my dancing lessons were a trial to me, for the steps and movements were strict and demanding.

At the end of one such lesson, I knelt at Farah's feet (I had got the habit from Samara, who always knelt before the Bey's senior wife, and somehow it seemed appropriate) and put my thoughts to her. Samara's eyes grew round as she translated for me. Obviously, such an idea was unheard of. Only an outsider, ignorant of proper protocol could have dreamed of it. To suggest that Tiliu be sent in the place of the woman actually chosen was outlandish.

Farah, though, was not so shocked. Though I was asking her to take something of a risk, she thought it possible. She ruminated, then nodded decisively. Yes, it would be done, and this very night. When I rushed off to tell Tiliu the news, she squealed and danced up and down and hugged me in her joy. Later, I did get some rather angry glances from the woman Tiliu replaced, but that did not signify compared to my Tiliu's happiness.

I was allowed to assist in her preparation, and I confess that when she was standing decked out with gold chains and bangles as I had been, she looked so ravishingly lovely I could hardly keep from kissing her myself. And the perfume that surrounded her, emanating from the oil that had been touched between her plump folds with the glass rod, was so soft and alluring I longed to bury my face in her and die from rapture. She kissed me a tender 'thank you' kiss just before her *chadoor* was draped about her, and my heart melted as Farah led her away.

I went to my chamber, but could not relax. Visions of my sweet Tiliu standing inside that draped portal, of the veils drifting from her body, of the Bey toying with her as he had with me, filled my mind with both joy that my friend was experiencing the raptures I had enjoyed, and delicious torment that I was not experiencing them again myself. I was hot and trembling. I walked rapidly around the garden-cloister, hoping physical activity would quiet my unruly condition.

I went at last to my sleeping chamber, determined to control myself and sleep. I had been there for half an hour, perhaps a little more, my lamp extinguished, trying to resist the temptation to touch myself, when a body slipped onto the divan beside me, drawing the soft covers up around us both. It was Samara. She whispered that Farah had sent her, and kissed me, and wrapped me in her soft arms.

Samara was the dearest of girls. Through her serving as translator, we had become close. Now, as she sought to comfort me, we grew closer. Her caresses were petals on my skin, her kisses soft and lingering. She would not allow me to caress her in my turn, but made me lie, moving my limbs to suit her purposes, loving me with gentle ardour. I drifted off on a rosy dream of sensation, forgetting Tiliu altogether as Samara delved in me.

When morning came, and Tiliu returned, there was a glow in her face, a liquid quality in her movements, a softness in her eyes, such as told me without words that her night with the Bey had been as moving as my own. She did not speak, simply stopped a moment in my doorway, half leaning against it in naked glory and, as I lay in Samara's arms, smiled down at me with a softness that bespoke more than any words could.

Later, at breakfast, Felicity looked at Tiliu quite sharply, guessing from her languid manner that she had not spent the night alone in our women's quarters. It was a little awkward, for Felicity had just come from another night of love with her 'Chamberlain'. When I had returned from my night with the Bey, I had not been able to wait to tell how glorious it had been. I hurried to forestall anything Tiliu might say, lest she upset Felicity unnecessarily.

I feigned unconcern at Felicity's pointed questions; told her that Tiliu had been with me, that we had lain together before, and would likely do so again. Felicity was shocked, stared at me open mouthed, leapt up from her cushion and rushed away.

'Ah, well,' I thought. 'Better for her to think ill of me than to learn the truth about her nights with the gardener.'

During our morning stroll with Sharpe and Donaldson, Felicity was all twitchings and sidelong glances. She did not chatter lightly and emptily, as she usually did. She was all sharp nerve-ends and wringing fingers. When Donaldson, as usual, found an excuse to get her alone she looked, for the first time, less than compliant, and when they returned she did not behave in that soft, simpering manner she usually adopted after he had shagged her.

I did my best to ignore her. So what if she became upset at the idea of two women pleasuring one another! So what if she was shocked! I was used to Felicity's hypocritical ways, and knew that she would soon get over it. How wrong I was in my judgement of the reasons for her tense behaviour became clear that afternoon.

She found me as I lay upon a divan in the bathhouse, relaxed from my bath and the massage Samara had given me, drinking coffee. Felicity was still fully dressed from our morning walk, and looked odd in this room of women in various stages of nakedness. I could almost feel the tension emanating from her as she stood beside the divan, picking at a fingernail, and avoiding my eyes. I moved a little to make room, and she sat down jerkily.

I girded myself. I was sure that she was about to burst into some kind of tirade, to lecture me on my lack of moral fibre, to launch into one of those mealy-mouthed diatribes about licentious behaviour beloved of acolytes of the two-faced moralists so common in our society.

She sat like a watch spring, trembling with whatever she was suppressing. I waited. She fiddled with a button, shifted her feet, took sudden breaths as though about to speak. Still I waited. If she was going to berate me, I was certainly not going to help her. At last, her head jerked around and she looked at me, but the expression on her face was far from the disapproval I had expected.

Instead, her eyes were huge and moist, her expression was of hurt rather than anger. I was disarmed. What on earth could be the matter? Several times her features contorted as though she were struggling to speak. I sat up, swinging my legs around so that I was beside her. She looked down at her hands, dragged in a breath.

'Why do you not like me?' she said in a voice so small

and choked I could hardly catch it. I was undone, incapable of even registering such a question. 'I know you do not like me,' she hurried on, her voice a little stronger. 'Nobody likes me. It is so unfair! I try, honestly I try, but I seem to get it wrong, and you do not like me, and I am so unhappy.'

I was confounded. Here I was, all ready to fend off some prissy lecture, and instead was faced with a hurt child. I *did* like Felicity. Oh, it is true there were irritating aspects to her, lots of them, but I had developed a fondness for her despite all her silly pretences.

For the first time, we talked as sisters might talk, and I was moved by the deep unhappiness she betrayed. She was pining for home and her parents. She did not know the uncle to whom she was being sent in England. She was afraid of Donaldson, and even of her 'Chamberlain', and only 'let them' so they would be kind to her. She had thought me her friend, and now . . .

Ah! Here we came to the nub. That she could still maintain that she only 'let' the men who shagged her betrayed that she still denied to herself her own sensuality, still convinced herself that she was only the poor victim of men who 'got carried away'. The vision of her kneeling between Jonathan's knees, sucking him avidly, that night he had deflowered her flashed across my mind. I had seen her with Donaldson, draped up against the corridor wall; with the gardener, arching her back in ecstasy as she writhed her loins upon him. How could she still think she 'let them'?

My reflections were interrupted, and it took a moment for me to register. Had she really said that?

'Can't you like me as you do Tiliu?'

She repeated the words. Did I understand aright? I glanced sideways at her. She was sat very still, her hands pressed together in her lap, a slight flush on her cheeks.

'May I be honest with you, Felicity?' I asked, touching her hand so she need not be afraid. 'I do like you. You are sweet and beautiful, and I do like you. At least, I like you when you are not pretending.'

'Pretending?' She cast a startled look at me.

'Come now, Felicity,' I put my arm about her shoulder. 'We know one another too well to prevaricate. I know you as a warm and loving woman, yet you hold yourself back. You delight in what delights me, yet you deny it. Here, at this very moment, you are denying it.'

She stiffened and stared at me, trying to find words to protest.

'Sshh,' I smiled. 'Look about you. We are in this lovely place, among only women, out of the sight of the world, yet here you sit, trussed up in frock and boots and corset, for all the world as though your clothing were all there is of you.' I took her hands and looked into her nervous eyes. 'Why cannot you relax? Why can you not lower your defences and be like other women? Can you not see that if only you did not hold yourself off so, people would welcome you with open arms?'

She was staring at me, doubt and bemusement in her eyes. I reached up and stroked her cheek.

'Especially someone as beautiful as you,' I added. 'Why do you not have a nice bath, and we can talk together.'

I had supposed she would leave me then, go off to the privacy she usually sought for her ablutions, and thus give me time to consider her unexpected outpouring. Instead, after a moment, she began slowly to unbutton her frock.

I was puzzled, and then a little embarrassed. I knew Felicity, despite the easiness with which she surrendered to any dominant man, as a rather prim young woman. A woman rather over-concerned to be seen to observe the proprieties. How often had she betrayed disapproval of what she regarded as my looseness? Yet now, she was undressing in front of me. More than that, there was in her air something which suggested she was undressing *for* me.

She stood, and shucked the frock from her shoulders, letting it fall to the floor. She pulled her chemise over her head. As she bent to tug down her drawers, she suddenly turned her face towards me.

'You will like me, won't you?' she whispered.

The strange, soft yet intense expression on her face quite undid me. What on earth could be happening? I could not reply; could only stare as she turned towards me, clad now in only her corset and stockings. She began to undo the tight lacing down the back of her corset, her face a little flushed, and her eyes shy. As she pulled off the boned and beribboned undergarment and dropped it onto the pile of her other clothes, the astounding realisation swept over me.

She *was* undressing for me. Standing there now, the splendour of her figure heightened by the black of her stockings, and by the few little marks on her breasts and hips bespeaking her nights of passion with the gardener and the tightness of her corset, she was doing nothing so much as to present herself to me. I was frozen. Was this really Felicity?

In an absolute reversal of our habitual ways of behaving, it was she who put her arm about me and rested her head on my shoulder, me who looked nervously about to see if anyone was watching. I was actually breathless with nerves at her sudden show of affection. I made flustered and, I am sure, clumsy excuses, and jumped up from the divan. The crushed expression which swept over her features gave me a pang of remorse. I patted her cheek.

'Go for your bath, my dear,' I heard myself saying. 'I will see you later.'

I did not mean to see her later. Wanted, in fact, only to hide myself away until the shock of the change in her had calmed, and I was able to think. You may well judge it peculiar of me to get into such a state. I have never shied away from any aspect of love before, whether it be with a man or another woman. Indeed, since being introduced to the delights of bodily pleasures by Talesi and his fellows among the Tukanna I have actively sought that rapture which physical closeness brings with it. Yet Felicity's sudden softness had entirely undone me. I was in no less mixed a state when she suddenly appeared in my sleeping chamber.

She had brushed her hair into a burnished cloud about her shoulders. She had put on the veils of the harem, rather than her European clothing. As she stood in the doorway, her eyes downcast, her fingers locking and unlocking at her waist, she took my breath away she was so lovely. The light from behind her turned her hair into a glowing halo of deep copper, and turned her veils into a white mist about her luscious body. As she moved hesitantly towards me the light silhouetted her long, enviably shapely legs, the roundness of her hips, her narrow waist.

By the time she stood above me, her eyes enormous with doubt and hope, her full breasts trembling from her quickened breathing, any decision had been taken away from me. Nothing existed save this vision of loveliness, and the hand which reached out to touch my cheek.

We lay together on my divan in silence. Words would have been an encumbrance now as her breath drifted over the curve of my neck, as her lips whispered across my skin like a flock of butterflies, as her breasts filled my hands. At times such as this the world becomes a dream, a trance of sensation, in which all is easy, in which one moves without effort, swims in scents and tastes and touches so pervasive, so consuming that the mind spins away.

My hands and mouth moved upon her, stunned and hypnotised by her lambent beauty, drawn on by her gentle responses, by the way her nipples hardened under my kisses, by the way she sighed and opened to me as my hand caressed between her thighs. Everything was warmth, softness, welcome.

Somehow, her mouth was at my centre, her hair trailing like a living shawl across my inner thighs. Her tongue delved, and I sighed as she moved between my parting legs, melting me with her breath and the insidious caresses of her tongue along my cunny-folds and around my straining cherry.

My eyes drifted open. Her thighs were close before my face. I buried my face in her. Her thighs parted to welcome me, the fabulous tulip of her womanhood opening in surrender to my mouth. Ah, the warmth, the softness of those delicate cunny-lips, the honey which welcomed my questing tongue. My arms went around her, my fingers digging themselves into the firm curves of her buttocks, as I buried my face into her ambrosiac depths.

Felicity's tongue lapped at my quim, and wave after swelling wave of rapture rolled from my writhing loins, to crash against my nerve-ends, and reverberate again and again until I was no more than spasm after sobbing spasm of joy, drinking her in, pressing against her mouth, desperate to consume every last part of her, and be consumed in my turn.

We lay together, deep in each other's arms, for a hundred years after that first overwhelming embrace. I was lost, adrift in cloud. Only slowly did my mind swim towards reality. Here in my arms, her eyes closed, on her delicately beautiful features an expression of ineffable peace, lay Felicity. Once the petty-minded, hypocritical Felicity who had so often irritated me, but now no longer petty, no longer hypocritical. I felt at that moment a swell of gentleness towards her. I could not resist placing a tender kiss upon her lovely brow.

Her eyes fluttered open. She looked up at me shyly, stirred a little, kissed my shoulder.

'Is it all right?' she whispered. 'You still like me, don't you?'

I could only hug her to me, in my heart a pang at her loveliness, and at how vulnerable her nature made her.

132

Nine

The Felicity who revealed herself to us after that afternoon
on my divan was a staggering transformation from the
woman I had known before. For the first time, she allowed
a warm, almost bubbling, side of her character to emerge.
No longer did she automatically feign disapproval of anything not allowed for by the conventions of her upbringing.
No longer was she reserved with Tiliu, nor did she treat her
as 'only a servant'. She turned out to have a sense of humour, now that she had lowered her guard of propriety
enough to let herself go in laughter.

She abandoned her prissy clinging to European clothes
and, except when we went on our morning walks with our
ship's officers of course, wore harem clothes with an ease
that was a revelation. She spent as much time as Tiliu and
I in the bathhouse, unembarrassed by her nakedness, or by
the attention that was paid to her by the Bey's concubines.
If they were interested in me, which in truth they had not
entirely ceased to be as an exotic European guest among
them, they positively drooled over Felicity, for she was
softness and sensuality personified.

So long as I approved, for she hung about me and constantly sought my reassurances, she seemed happy to accept
things she would have formerly shied away from as awful. She
let herself be massaged by the other women; let herself, after a
glance to ensure that I was content, be led off to little side
rooms with divans in them; surrendered, to be brief, to whatever sensations were offered her. And she told me everything,
poured out to me descriptions of every detail, as though she
was compelled to seek my approbation for everything she did.

This change in her was double-edged. It was a joy to have Felicity so open now, so fond, so softly willing. At the same time, it soon became a burden, for she focused everything upon me. It was as though, in describing to me in such detail exactly what 'the Chamberlain' had done last night, or what some woman who had taken her off after her bath had wanted, she was in reality seeking my consent.

I was torn. This new Felicity was a much more likeable person than the old one. And when, as often now, she sought me out in my chamber, and came to me, and made gentle love with me, it was wonderful beyond description. In truth, she was in looks and in nature a goddess of passion, and I could not get enough of her. Yet at the same time this dependency, this revelling in her body only when I permitted, was a proof, if one were needed, that the change in her was only partial.

It seemed to me that this seeking of my consent for her actions was merely a different face of her earlier self-deceptions. Instead of she herself 'having to let them', she had surrendered herself to me and it was *I* who now let them.

The way she had surrendered to Jonathan, that night we plotted her seduction, was not in essence different from the way she surrendered to me now. The way she submitted to Donaldson, when he got her aside and pushed her up against a wall and shagged her, was the same as the way she now went off with some woman or other, only to return and describe to me, unasked, what had transpired.

She was a puzzle. I cannot say that my reflections were unselfish, for when she came to my bed there was rapture. Her loveliness, her desire to please me, her instinctive understanding of how to drive me to madness, the taste and touch of her, all conspired to make me selfish. But when, was it the third, perhaps the fourth, time we made love on my divan, she raised her head from between my thighs, and kissed my mound, and whispered 'I love you. I love you,' a dart of nerves entered my heart.

* * *

This was the obverse side of the new Felicity. It was as though she were besotted with me, wished to be with me every moment; as though I were the entire focus of her being. It was very flattering, but also somewhat irksome – not least because of her strange, blinkered possessiveness. She would hurry back from her nights with her 'Chamberlain', and tell me every detail of what they had done together. She would blushingly confess to me how this or that woman in the bathhouse had taken her aside and enjoyed her. She even gave me graphic accounts of the times Donaldson took her aside from our morning walks, and shagged her up against a tree or a wall or in the dust behind a wagon. Yet if she saw me so much as hold Tiliu's hand, or throw my arm around Samara's shoulder in friendly laughter, she came over in a pet of sulkiness.

She drove me to distraction. I had to find a way through this dilemma, find some means, without hurting her fragile new personality, of showing her that it was not *me* but her own senses that were the source of her pleasures, of opening her, as it were, to the real joys of the body, without the emotional trappings she dragged into the equation.

I made her admit that Donaldson and her 'Chamberlain' gave her comes, tried to get her to agree that she delighted in feeling their cocks inside her. But she would only blush, and say she 'couldn't help it' and that she could not stop them when they 'got carried away'. I made her confess that she liked being taken aside by the other women of the harem – she did so, but only with a coy glance and a whispered hope that I did not mind. How could I make the silly girl realise that not only did I not mind, I was anxious to encourage her.

The impasse was broken by the wisdom of Farah. What a deep and perceptive woman she was! Farah did not tell me of her plan, but simply let it unfold. The first I noticed of it was that Felicity was no longer by my side from before breakfast until we left for our morning walk dressed as Europeans. Then one morning she was not with us for our walk. Neither Tiliu nor I could fathom her absence, and Samara professed ignorance. I was for going back for her, but Samara said she would look after things, and anyway our officers were waiting, and so we went without her.

On our return there was still no Felicity. The first glimpse I got of her was when I emerged from the hot tub room on my way to the waterfall-cum-shower. She was coming out of one of the little side chambers, drifting languidly on the arm of a tall Nubian woman, whom I learned was the Bey's third wife, her head resting on her companion's shoulder, and a soft glow on her features. To any observer it would have been instantly clear that Felicity had just come from some very moving experience.

I was surprised a while later, as I lay on a divan after my bath and massage, to see Felicity emerge from another side chamber on the arm of another woman, and looking even more languid and unstrung. And when, almost before she had time to register my presence and give a weak wave in my direction, Felicity was approached by yet a third woman, who took a good grip on her arm and obliged her to go off towards the hot tub room, I became positively curious.

Farah's plan was so simple. Seeing into Felicity's real nature, she had arranged that whenever Felicity was not with her 'Chamberlain' (for she still went to him nearly every night), one, and sometimes more, of the women would demand her services. When one woman was finished with Felicity another would come for her, and so on, in a round of constant, unremitting stimulation. Farah saw that Felicity always responded to being commanded, and chose this way to draw her beyond her equivocations.

By exhausting her with sensation, forcing her, as it were, to own that it did not matter *who* made love with her, or even how, she would show Felicity that it was herself, her own body, that was the key. By learning that, Felicity would learn to know herself, and live honestly and comfortably with the woman she was.

Having heard from Farah's, or rather Samara's, lips

what was afoot, I became enthralled. There were, of course, moments when Felicity and I met, briefly and in passing, for she was always on the arm of one woman or another. In those moments, the eyes Felicity turned up to me were meltingly deep. Her gaze would meet mine, she would look down, then glance again as she was taken past me, her expression a confusion of beckoning and asking and (I have to say it) fulfilment.

Some change in Felicity was apparent on only the second day. As she was led towards the hot tub room by the same tall Nubian woman she had been with yesterday, whose name I learned was Solfina, and who was indeed the Bey's third wife, she protested, though quietly. But the timid glances she cast up at her were as warm as they were submissive. By the next afternoon the change was quite dramatic. Now, Felicity was melting in Solfina's arms, her own arm around her companion's waist, her eyes soft and enormous. I followed them, as though drawn on an invisible string.

Solfina was a splendid figure, tall and broad in the shoulder, with clipped hair, a long, graceful neck, and full, proud breasts. She towered over Felicity, the gleaming ebony of her body only emphasising Felicity's paleness. As I looked around the edge of the doorway, she scooped Felicity up in her arms as though she were a doll, and lowered her into the steaming tub.

Felicity gasped a long sigh, and her head fell against Solfina's arm as the hotness engulfed her. Her eyes were closed and on her face was an expression of such soft surrender as the woman began to wash her that my heart gave a tiny lurch. She did not resist, sitting forward so that her back could be washed, lying back again to allow her breasts and tummy to be sponged.

She lay her head against Solfina's shoulder as she was lifted out of the bath and carried into the waterfall room. The shock of that icy shower would revive a fossil, and Felicity jerked alive at its touch. With a squeal she threw her

137

arms about her companion. Gasping and puffing, she buried her face in Solfina's neck. Solfina set Felicity down on her feet, standing behind her, and ran her hands down over her flanks and up again to heft her breasts.

Felicity shook her head as though to clear it. She placed her own hands over Solfina's, and turned her head, glancing softly back. Solfina turned her around, hugged her, pressed a kiss to her lips, raised a muscular thigh between Felicity's slack knees. Felicity's arms were about Solfina as she returned the kiss.

As the magnificent Nubian woman once again scooped Felicity up into her powerful arms, the muscles of her thighs and buttocks flexing as she walked, I heard Felicity whisper – so faintly it might have been my imagination – 'No. Please don't. Not again. Not so soon.'

Solfina did not wait even to dry Felicity or herself. She carried her to a side room. I hurried to follow. There in the room, as I gazed in fascination, half-hypnotised, Solfina set Felicity on her feet. It was strange, because Felicity stood for all the world like a schoolgirl awaiting instruction, her eyes downcast, her hands fiddling together at her waist, the great toe of her left foot twisting upon that of her right. Had she not been stark naked and wet from the bath, one could have imagined her to be awaiting instruction from a stern schoolmistress.

Solfina stood before Felicity, almost a head taller, her back straight, her feet planted a little apart. She said something in what I supposed was her native language, and clapped her hands. Both the tone in which she spoke and the attitude in which she stood bespoke command. Command which, to my astonishment, Felicity instantly began to obey.

Clearly they had done this before, for at once Felicity moved very close to Solfina. To my amazement, she reached up with both hands, bent her head, and began to dry Solfina's glistening wet body with her hair. It was like a scene out of some voluptuous fantasy.

Solfina stood motionless, her ebony skin tight over her muscled back and thighs, her full breasts high and firm, as Felicity rubbed handfuls of her glorious copper mane across Solfina's shoulders and arms. Necessarily, her face was very close to Solfina's body as she worked – and work she truly did. I watched spellbound, as Felicity attended to every inch of Solfina's glossy skin, her hair a towel, her nose and lips never more than an inch or two away from that powerful body, her own body arching and straining as she worked.

I held my breath as Felicity moved down from Solfina's shoulders and arms towards her breasts. With her face close between the two voluptuous mounds, she rubbed over and around both breasts at the same time with great handfuls of her locks. I was acutely aware that Solfina's nipples had hardened with arousal, because so had mine.

Felicity moved further down, her copper tresses wiping over Solfina's firm stomach, on her face an expression of such concentration she reminded me of a painting I once saw of a maidservant desperately polishing her master's riding-boots while he tapped his crop against his palm, obviously impatient to be off to the hunt.

Indeed, by the time Felicity had completed her task, the image was not so much of servant as of slave, for in drying Solfina's feet, Felicity had come to a kneeling position, her face close to the floor, and resembled nothing so much as a slave begging for something.

She was kneeling low, her hair now a mess, her breasts crushed against her knees, her round bottom towards me, as she gave a few final rubs at Solfina's toes with her hair. And then, as if to confirm that 'slave and mistress' impression which had begun to grow in my mind, Solfina raised a foot and tapped it upon the back of Felicity's lowered head.

At once, Felicity knelt up. She did not rise, but knelt straight-backed, gazing up at Solfina as though waiting. I can only describe the expression on her face as that of a person nervously hopeful.

* * *

139

It became more nervous than hopeful when Solfina strode across to a small chest near the wall, rummaged in it, and returned. In her hand she carried an object like that which Tiliu had shown me some days earlier. One of the objects with which the women of the harem assuaged the pangs of waiting to be chosen by their master, the Bey.

Solfina clicked her fingers. Felicity instantly knelt forward again, her brow to the floor, her buttocks raised. I found that I could hardly breathe, for I somehow knew what was about to happen, and was staggered by it.

Solfina approached the abased figure of my friend Felicity. Could this possibly be the same Felicity who so disapproved of impropriety?

Solfina's hand descended. She cupped the offered moon of Felicity's left buttock. She kneaded it, moved to the right buttock, explored the tender cleft between. Her hand moved down to touch on, to fondle Felicity's offered cunny.

Slowly, her other hand approached. In it was one of those artificial cocks I gather are called dildoes. I could not breathe at all as I watched the dominating Solfina part Felicity's soft folds with the fingers of one hand, while with the other she slid the head of the ivory cock back and forth.

She found Felicity's entrance. Felicity's hips gave a jerk as Solfina pressed. Slowly, as Felicity wriggled her luscious bottom, Solfina pressed the device into her cunny. She did not pump it in and out in imitation of a genuine shag, as I had seen Tiliu's partner doing the first time I ever saw one of these devices. Instead, having thrust it as deep as it could go, she moved to lie on the divan, her weight on her elbows, her hips over the edge, and her legs splayed wide.

There was no sound except a slight panting from Felicity. I watched enthralled as she crawled on hands and knees towards Solfina's recumbent body, her movements made awkward by the device filling her sheath.

Felicity knelt between Solfina's thighs. She slid both her

140

pale hands along Solfina's muscular legs until they met at the Nubian woman's offered vulva – which I suddenly noticed appeared to have been shaved, for it was quite naked of hair. Felicity parted the plump and glistening folds, slid her fingertips along their length and then, with a quick glance up to where Solfina watched, lowered her mouth.

I know that being licked and nuzzled as Felicity was now licking and nuzzling Solfina is the most transporting of sensations and the sight of this ravishingly lovely, and once so haughty, girl kneeling humbly between the Nubian's thighs, her hands and mouth and tongue striving to give the most exquisite of pleasures, aroused me greatly.

Solfina lay back, her thighs opening wider to give Felicity's bobbing head more room. As she moved to cup and caress her own breasts, mine felt full and tight and that hot tension I knew so well was growing in my tummy.

The sight was stunning. Part of me knew I should not be watching; should depart and leave them to their pleasures in private, but I could not. Could only gaze in wonder as Solfina's magnificent body began to move under Felicity's ministrations. The muscles of her belly began to flex and tense. Her hips began to move in that inexorable rhythm which betokens the rising excitement towards the climax of sexual delight. She was kneading her breasts almost frantically, and her head was rolling from side to side.

Suddenly, she began to gasp and pant, and her hips bucked and writhed, bouncing Felicity's head. Felicity became voracious. Her fingers pulled Solfina's folds wide apart. She crammed a thumb into the panting woman's glistening opening. Her lips and tongue writhed greedily all over the oozing folds. Suddenly, Felicity clamped her mouth over Solfina's straining cherry. I could see by the movements of her jaw and throat that she was sucking avidly.

Solfina cried out, and bucked and writhed and shuddered into such a come as dreams are made of. On and on it went, for Felicity did not let up on her sucking. I found that my own hand had clamped itself between my legs, and I was almost in a come myself.

After an eternity, Felicity eased off. As Solfina's spasms calmed and she lay gasping, Felicity raised her head, her face glistening with Solfina's ambrosiac juices. She glanced up, bent again to plant the tenderest of kisses upon Solfina's swollen cunny-lips, then sat back on her heels.

Felicity gave a little gasp and her hand flew to her own cunny. I suddenly realised that she still had that dildo device crammed into her. It must have been a strange torment to her to have the thing stuffed inside her and not moving except to her own wrigglings. She did not remove the device, though. Indeed, she snatched her hand away as if it was forbidden to her to touch it.

Awkwardly, for the device must have made movement difficult, Felicity rose to her feet and moved to stand beside the divan on which her sated partner lay. To my intense puzzlement she did not lie down, but instead stood quite still, her feet apart, and placed her hands upon her head.

It was most peculiar. As Solfina lay recovering from her transports, Felicity stood perfectly still in her strange pose for all the world as though she were waiting. And indeed, waiting she must have been, for after some time Solfina rolled onto her side on the divan. She smiled up at Felicity, but it was not the soft smile of a lover. Rather, it seemed more the smile of some kind of predator.

She reached out a hand towards Felicity's belly. Felicity had her back towards me, and I could not see what Solfina did. Whatever it was, the effect was instant and electric, for Felicity cried out, and her body squirmed and arched as she thrust her hips forward. She did not change her pose nor remove her hands from her head, but it was obvious from the way she gasped and the way her ripe buttocks clenched and squirmed that she was having a most intense come.

Solfina still had that wolfish grin on her face, and Felicity was still writhing and gasping, indeed almost sobbing, as I dragged myself away, my emotions in turmoil. That women should make love one with another was not shocking to me, but in my experience it had always been as partners. What I had seen was more like mistress and servant. How far had Felicity come in the ways of pleasure!

My own daily life continued, even though what was transpiring with Felicity was a decided distraction. To see such a gloriously lovely girl blossom from a mealy-mouthed prude, incapable of admitting her own sensuous nature, to a wholehearted woman who not only accepted but now actively sought the delights of lovemaking was heartwarming and, I confess, arousing.

I know as a fact that she did indeed seek physical delights, for I saw her once. I was about to enter her little sleeping chamber one afternoon when I beheld such a sight as froze me on the spot with wonder. Felicity was alone on her divan, her head and shoulders propped up by a large cushion. Her head was lolling. Her legs were bent and parted. Between them, her hands were busy. With the fingers of one hand she held the swollen lips of her quim open. With the middle finger of the outer, she was rolling and teasing her cherry.

That flush of redness which spreads between her breasts and over her collarbone when she is aroused was glowing now. Her breathing was quick. Her nipples were like pegs. I crept away. I have myself engaged on occasion in just such self-excitement. I did not wish to disturb her.

Not the least exciting of the changes in Felicity was when she came to me, perhaps in the small hours, perhaps in the bath, and made love to me with such simplicity, such gently open pleasure, that I knew for a fact that her self-deceptions were gone for good. And I loved her for her new honesty. For so long she had pretended, had told herself that she was only 'letting them', whoever they might be. Now, at last, she was admitting even to herself that the joys of the body are joys to be delighted in, not quibbled about.

And if she could have seen the effect her transition had upon her appearance, which perhaps she might for all I know, she would have been as moved as I. If she had been lovely before, now she became the very personification of womanly glory. Her hair took on a lustre which outshone any lamp. Her smile became so deep and soft one longed to swim in it. Her skin took on a glow. Her breasts, always lovely, filled and grew proud, her nipples became roseate medallions that positively demanded the hand or mouth. Her very walk became a languid moving of waters, as smooth and rippling as any swell upon a tropic sea. And her eyes! She was shy of herself and her new awareness, and I swear there is nothing in the universe so enticing as eyes that *know*, as hers now did, but are shy at the knowledge.

Sharpe certainly noticed the change in her and on one of our morning walks, after Donaldson had taken her aside as he always did, and Tiliu had given the purser himself an eager sucking, he waxed enthusiastic about her charms. I wondered how the new Felicity would react to the immensity of his organ. She never got to know of it, though, for even more staggering changes were to overtake her very soon.

After our daily walk, as I have said, we would bathe and change into harem clothes. Felicity would go off, usually, though by no means always, with Solfina, and Tiliu would watch me at my dancing lesson. The dance I was to perform was rather intricate, with many hip and arm movements, and Farah was a very strict task-mistress, so that I always needed a second bath afterwards. Then we would take some coffee and sweetmeats, and try to find something to do to while away the evening.

Felicity was, of course, fully occupied with her 'Chamberlain' and her women friends. For Tiliu and I, however, the joys of female company – delicious though they are from time to time – soon palled. It occurred to us both that although we were living in the seraglio, and had both spent a night of concubinage in the Bey's bed, we were not actually part of the harem, and so should not be subject to all its rules. If we could go out with our ship's officers in the mornings, why could we not go out alone at other times?

We knew such a thing would be frowned on, especially by Farah, but that only gave the idea an extra excitement. We decided to purloin a couple of the black, all enveloping *chadoors* and sneak out one night in an effort to alleviate our boredom by a little exploration. We succeeded almost too well.

I had found a little door in a far corner of the garden-court on one of my solitary strolls. Though it had a large padlock, I noticed that the wood of the frame looked rotten. Using a fruit-knife I had borrowed, we chipped away at the frame so that the metal plate to which the padlock was fixed came loose. I had poured some oils from the bathhouse over the hinges to prevent them squeaking, and it was now possible to open and close the door without anyone detecting that it had been tampered with.

Ten

Tiliu and I were entering a part of the palace we had never seen, for we only knew the women's quarters and the main entrance we used for our morning walks. It was a maze of passages and little rooms, much simpler in decoration than the palatial harem, and was clearly the servants' area. We found any number of storerooms containing wines and sacks and barrels of foodstuffs. We peeped into a vast kitchen, fortunately unused at this time of night, and crept past sleeping chambers and a sort of mess room where several men were drinking and playing dice, too engrossed, luckily, to see us flit across the doorway.

It was vastly exciting to get this back stage, as it were, glimpse of the Bey's palace, and I suppose we got a little too excited and over-confident. Otherwise, we would never have made our two dreadful mistakes. The first was to take off our *chadoors*, although at the time it seemed entirely sensible, for they were rather voluminous, and restricted our movements somewhat. The second was to be in that blind passageway, with nowhere to hide, when a group of palace guards came along.

How were we to know that the passageway led only to the guards' quarters? How were we to know that, in this strange society of separate worlds for men and women, and strict and fearsome rules, any woman appearing outside the women's quarters without a *chadoor* was regarded as no better than she should be, and invited whatever might befall her? And to make matters worse our faces were not veiled, an offence only the loosest of women ever committed.

* * *

The group of guards, whose loud talking and laughing as they approached had forewarned us, froze into stunned silence as they rounded the corner and saw us, pressed against the wall as though we might melt into it and escape. Their faces were almost comical masks of astonishment, and a long space passed before anybody moved. Then, in complete silence, but moving as if rehearsed, they formed a half-circle around us as we pressed ourselves against the wall.

The guard with their lamp, a thick-set man with a huge moustache, held it forward, close to each of us in turn. As he moved the lamp slowly down, then up again, I could feel their eyes moving over me.

I could hear Tiliu breathing tensely beside me, and from the corner of my eye I followed the lamplight as it moved over the body her veils did so little to conceal. There was a shuffling among the men surrounding us. Their intentions became obvious, though they did not leap upon us as I dreaded they might. Instead, moving as a group, they shepherded us along the passageway and through a door. It was clearly a guard room of some sort, for as well as a stove, table and stools, there were a number of narrow beds. I expected them to leap upon us, to rip off our veils, throw us down, and fuck us wildly – for had they not found two easy victims late into the night, and were they not all healthy men? They did not. For long moments they simply stared at us, and I could veritably sense their eyes investigating my body beneath my veils. I cast a quick glance at Tiliu. She was staring back at the group of men, her eyes wide, her lips a little parted. She was breathing rapidly, as though readying herself for some kind of contest.

Still without yet touching us, the guards edged Tiliu towards one of the beds, myself towards another. There was no sense in resisting. There were too many of them. I counted at least eight. A hand reached out and tugged at one of my veils. I could see Tiliu in similar case to myself, hands reaching out, her veils being pulled off as rapidly as

148

my own. Then I became unable to think of Tiliu as hands reached for me.

In an instant, I was borne off my feet and carried to the bed. Several mouths sought mine as hands found my breasts, and pulled my legs apart. I do not know where the inspiration came from, perhaps from some vague memory of the times among the tribe when a number of men had come for me at the same time. However it may be, I found myself grabbing the head of the nearest guardsman, and kissing him, and pulling him to me.

This display of apparent willingness may not have calmed their eagerness, but I am sure it did at least make them less rough. The man I was kissing pushed some of the other hands off me, and scrabbled at his loose trousers. I clamped my legs around him as he thrust into me. Other men were pressing close, tearing at their clothes and trying to get at me. I reached up and took hold of a cock that waved close above my face. Another bumped against my cheek, and I opened my mouth to it.

The man shagging me was very quick to reach his climax. Another man took his place in an instant. Someone climbed astride my ribs and placed his stiff cock between my breasts, squashing them over it, and rutting as though he were in my cunny. There were now four men having me. I had been in such a situation before, while I was with the Tukanna, and so I was no longer apprehensive. I knew that one woman could out-shag many men, so long as they were not rough. Their first clumsy excitement would soon be over, and if we were sensible, Tiliu and I, we would get out of here without too much harm.

That first rush was indeed quickly over, but it was quite a while before we got out of that room. The man in my mouth took longest, even though I put all the skill I could muster into sucking him. Long before he grunted and jerked his heat into my throat, the man between my breasts spurted over my chest and neck, and the one I was rubbing with my hand shot his essence up my arm and over my

149

hair. I suppose the staying power of the man I was sucking gave them time to recover, for by the time he pulled out of my mouth they were ready for me again.

It was less frantic now, but just as intense. Perhaps they realised I would not resist, for though they had every part of me in every way they could, they were purposeful rather than frantic. I had been on my back, my legs open wide. I was rolled over, and found myself on my side, pressed face to face on one of the men. My leg was lifted and draped over his thigh, and he entered me with a single thrust. A second man lay close behind me, his hand reaching over to grasp my breast, his cock searching for me. He found my already occupied cunny, moved back a little and thrust instead into my bottom, making me groan, for the delicate bridge of flesh between my rose-hole and my cunny was stretched quite painfully. As if my groan had been an invitation, a third prick slid deep into my mouth.

Helpless, impaled on three thrusting cocks, I could only submit and pray they would be easy with me. It was as though they were working in time with one another, thrusting alternately into my cunny and rose-hole, the third man setting his own rhythm, pushing for my throat, and hardly pulling back at all. Instinct took me over. I was once again the girl of those times with the tribe, at Mallani's wedding perhaps, or Tiliu's initiation, when all rules were abandoned and the tribe became one whole mass of orgiastic excitements.

What surprised me a little and, if I am honest, served to magnify the sensations washing over me, was that, after that first rush, these men were strangely orderly in their having of us. True, we had perforce to accommodate more than one at a time, and our mouths and bottoms were as actively ploughed as our cunnies, but there was little pushing and shoving to get at us. Indeed, they seemed entirely content to take turn and turn about.

I gave myself up to sensation now – not absolutely, for the mind does not entirely blank out in such circumstances. Even being as energetically fucked as I was, a part of my mind still was able to retain distance from what was happening, to check occasionally that Tiliu was all right, and to wonder how soon these men would be satisfied so that we could escape back to the women's quarters. The rest of me was inevitably swept up by voluptuous sensations which always overtake a girl, or me at least, when she is being repeatedly and enthusiastically fucked by several men.

They were only a little rough, though I confess my bottom was rather sore, and my jaw ached a little, and there were a few slight bruises on my breasts and hips the next day. The brief glimpses I was able to get showed me that Tiliu, too, was having an active time of it. Once, she was on all fours across the bed, one man grasping her hips while he pumped at her from the rear, another deep in her mouth. Later, she was lying face down on one man, with another atop her, all three grinding and writhing like a nest of snakes, while both her arms were pulled wide and a third and fourth cock filled her hands.

How many times they had us I cannot say. I know that the sight of a naked girl being thoroughly shagged stirs up a man even if he has only just enjoyed a fuck himself, and these guards had plenty of stamina. It was the early hours of the morning when we limped naked and perspiring, Tiliu as weak and stiff as I, along the passages back to the harem, led by two of the guardsmen. And would you not know it, they insisted in getting us up against the wall for a last quick fuck before they let us go.

We were both of us, Tiliu and I, in rather a sorry state. Clutching the remnants of our veils in our hands we crept naked across the garden courtyard. As you can imagine, we were rather weary – not so much from lack of sleep as from the very energetic attentions of the guards we had been obliged to entertain. For myself, my jaw ached, my bottom felt tender, and I was all over sticky from perspiration and the men's effusions.

Tiliu was in the same case, and without consultation we

both headed for the bathrooms. At this hour there was no-one else about, so we were able to bathe quickly and scurry off to our bedchamber, anxious lest anyone see us and ask what we had been up to.

Fortunately, the only consequences of our hectic adventure were that we were rather less than lively company on our morning walk (although Sharpe did not fail to get Tiliu bent over in our little glen and shag her very thoroughly from the rear), and I performed rather wearily at my after-noon dance lesson.

Farah was very concerned at this, for the Prince's ban-quet was only a couple of days off. She fussed and flustered, worrying lest I was unwell, then scolding my clumsiness. It was impossible for me to tell her the true rea-son my movements were stiff and halting, and so I just had to bow my head and try harder.

Eleven

As the time of the banquet drew closer, the level of excitement among the womenfolk grew and grew. It seemed that every single woman was engaged in some way or another. Groups sat around busily sewing drapes and hangings. Vast quantities of plates, huge silver dishes, piles of knives and spoons, whole boxes of goblets and flasks appeared and were eagerly washed and polished until they gleamed fit to blind.

I noticed much work was also being done on veils and costumes, and learned to my surprise – for I understood that the Bey's women were always kept hidden away – that every member of the harem was to take some part in serving at the banquet. It seemed, when I enquired, that the seraglio was indeed kept exclusive except when the Prince or some official higher than the Bey was visiting. On such visits, the whole band of women was brought out as if to display the Bey's wealth and taste.

And, I guessed from Samara's coy blushes, were brought out for rather more than just display.

Another surprise was that, despite not being real members of the harem, both Tiliu and Felicity were to take part. With Tiliu's adventurous nature, I knew it would have been hard to keep her away once she knew I was myself to dance at the banquet. In Felicity's case it was much more of a surprise, and a delightful demonstration of her newly open nature.

Both had worked hard on their costumes with the help and guidance of Samara and Solfina. I was not to have the opportunity to see my own costume until Farah prepared me for my performance, and as I watched those of my two friends take shape with fitting after fitting I only hoped that mine would be as delicious.

Though different in colour – Felicity's being mainly pale green to set off her copper tresses, while Tiliu's was entirely white to contrast with her glossy darkness of skin – they were basically the same. Each began with what was nothing so much as a very small pair of drawers with the legs cut off. They tied at the waist as drawers do, but were not joined at the sides, so that they were only a strip of silk drawn between the legs, hardly more than the provocative little loin cloths the girls of Tiliu's tribe wore. When pulled tight, as Tiliu did with hers, they actually outlined rather than concealed the shape of the treasures they covered, and looked very provoking.

Over these scraps of fine silk were worn loose muslin pantaloons composed of two separate legs, and tied at the waist to give the appearance of a single garment. Cunningly, the muslin was thicker than usual so that, while it was still somewhat translucent, the shape of the legs within was suggested rather than revealed.

Above the waist each girl was clad in a strange sort of abbreviated waistcoat – I can think of no other way of putting it. Like a waistcoat, it fitted across the shoulders, with wide holes for the arms, and was short. Unlike any waistcoat I have ever seen, though, it was very short indeed, reaching hardly lower than the undercurves of their breasts, and had very narrow shoulder straps, hardly more than an inch wide. It had no buttons either, but was linked in front by a tiny golden chain. Linked but not closed, so that through a gap at the front of perhaps two inches one could glimpse the valley between the breasts.

Like the pantaloons, the effect of the little waistcoats was to draw attention to what they pretended to hide, to suggest delights while half-concealing them from the eye. In fact, to tease any observer – an effect only emphasised by the loose blouses of muslin with which they then draped their torsos.

The final effect – and I now realised how deep and subtle was the Eastern knowledge of the arts of titillation – was the donning of the *yashmak*, which is the name of the little veil that covers the face below the eyes.

Both Felicity and Tiliu are, each in their own way, beautiful. Now, as they placed circlets of wide silver chain about their brows, and from them hung opaque *yashmaks*, one pale green, the other pure white, the effect was to draw attention to their eyes. There is a saying that the eyes are the mirrors of the soul: for me, the eyes are the centre and the epitome of beauty and promise. Now that their faces save for their eyes were entirely concealed, the individual loveliness of each of my oh, so different friends was revealed.

Felicity, her mane of copper hair flowing about her shoulders, her voluptuous figure half hidden by her costume, became by the greenish-brown glow of her eyes an island waiting to be explored, a treasure house of nervous yet eager promise. In contrast, Tiliu became a cat, a lissom, almost predatory creature whose eyes said 'Here I am – if you are bold enough to dare.' Though each stood absolutely still and kept entirely silent, one could see from their eyes alone the depths of their natures – Tiliu's open, knowing, even challenging; Felicity's tentative, knowing but nervous of the knowledge, inviting conquest.

'Oh, heavens!' I thought at the time. 'If there are rules of behaviour for the men at the banquet, these two visions will put them to a sore test.'

And so it indeed proved.

My own preparation for the banquet, apart from the dancing lessons I had endured each day for the last week or more, began quite early on the morning of the day itself. Called for even before I could have my morning bath, I was taken off to a chamber I had not seen before, and was kept secluded there for the whole time until the banquet.

Not that my seclusion was solitary or idle by any means. Indeed, I was kept very busy, and surrounded by women the whole time.

My preparation took an inordinately long time, and might have become tedious had not each separate step been so luxurious or so novel, or both.

First came a long and very careful bath at the hands of Farah and Solfina, after which my bush was trimmed very close and I was massaged all over with aromatic oils. Ever since Motallo gave me my first ever massage, after that hectic night I was inducted into the Tukanna tribe, I have loved being massaged. Few experiences in life are so easeful and relaxing as to have expert and gentle hands smoothing over one's skin and kneading one's muscles into a warm softness.

Inevitably, Solfina turned the massage into something of a game, and a rather naughty one at that, fondling my breasts rather more than was necessary and, when she moved down, slipping a fingertip between my cunny-folds. I would have quite enjoyed it, but Farah became very stern and scolded her, and she became more businesslike.

After the massage, my fingernails and toenails were filed and buffed, and then painted with a deep red lacquer which made them shine like jewels. The lacquer took a while to dry, and I had to keep very still lest I touch against something and ruin the shine. Meanwhile, as I sat with my hands out and my feet spread to give the lacquer time to dry, my hair was combed and brushed until it was positively gleaming. I puzzled briefly that it was not set in any particular style, as it had been on my visit to the Bey's bedchamber, but learned the reason soon enough.

My hair done and draping like a shawl about my shoulders, my eyes were kohled and my cheeks and nipples rouged. Then my lips were painted with a deep red, waxy substance, which, to my surprise, was also smeared between the lips of my quim.

I caught sight of myself in a long looking glass fixed to

a wall, and was struck by the strange, alluring figure I saw before me. Her hair shone about her shoulders, her eyes were made huge by the cunning way the kohl outlined them. The rouge on her nipples accentuated the firm fullness of her breasts, and the close trimming of the fuzz upon her loins served to draw the eye to her plump cunny-lips, which were clearly visible even though her thighs were pressed together.

It took me a moment or two to recognise that this vision was in fact me, and I blushed with surprise to realise that, like Tiliu and Felicity, I too was beautiful. That this was not just vanity was confirmed by the shining eyes and wide smiles of the women around me, who now proceeded to get me into my costume.

First, bands of black satin with tiny gold bells dangling from them were fixed about my wrists and ankles, so that from then on my every movement was accompanied by a gentle tinkling.

I did not have a circlet about my brow as Felicity and the others had. Instead, a cap of fine-spun gold thread was placed upon my head. From it hung dozens and dozens of long, fine threads, which were combed and plaited into my hair, making it seem thicker and more golden in tone. The style they set my hair in was unlike any I had ever seen. First, a thick swathe was plaited behind each ear, and rolled and pinned in a sort of disc which covered almost the whole of each ear. The rest, the whole of the back of my head, was woven into dozens of thin, tight plaits which hung down to my shoulder blades. Into the ends of the cord-like plaits were fixed yet more tiny golden bells, which made my hair feel strangely heavy, and caused me to concentrate on keeping my head still.

Felicity told me much later that keeping my head thus still had given my dance an added dignity and elegance, so I can only conclude that Farah's choice of hairstyles was deliberate.

* * *

After my hair was dressed (which took well over an hour), my attendants continued with my costume. First, a wide sash of black satin decorated with gold rings and medals was placed about me so that it hung loose around my hips. From it was hung a tiny skirt of silken muslin, which reached hardly lower than the very tops of my thighs. A band of the same muslin was draped around my bosom and tied loosely with a fine string, so that it was only the swell of my breasts which kept it from falling off me.

The effect of these two skimpy garments was, if anything, to make me feel more naked than had I actually been so, for the material was almost entirely transparent, and served only to draw the eye to what it purported to cover.

Next came pantaloons, like those the other women would be wearing, in fine muslin, with separate legs. Over these, tucked into the sash about my hips and draping to my ankles, were hung a dozen or more lengths of organza, giving the effect of a full, though very light, skirt which swayed and drifted as I moved.

My torso was draped with half a dozen loose shawl-like veils, each made up of two squares of organza similar to that draped about my legs, and tied at the shoulders so that they hung lightly front and back, but were open at the sides.

Last of all came a pair of brocade slippers as soft and comfortable as gloves, and my *yashmak*. This was a square of heavy white silk edged with gold thread, and was held on by two loops which fixed around my ears, and were concealed by the swirls of my hair.

Looking at myself in the big looking glass I was amazed at the strange, exotic figure before me. The effect of my hair-style was as of a golden helmet, and the opaque *yashmak* combined with the kohl around my eyes to make them seem larger, and quite cat-like. The many layers of veils about my legs and body made me seem almost shapeless, yet when I moved even a little the material swirled and drifted, and gave brief glimpses of my figure.

I essayed a few of my dance-steps, and the cunning suggestiveness of my costume was instantly apparent. With each movement, each shift of a foot or tilt of a hip, the veils swayed and parted to reveal a suggestion of my legs. Every time I turned my shoulders or raised an arm the veils about my body wafted like mists, displaying glimpses of my torso and the sides of my breasts. Obviously, it would not be just the steps that were the focus of my dance.

Then, with a smile to Farah, Solfina casually reached out a hand and tugged at the outer veil about my torso. At even that slight pull, the knots at my shoulders came undone and both front and back veil drifted to the floor. At once, she did the same to part of my skirt and it, too, fell from me. Solfina laughed aloud, a deep, rich sound, while the other women smiled and clapped.

On the instant, I understood. Though Farah had not told me so, I knew now that during my dance these dozens of veils, which transformed me into an almost shapeless figure would not stay on me for long. They would be tugged off. Now the careful trimming of my bush and rouging of my nipples and cunny-lips made sense. I knew that I was destined to end my dance more naked than if I had been naked.

All the other women of the seraglio, and Tiliu and Felicity too, of course, went off about their duties long before I was to be required. The wait was irksome, and made the more so by a combination of the warm glances Solfina kept casting at me, and the new knowledge that I was to be stripped as I danced.

I had seen Solfina with Felicity. Knew that she had become my friend's dominating lover. What I saw in her eyes as we waited gave me pause. Solfina was a strikingly handsome woman, tall and broad shouldered, with an erect bearing and a proud, though not haughty, air about her. Though she was now fully dressed, visions of her naked,

159

powerful form carrying Felicity towards a divan entered my mind. Her high-breasted posture, the easy way she had gathered Felicity up in her arms, the flexing of her back and thighs as she carried her willing burden, only added to the sensations my other train of thought was causing in me.

Perhaps I am unusual in my responses to circumstances such as those I now found myself in. Perhaps not. However it may be, the new realisation that my dance was to be more than a dance, that the Bey's, and Farah's, intention was that I should end up displayed naked before whoever was at the Prince's banquet, had begun to stir me up.

I was committed, and for pride's sake as well as Farah's I could not now back out. And the knowledge that I had thus committed myself to such an exhibition for the delectation of unknown men had a very arousing effect upon me, but at the same time made me nervous.

160

Twelve

The scene which greeted my eyes when at last I saw the banqueting chamber took my breath away. I had suffered a long wait before I was taken there, and was conducted there entirely concealed behind a sort of screen of black cloth held up by Farah, Solfina and the Bey's two other official wives. Both these things only served to screw my nervousness tighter.

At last, there came a crash of cymbals and my screen was whipped away. Farah had instructed me that when the screen was removed I was to pose absolutely still until my accompanying music began. She had not told me that the sight which met my eyes when the black cloth dropped away would stagger me.

The chamber was large, and crowded with any number of gorgeously clad men. But what froze me, what drove any thought of my dance-steps or anything else from my mind, was the sight of the people seated around the Bey. To his left, in a rich jacket of silver and black, on his head one of those caps called a fez, sat the Egyptian from the ship. Next to him sat Tiliu's mysterious stranger – and to judge from the richness of his apparel, and the thickness of the cushions which surrounded him, he was not the body-guard I had thought him to be, but someone very important.

The sight of these two men from the ship drove every-thing from my head except the appalling thought that I would be recognised – that Felicity and Tiliu, too, would be known. Our reputations would be destroyed.

I heard my music begin, but I was in such a tizzy I could

not remember my steps. But I could not just stand there, posed with my arms up like some statue. I made myself move. All that came into my head was the dance Tiliu and the other virgins had performed at the tribal initiation ceremony I had witnessed so long ago.

I found that my body could perform the movements separated from my mind and my eyes, which darted about the chamber. Moving in time to the rhythm of the drum and cymbals, with the flutes soaring up in the strange tones I was becoming used to, I swayed my hips, stepped forward with my left foot, giving a forward thrust of my loins just as Tiliu had, then my right foot and another thrust. Every move of the dance became centred on my hips and pelvis. A step, a wriggle, another step, another wriggle.

What I was doing with my arms I know not, for my eyes were racing about the hall. There were perhaps twenty-five men in all, each attended by one of the women of the seraglio. The circle centred on the man I guessed to be the Prince, a corpulent, round-faced man, clean-shaven, and dressed very richly in a gold brocaded jacket and silk pantaloons. The women of the harem, eyes lowered, were busy proffering plates or cups or cuts from the vast joints of meat that sat in silver dishes on the tables.

I cast my eyes about as I circled the clear central space in my improvised dance. Where was Tiliu? Was Samara here?

Felicity I knew instantly, from the colour of her lovely copper hair and the paleness of her skin. But she was not serving food or drink. Instead, she was kneeling with bowed head close beside the Egyptian. His arm seemed to be behind her, and to judge by the way she occasionally twitched or wriggled his hand was somewhat busy.

While dancing I had to circle around the room, the circles slowly getting wider to take me closer to the seated guests. When I got close enough, I now knew, they would begin to pull off my veils. That, though, was now the least of my concerns, for my mind was still spinning with the thought that the Egyptian and the stranger would recognise us, and expose us. Then two wonderful thoughts struck me. We each had on our little *yashmaks*, which concealed our faces save our eyes. We might not be recognised after all. And on top of that, to judge from their easy manner here, the two men were not likely to be returning with us to the ship. We were safe.

My nerves fell off me. Suddenly I was able to think about my dancing, and to look about me without the blinkers of fright. To judge from the way the men's eyes were following me, my movements were meeting with approval. I exaggerated them, swaying my hips wider, taking longer steps, circling and wriggling my pelvis. I realised even as I did so that my movements were pretty close to those a girl's hips make when she is actively shagging. The thought lent spice. I was beginning to enjoy myself, and enjoy the way the men's eyes began to glitter as they stared at my swaying body.

At the same time, I was able to watch the women. Though some were still passing dishes or goblets of wine, others had become engaged in activities which indicated that food and drink were not the only things on offer at this exotic banquet.

A bottom, which I thought I recognised as Tiliu's, was jiggling prominently while its owner's bobbing head was busy in a man's lap. A woman was kneeling on all fours, her knees apart, while the man she had been serving was doing something very active with his hand between her legs from behind.

I circled wider, more rapidly, to come to a halt close to the Prince. I hovered above him, circling and writhing my hips close before his eyes. His eyes moved slowly over me, and I was thrilled at how excited he seemed to be. He reached forward. The first of my veils was removed.

As if it had been a signal, all the other men reached forward whenever I got anywhere near them. Soon flimsy veils were falling off me like leaves in autumn. In only a matter of minutes, I was down to the little veils draped about my hips and my breasts, which were so transparent they left nothing of me to the imagination.

By now I was myself considerably excited, and became more so at the sight of what was happening around me. Any pretence at eating a meal was rapidly disappearing. The veils of the other women were now being torn off, and less ritualistically than mine had been.

I heard a muffled squeal, and saw Samara being pushed over onto her back as a tall, obviously excited man threw himself between her flailing legs. Several other women were in similar case. Others had their heads or their hands inside men's pantaloons as the men started their pleasures of the evening. It became just like one of the celebrations among the tribe, with curling, writhing bodies all over the place.

Only the Prince, the Bey, the Egyptian and the stranger had not joined in what was now an orgy, and growing wilder. The music had ceased and I stopped dancing and stood still in the centre of the room. Beside the Egyptian knelt Felicity, now stark naked save for her *yashmak* and slippers, her head bowed, waiting for what she knew was going to happen to her soon. I saw with some surprise that behind the Bey sat Solfina, looking superb in white veils, with a gold band around her forehead. The Prince and the stranger were alone.

With a clap of his hands, the Prince suddenly stood up. The others followed suit. Last of all, the two women also rose to their feet. As the group turned and began to follow the Prince out of the chamber, Tiliu's mysterious stranger beckoned to me imperiously. I found myself following.

I guessed what they were taking us off for, but was a little puzzled as to why there were only three women to four men, and even more why they had not simply joined in the now pretty frantic activity going on all about the banqueting chamber. Why they were taking us away when they could have fucked us then and there seemed odd to me. That there was more to it soon became clear.

* * *

Walking with slow dignity, as though taking part in some ceremony, the Prince led us along a wide corridor and into another chamber. A heavy, crimson curtain hung across the entire width of one end, and three thickly cushioned divans almost filled the main part of the room. Felicity, Solfina and I were motioned to kneel one beside each of the divans. The Prince stood in the centre of the room facing the curtain, with the Bey a little behind and to his left. The Egyptian and the stranger moved to stand near the middle of the curtain, facing the Prince.

They both bowed and made short speeches which, of course, I could not understand, then bowed again. The Prince said something and gave a cursory bow before placing a hand upon his sash and standing as tall and proud as his round figure allowed. There was a pause. The two men at the curtain bowed again, turned, gripped the curtain, swished it aside.

The sight that met my eyes was out of a fairy story. Behind the curtains, lit by brass lamps and hung all around with muslin drapes like some magical tent of clouds, stood another sumptuous, silk-upholstered divan. On it, like some fabulous eastern statue, was the most lovely woman you could ever wish to see.

She sat cross-legged, her delicate hands resting palm-upwards on her knees. She was naked save for an abundance of gold and silver jewellery, glistening with gems of all kinds, which set off the warm coffee-colour of her flawless skin. Between her legs was entirely hairless (I supposed she had been shaved) and her crease like the nipples of her full breasts had been rouged a deep, glossy red.

Her head was bowed, and her straight, raven-black hair gleamed like polished metal in the lamplight. She sat motionless, and her beauty cast a hush over all of us.

After a long, breathless pause, Tiliu's stranger clapped his hands, making me start with the suddenness of the noise. The girl on the divan slowly raised her head, and took my breath away again, for her face completed, no, added to the vision of loveliness.

165

She wore no *yashmak*, indeed wore no garment of any kind. In the middle of her high, flawless brow was a round mark in the same glossy red as her nipples and between her legs. Her eyebrows were narrow and arched. Her dark eyes seemed almost too large for her face. They were outlined in kohl, tilted up at the outer corners, and her lashes seemed almost unnaturally long.

Her nose was small and straight. Her high cheekbones gave her a slightly feline look, as though she were half Oriental, half African. Her lips were soft and full, and her chin a perfect curve that almost cried out to be caressed.

There came another clap, and she rose from the divan so smoothly, so gracefully that it almost seemed she was being lifted up by some magical force, rather than rising by her own efforts. She stepped off the divan and moved to kneel at the Prince's feet with such grace it was as if she floated rather than walked.

Later on, for everything that was said was strange to me, I got Samara to help me question Solfina. It seemed that this divinely beautiful girl was a present to the Prince from some distant ruler. The Egyptian and the stranger were emissaries, and had been her guardians on the journey from somewhere called Malagasy, which is apparently a large island off the coast of southern Africa, recently claimed by France.

As the girl knelt before the Prince he moved one foot a little forward. To my utter surprise, the lovely girl bent forward and pressed a kiss upon it. He pulled it back and pushed the other forward. Again she kissed his slipper. To me, such a show of submissiveness seemed outlandish, even offensive, but I supposed that in this society, where women were the property of men, it was perfectly normal.

The Prince then strode across to the divan. The girl rose and followed him with that same ineffable grace, and knelt at his feet again, pressing her forehead to the floor. The Prince raised his right foot and placed the sole of his slipper on the back of the girl's head, for all the world as though he were taking possession.

He stepped back. The girl rose and climbed onto the divan. In its centre was a large cushion of white silk. The beautiful girl lay down carefully, ensuring that her hips were on the cushion. She raised her long, slender legs, gripped them with her hands behind her knees, waited, offering herself. The sight was so sensual, so provoking, that I felt my own body becoming aroused. If only I could look so ravishing when readying myself for a man.

The picture was spoilt rather when the corpulent prince climbed onto the divan, his weight bouncing the waiting girl about. Though he was a round man, and far from handsome, the cock he hauled out through the split in his pantaloons as he knelt between the girl's raised feet was handsome indeed – and very ready for the task at hand.

I felt myself breathing rapidly, my folds moist and tingling in my excitement at the erotic tableau before me. Even the incongruity of the girl's graceful loveliness contrasted with the Prince's rotund clumsiness as he leant forward, resting with his hands on either side of his bed-partner, his large body poised above her slender form, could not detract from the stirring nature of the scene.

I had expected him to plunge into her as soon as his gnarled and rampant member was above her pouting cunny. He did not. To my astonishment Solfina, of all people, suddenly appeared, kneeling beside the divan. She reached out a hand and parted the girl's folds. With the other, she grasped the Prince's member. She guided it. Slid its purple bulb along the girl's crease. Located her entrance.

The Prince instantly thrust down upon the girl, impaling her with a single, fearsome movement. The girl cried out. The Prince rutted on her like a wild thing. It was over in less than two minutes – two minutes in which the girl's body was crushed beneath the Prince's weight, in which her head rolled wildly from side to side, in which she lost the grip on her knees and her legs fell apart as she clenched her fists and pressed them to her brow, her eyes screwed shut as though in agony.

Then it was over, and the Prince hauled himself off the prostrate girl and moved to sit near the head of the divan. Solfina at once hurried up. She peered down between the girl's still-splayed thighs. She smiled softly, said something to the girl, stroked her hand across her forehead. The girl gathered herself and climbed off the divan. She once again knelt at the Prince's feet.

Solfina picked up the white cushion and held it out, showing it first to the Prince and then to the rest of us. Its pristine whiteness was speckled with red. The Bey, the Egyptian and the stranger shouted and clapped their hands enthusiastically. The Prince smirked and bobbed his head as though accepting applause. I was astonished. How could he be so smug and proud? All he had done was deflower a young virgin, and clumsily at that. It was the girl who should be applauded. How odd, how shallow men are!

Of what followed I had only a series of brief and increasingly confused impressions.

I saw the Prince lie down on his back on the divan and the glorious girl he had just deflowered climb astride him. She gripped his still-rampant cock in both her tiny hands and lowered herself upon him, an expression of fierce concentration on her lovely face.

I saw Solfina move to sit beside the Bey and his hands cup her voluptuous breasts as she slowly sank back on the divan.

I saw the naked Felicity, already on her back, raise and spread her long legs as the Egyptian moved between them, his cock poised over its moist target.

I was kneeling beside the divan on which Tiliu's stranger had seated himself. My arm was gripped. I felt a sharp tug. I looked up. The stranger was hauling me up from my knees towards the divan.

Perhaps I was too slow to move. Perhaps he saw a momentary reluctance in my eyes. However that may be, he moved with sudden swiftness. With the hand not gripping my arm, he reached down and grabbed the black satin sash about my waist. I was hoisted bodily from the floor, swung through the air as though I weighed nothing, dumped on my back on the divan. It was so quick, so decisive, that for a moment I was startled out of my wits. By the time I recovered myself it was too late.

He had pressed the flat of a hand to my brow, holding my head immobile. His face was close above mine, his eyes staring into my own. His face was absolutely impassive, and he moved with an assurance which made me suddenly feel as helpless as I have ever felt. Perhaps Tiliu was right – perhaps he did 'have juju'.

Unhurriedly, he gripped and tore off the skimpy veil that covered my breasts. He did not look at them, but kept his eyes fixed on mine. Then he tore off the veil about my hips. He did not touch me yet, except with the hand on my brow. I did not know what to do. I was as if mesmerised.

I could not look away from his eyes, could not move even when he released my forehead. He stood and looked down at me, his eyes flicking over me from head to toe. It was a very strange experience. I knew that in the banqueting chamber we had so recently left, the Bey's concubines were wildly and erotically entertaining his guests. In this very room three other couples were fucking with various degrees of abandon. Yet there seemed to be a stillness around me, a strange tension between me and the hypnotic man gazing down at me that cut out all other sensations.

Tiliu had said she felt this man could see into her mind. I felt exactly the same thing. And not only that he could read my thoughts, but that he could command them. He said nothing, did not even gesture, yet I found myself reaching up to him. It was as though I was a spectator to my own hands as they touched against the silk of his loose trousers, one on the outer side of each knee.

I sat up as though drawn on strings. My hands slid up

his thighs, fumbled a moment with the material that shrouded his loins, reached inside. I drew him forth, my fingers fluttering around the shaft which reared before my eyes.

It stared back at me, its bulb round and glossy, the folds of skin where it joined the shaft crinkled and brown. My fingers slipped up and down that shaft as though eager to caress it, yet nervous of doing so. He stood absolutely still. As in a dream, I leaned forward. I kissed him. I parted my lips and slid my mouth upon him. He was hot and smooth, and tasted of musk and exotic spices.

Though he was not moving, it was as though I was not setting my own rhythm, but responding to some unheard commands. Slowly, my mouth slid further and further onto him, my tongue writhing. Then just as slowly my head moved back, my mouth sucking and licking ravenously, until only the very end of his plum was between my lips and the tip of my tongue was lapping at his eyelet. Then down again until he almost plugged my throat, and back to kiss his tip.

Never had I served a man with my mouth in quite that manner. Never had a man willed me to. All the others, before and since, want quickness, voluptuous suckings, and to pump their comes as deep into my throat as I will allow. This man did not. It was as if he willed the slow descent of my lips along his shaft, and the equally slow sucking back, to serve as gestures of submission rather than attempts to bring him off. And he did not require to come.

After perhaps a dozen strokes of my lips along his member, I felt the lightest of touches on my brow. Somehow, I knew he willed me to stop. I lay back upon the divan, once again staring up into his compelling eyes.

My legs parted themselves. My arms raised themselves above my head. I can describe it no other way. I was like an automaton, yet one with senses that raced and whirled. My body was nothing else than an offering, a longing to be touched, to be taken. I could not breathe as he moved to kneel between my trembling legs. My folds were oozing for him, yearning to be stretched and penetrated.

He placed his hands on either side of my breathless body, lowered himself. I felt his hotness touch against my cunny-lips and shocks went through me. He pressed, found my seeping entrance, pressed again, parted me, thrust into me in a long, slow movement that pierced my essence and drove me beyond thought.

Nothing touched me save his magnificent penis and his pelvis as he reached my depths. No hands reached for my breasts. No lips sought my own. Nothing touched me save the member filling my burning sheath as he pressed and withdrew, pressed and withdrew, in an awesome rhythm which had nothing to do with my needs, yet drove me to madness.

I was no more than a fish on a spear, a receptacle on which this man was taking his pleasure – yet never had I been so deeply stirred, so overwhelmingly aroused. Nothing existed in the universe except the baton ploughing my body, the eternity of uncontrollable sensations it was driving through me. I think I had begun to come at the very instant he penetrated me, and was driven higher and higher until my head was bursting, my lungs were on fire, my body was an earthquake.

I know the man had a come, because he moved quicker, more strongly, violently almost, and I felt him flood me – but then, suddenly, he was gone. My helpless body was still pulsing, still cramping, but it was empty. I spiralled dizzily down, panting, feeling suddenly chilled and bereft. I looked wildly about. Where was he? He was nowhere in sight.

Slowly, feeling as though I was dragging myself out of some shattering dream, I gathered what I could of my wits. He could not have taken the eternity it had seemed, for the Prince was still bucking beneath his new concubine, the Bey was firmly embedded in Solfina's luxurious body, and

171

Felicity was now lying prone on her divan while the Egyptian rutted on her from behind.

I could scarcely believe what had happened. What an amazing, incredible man. On the ship he had taken Tiliu aside, fucked her to a finish without speaking a single word, and at once disappeared. And now he had done precisely the same with me. Had silently driven me to madness, fucked me like I had never been fucked, and vanished.

I never saw him again. Never even caught a glimpse of him from a distance. I could not even find out who he was, not name, nor rank, nor function. It was as if he had never existed.

I sat up and shook my head to clear it. The three couples around me were too busy with each other to have noticed anything. I sat for a while, getting my breathing under control and allowing the heat in my body to die off. I felt quite weak and distracted by my overwhelming experience. I got up and wandered out of the chamber.

I found myself back in the main banqueting hall. The scene around me was as wild and strange as ever one could dream of witnessing, yet I felt oddly detached, as though I was looking at some giant Zoetrope rather than at real people.

I saw with dispassionate clarity that Samara was being kept very busy. She was kneeling astride a huge African, her hips writhing wildly as she shagged him, while a second man, an Arab I thought, ploughed her eager mouth, and yet a third bounced and kneaded her full breasts while her hand rummaged inside his pantaloons.

One of the Bey's African concubines, whose name I never learned, but whose slight form and delicate features had imprinted themselves on my mind, was supporting herself on her hands while a rather corpulent man held her up by the hips and rutted in her pert little bottom.

A man stood leaning his shoulders against a wall while a slender girl, her head thrown back in abandonment, hung onto his neck and pressed her feet against the wall to bounce herself on his prick.

Two women lay in a curled and writhing ball on the floor as their mouths nuzzled greedily between each other's thighs.

I saw Tiliu rise from the exhausted body of one man, mop her cunny and between her breasts with a napkin from a table, then move to where several men were eagerly mauling at a woman's splayed body. With a wicked grin, she reached in, grabbed one of the men by his cock, and pulled him away. Greedy minx!

I was still in this odd, dispassionate state when I felt hands on my breasts. I could not see who the man was, for he had come up behind me. I looked down and watched the hands as they hefted and squeezed me, rolling my nipples with their thumbs, digging their fingers into my softness.

It was for all the world as though I were not actually there. As though there were a gap of some kind between my body, which could feel exactly what was happening to it, and my brain, which seemed merely to observe.

My breasts were squeezed and jiggled. One of the hands disappeared, and I felt it alight on my shoulder to push me forward. I bent. Both hands had now left my breasts and were on my bottom. My cheeks were parted. Fingers toyed with my quim and my rose-hole. Looking between my parted legs, I saw a hand rummage in pantaloons. An erect cock appeared, was pointed towards me. Clearly, I remember thinking as it moved forward, this man prefers what girls have in common with boys.

He was not especially big, and my bottom was able to accommodate him without discomfort. I wondered, as his fingers gripped my hipbones and his belly slapped against my buttocks, how long he would take, how soon I would be able to wander back to the quiet of my chamber in the seraglio.

It was not to be, for as soon as whoever it was jerked

173

into his come and withdrew from me, other hands reached for me.

I suppose it was because I was the only European that made me so popular. My strange mood of detachment continued as I was taken towards a pile of cushions. The man who was tugging me was shorter than I, and I noticed that his brow and his bald pate were bedewed with perspiration. I lay down on the cushions, remarking to myself how silly he looked as he tore eagerly at his pantaloons.

The prick which he waved triumphantly above me was not large, and his keenness ensured that the fuck which followed was not particularly exciting. I remember hoping that the way he jerked my body with his wild humping would not cause the cushions I lay on to part and deposit me on the floor.

Before he finished and bellowed out in his little come, another man joined the fray, and required the use of my mouth. Automatically, my hands reached to grasp this new cock. I might as well get it over. Instinctively, for my mind was, as it were, five paces off from me, I gave him as good a sucking as he could have wished for.

My mind stayed distanced as my body was sought and enjoyed over and over again. The two men who'd had me on the pile of cushions having finished and moved away, I sat up. Someone pulled me to my feet. I felt the cool tiles of the wall against my back as he fucked me in the way Donaldson preferred to fuck Felicity. Then I found myself lying on top of one man while another lay on top of me, as I was plugged front and rear at the same time.

I was on my back, legs raised, being enthusiastically shagged. I was bending over, one cock in my bottom, another in my mouth. At some stage, a man even shoved his cock between my breasts, and brought himself off by squashing them onto it and rutting like a wild thing.

And all the while my passive body was being twisted and turned, and pulled and probed, my mind was getting further and further away. Quite what would have become of me I cannot guess. Perhaps, divorced from myself as I so strangely was, I would have allowed the whole corps of men to fuck me until I was no more than a rag. As it was, Tiliu, my beloved Tiliu, came to my rescue.

I felt my arm being tugged. Wearily, I rolled over, prepared to accommodate yet another sweating, fumbling stranger. Instead of the grinning, bulge-eyed features I expected, my eyes focused on Tiliu's sweet face, looking anxious and concerned. She tugged harder at my arm.

'Come, Ridja. Come.' Her voice was a hiss, and I came to myself the instant I realised that she was actually scared about something.

'This is not good,' she whispered, her mouth now close to my ear. 'Come with me. We get away from here.'

From somewhere, Tiliu had found a couple of *chadoors*. She threw one over me, donned the second herself, and holding my hand fast in hers half fled, half dragged me around and over writhing bodies and away from the banqueting hall.

I was still in a peculiar state, part of my mind detached from me, part of it anxious about Tiliu's concern. I was worried for her, concerned that something unfortunate had happened to hurt her. By the time she got me back to the women's quarters I was in a considerable panic.

The moment we reached my sleeping chamber that part of me which was not off in its strange detachment grabbed Tiliu and demanded to know what had scared her. She span to face me. She gripped my shoulders with both hands. She stared into my eyes, such love and concern burning in her own eyes that suddenly I was undone.

She *had* been scared, but scared for me. I knew on the instant that she had seen my weird state, seen the way I had let all those ravening men use me without response, and determined to rescue me.

Suddenly I was overcome with tears. I did not know where I was, even who I was. All I knew was that I was wracked with sobs, and that dear Tiliu was holding me,

saying nothing, just hugging me and smoothing my forehead.

I know now that I was, to coin a phrase, 'having hysterics'.
It had never happened to me before and has never happened since. It is not something that a sensible woman
allows to happen. I can only conjecture, thinking back,
that my nerves at the task of dancing for the Bey and the
Prince, the sight of that beautiful, unknown girl so humbly
submitting herself to being deflowered, and most of all that
strange, dominating man who had so taken, ravished and
reduced me had combined to drive me from myself, and
reduce me to a sobbing wreck.

Tiliu comforted me, gave me wine, sponged the burning
tears from my face with cool waters, and cuddled and
soothed me. Mercifully, exhaustion – perhaps more emotional than physical – overtook me, and I dropped into the
sleep of the dead.

I awakened next morning still enfolded in Tiliu's warm
arms. My bleak mood of last night had eased, but not entirely disappeared. Tiliu's sweetly sleeping face and the
fluttering of her gentle breath against my cheek were so
soothing that I did not want to arise yet.

My thoughts returned to the strange things I had experienced last night. To the graceful loveliness of the girl the
Prince had so harshly and smugly deflowered before our
eyes, and what her fate might be as his possession. More,
though, to the extraordinary man who had reduced me to
an automaton, and had his way with me, and shattered my
senses with his hypnotic presence.

The way he had commanded me without words, the way
he had seemed to see inside me and have the power to control what he saw, plagued me. That I had knelt at his feet
and offered my mouth not for my own pleasure, but simply
as a receptacle in which he could stimulate himself, for all
the world as though I were no more than a puppet, disturbed me. The way, then, he had hoisted me onto his bed and

calmly and awesomely shagged me into a state of sobbing wreckage, was like nothing I could ever have imagined.

I now really understood the state Tiliu had been in that first night on the ship. I was in that state myself now. Truly, as Tiliu had said, he 'had juju'. That he had vanished as soon as he had erupted into his come made him seem all the more mysterious and disturbing.

Would we see him again? The very thought chilled me.

I roused myself. It would do no good to wallow in this mood. A bath would make me feel better.

Tiliu awoke the instant I moved, and together we went to the bathhouse. By the time we had soaked ourselves in the hot tubs, and stood breathless beneath that wonderful waterfall-cum-shower, and lay relaxing in the main bath, I was more or less back to myself again.

...long and ... Susan ... more ... of ... in
...regret ... the matter, I could not have imagined.
...are ...at the...? This had been in that
...might ...to do this. I saw ...that...one more
...Hotel ... ...and ... and ...The ...had ...and
...as ...had ...up... the distance might, and ...all
...Oh ...in ...the ...

...would ...him again. The ... ...
...called me on ...to ... ...do...you...the
...shock. A ... ...along ...the ... her before.

...This ...on...the ...when ...went...chatter ...what
...another ...night ...Before ...time ...we had ...world...was...in
...Of ...not...be...different ...were ...in...that world ...the
...water ...something ...and I knew ...to ...to the ...before...
...was not too...far...to...start...again.

Thirteen

The first and most noticeable consequence of that bizarre banquet-cum-orgy was that all the women I saw that morning had something of an air about them – an air part the softness of satisfaction, part the stiff weariness that follows a strenuous night of shagging. If I had thought the women of the harem were for the exclusive use of their master, I was wildly wrong.

When I found Samara, she exuded that air to a high degree. She blushed and giggled, and there was a suggestion of shy pride in her manner as she told me something of her wild night. She had never been with a man before. She had known what to expect, of course, for the women coached and instructed each other as a matter of common practice. But she had been in the seraglio now for almost a year and the Bey had not selected her. She was beginning, she said, to worry that she was plain and unenticing and would never 'become a true woman'.

Last night she proved otherwise. Lots of men, she told me with a proud blush, had wanted her. Oh yes, she was a little sore in her bottom, and her jaw ached, and her hips were rather stiff, but it was worth it. Some of the men had been rough, and there were bruises on her breasts and thighs, but oh, she was truly a woman now! Perhaps, if she was lucky, the Bey himself might even select her now.

She was so filled with delight and happiness that it communicated itself to me, and I hugged her for joy. I looked about me with brighter eyes. The bathhouse was more crowded than usual, and there was a buzz of whispering and giggling among the score or more naked women, as if they were comparing notes about their night's escapades. Clearly, being part of what can only be described as an orgy met with their approval.

It was only after some time that I realised that I had not seen Felicity anywhere. I looked in her sleeping chamber. I searched all three bathrooms, and then the garden-court. She was nowhere to be found. I hurried to Farah, but she did not know where Felicity was either. She did not appear until the middle of the day, by which time I was becoming quite disturbed. When at last she appeared, my perturbation turned at once to wonder and curiosity.

A figure in a *chadoor* drifted through the bathhouse portal. The voluminous garment was discarded with a languid motion to reveal the naked form of Felicity. Without a word, without even looking about her at the assembled women, she moved towards the room that housed the hot tubs. The way she moved was strangely different from her usual elegant walk, but it was rather the expression upon her face that struck me.

It was as if she was moving through some heavenly dream. Her eyes were soft and enormous, and she seemed to be gazing at some paradisal vista rather than at the chamber she was moving through. Her face was lit with such a gentle half-smile that her beauty was doubled and redoubled.

What could have happened to her? What wondrous experience could have so transformed her?

I went to her as she lay in a tub of steaming water, her voluptuous breasts swaying as she moved her arms gently to stir the aromatic oils. She seemed not to notice me until I spoke, and when she looked up at me I could have drowned in her eyes.

'Oh, Lydia!' was all she said, in a voice so soft it was hardly even a whisper. 'Oh, Lydia!'

That whisper proved to be the start of the oddest, and in its way the most difficult, situation in which I have ever become involved. I did not know it at the time, but Felicity's melting state was to cause problems which engaged not only myself, but the Bey and numerous others, and which might well have caused a diplomatic incident.

As usual in the harem, it was Farah, through Samara's offices as translator, who apprised me of the problem – and for the only time in the brief spell I knew her Farah was flustered and at a loss. It seemed that the consequences of the night's orgy were deeper than simply a bunch of women comparing notes, for the Egyptian gentleman, on recovering from his night of love with Felicity, had straightaway gone to the Bey and demanded to buy her.

He was, I came to learn, a very important man in relations between the British military powers in Cairo, and thus our Government at home, and the Ottoman rulers in Istanbul. As well as that, he was uncountably rich in his own right. Both these things gave him great power, even over the Bey.

Since she had been represented to him as one of the Bey's concubines the Egyptian, whose name I learned was Tapak Nasseri, had assumed that she would be available for purchase. Price was not an object, for he was besotted with her, and determined to have her.

Of course the whole thing was ridiculous. Felicity was an Englishwoman, and not to be bought by anyone, no matter how rich or powerful. Unfortunately, there were two other considerations which made the whole situation even more bizarre.

The first was that apparently Mr Nasseri was powerful enough to make it difficult for our ship's repairs to be completed, and thus at least delay our sailing: powerful enough even to wrest Felicity from the Bey's palace by main force. The second, which I learned when I told Felicity of our problem, was that she *wanted* to be bought – longed desperately to stay with him.

Quite what had happened between them during that orgiastic night I could not imagine, but whatever it was Felicity was indeed infatuated with her new lover. At first I chided her. Had she forgotten Jonathan Andrews, for whom she had professed undying love such a short span of weeks ago? Had she not even declared her love for *me* only a few nights earlier? And what about her 'Chamberlain'? How would he take her change in affections?

She cast my objections aside without a thought. She belonged heart and soul to her wonderful Tapak, and would never leave him.

I had to become practical. I pointed out the impossibility of her father, back in Africa, consenting to such an outlandish arrangement as his only daughter becoming the concubine of an Egyptian. I reminded her that she was not yet twenty-one, and thus a minor in the eyes of the law. I told her of the scandal that would be caused – and not just a local scandal either, but spreading from here all the way to England and Africa.

Nothing would move her. She was absolutely adamant. She would, she said, sweep aside any barriers. Why, if necessary, she would run away with him!

I was horrified. I loved Felicity enough to want her happiness, but was aghast at the problems her new passion would stir up. I conferred with Farah. She could think of nothing save virtually imprisoning the girl until our ship departed, and preventing her ever seeing the man again. I thought there must be a less cruel solution. I asked her to arrange an interview for me with the Bey. Surely he would be able to help.

I dressed carefully in my European clothes for our meeting, thinking that formality would keep things businesslike. It was lucky I did, for the moment I saw him as I entered his chamber my tummy lurched and my breasts tingled, and I am sure that had he made the slightest move for me, I'd have been on my back with my legs up in an instant.

He did not, and our meeting was indeed businesslike, though fruitless, for the Bey confirmed that Mr Nasseri was as besotted as Felicity, and as determined to have her.

What was worse, he was a man of considerable power, and might well carry out his threat to bear her off by main force.

Suddenly, a very flustered man burst into the room. He threw himself onto his knees before the Bey, touching his forehead to the floor and gabbling frantically. The Bey gave a bellow, and leapt to his feet, his face flushed with anger. I stared from one to the other. I had no idea what was going on, and found the angry Bey a rather frightening sight.

He rushed to the door, shouting what seemed to be a stream of orders. There was pandemonium. Uniformed men rushed hither and yon; the Bey shouted; I heard a bugle sounding. I hurried over to the Bey, grabbed his arm, demanded to know what was happening, what all this noise and rushing was about.

When he told me that Felicity had dressed up in her European clothes as though to take a walk outside the harem, but instead had flitted and was last seen going off with Tapak Nasseri, I felt like to swoon. But when the Bey told me he was sending out an armed party to bring them back, I came to my senses. What of the scandal! All I could think of was the public furore such a thing would stir up, of the appalling after effects there might be.

I grabbed the Bey's hands, tugged him willy-nilly back into his chamber. There must not be a fuss. We must deal with this quietly. To send out troops would stir up a hornets' nest. Besides, if Nasseri really was powerful, would it not bring down greater trouble on our heads?

Somehow, I persuaded him that it would be better if he took me to wherever the two elopers had gone. I would talk to Felicity, find some way to pull her back from this rashness. Actually, I had no idea what I was going to say to the impetuous girl, but nevertheless I managed to sway him to my way of thinking.

Instead of troops, the Bey sent out runners charged with finding out where Nasseri had taken Felicity. It transpired

183

that they were in a house on the far side of the town. Conveyed in a closed litter and accompanied by the Bey and half a dozen retainers, I was hurried over there.

It was not easy to get to see them, for Felicity was reluctant and knew we would try to get her away. At last we managed it though, and the sight of Felicity clinging wide eyed and nervous to Nasseri's arm caused my heart to soften. She had discarded her European clothes, and was dressed again in harem style. She gazed from Nasseri to me with such pleading in her eyes that I knew in my heart of hearts it would be too cruel to part her from this man. Nevertheless, something had to be done.

'Felicity,' I heard myself saying. 'This is silly.'

'I will not leave him.' She clung tighter, and her voice quavered, for she seemed close to tears. My mind was racing.

'You do not have to lose him, my dear, but there must be a better way than this,' I said. 'Think of the scandal. Think of the repercussions. Why our Government might even get involved!'

It took long persuasion, for Felicity was ready to face anything rather than lose this new love. Verily, she was mad for him. At last, though, a plan was concocted – complicated, and with some risky aspects, but a plan none the less.

Tapak Nasseri agreed to abandon any other arrangements, and book a passage on our ship all the way to England. In the meantime, until the necessary repair in the engine room had been completed, he would take up residence in the Bey's palace. That way, the couple could be together as much as they wished (though how we were going to keep their relationship from Captain Prendergast I had no idea) and make love to their hearts' content.

In the meanwhile, a message would be sent to Captain Mackay back in southern Africa seeking permission for them to marry. I thought privately that such permission

184

would almost certainly not be forthcoming, but the ploy would give us time, and who knew but Felicity might cool down in the meantime.

It was a complicated plan, and took long and difficult negotiation. Felicity alternately sobbed and clung wide eyed to her lover's arm. Tapak bridled, grew angry, calmed, talked. He and the Bey from time to time conducted intense exchanges in their own languages.

I stuck to what proved to be my most telling argument. There would be uproar. Governments would get involved. We had no choice but to follow my suggested plan. They could still spend time in each other's arms, albeit sneakily. They could eventually be together for all time. And my way, they could avoid an explosion of scandal and diplomatic uproar.

At last, I prevailed. All was agreed. Felicity was in a transport of happiness. Nasseri was smug. Wine was produced, and we celebrated.

Our discussions had taken hours. It was now well into the night. With a sidelong glance that sent my blood a-flutter, the Bey suggested that it was too late to return to his palace. Were there, by chance, accommodations Nasseri could offer so that we did not need to journey back through the darkened town?

There were. The Bey glanced at me, a smile on his face as his eyes moved from mine down to my bosom, and back again. I felt my nipples perk. Clearly he did not intend that his accommodations and mine should be separate. Felicity looked at me with arch understanding in her beautiful eyes. She knew that she would spend the night with her beloved Tapak, I with the Bey. There was an air of happy complicity as Tapak Nasseri sent for more wine.

We took supper together, and it was the only occasion in the weeks we were in the little port town that we women ate in the company of men. Even at the Prince's banquet, only the menfolk had dined, while the women served them.

The atmosphere, already high with Felicity's happiness

and my own excitement that I would be spending another night with one of the most skilful and sensitive lovers I have ever known, grew more tense with unspoken eagerness as we worked our way through mutton, rice-filled vine leaves, various pastes we dipped flat breads into and wine and coffee.

By the time we got to the fruit I was almost blushing at the intensity with which the Bey was looking at me. Though he had shown delicate table manners at the start of the meal, by the end he was biting so eagerly on his peaches and grapes that juice was positively pouring down his chin as he chomped as though in a race.

Mind you, so was Tapak Nasseri, though Felicity hardly ate a scrap, for she simply sat gazing with adoration at her new love. When I reflected on it later, I could not for the life of me see why she had been so suddenly struck all of a heap.

He was by no means an unattractive man, but neither did there seem to be anything about him which could send a girl off her head – at least not so far as his face and figure suggested. He was a neat man, quite slight in stature, with short, very black hair and sharp eyes, and the habitual expression on his face was rather serious. His voice was surprisingly deep, though rather quiet, and for a supposedly rich and powerful man he seemed oddly diffident. It was obviously something other than his outward appearance that had so struck Felicity.

Those reflections came much later, however. At the time, my only thoughts – other than what was soon to happen with the Bey – were that Felicity's 'Chamberlain' would be out of luck from now on. And probably Solfina, Donaldson and anybody else for that matter.

Supper being over, Nasseri and Felicity lost no time in ushering us off to our chambers so that they could hurry off to their own. My earlier eagerness had changed to an odd nervousness, and a veritable flock of butterflies rose up in my tummy as I preceded the Bey along the passage.

There was no servant with us to necessitate circumspection, and we had hardly left our supper companions when the Bey's hand alighted on the small of my back, and descended to my hip.

We had been given a room each, but it never occurred to either of us to use more than one. The chamber we both entered was large and prettily furnished, with several spindly but beautifully carved chairs, and an enormous bed.

The very moment we stepped through the portal, the Bey's hands slid round me from behind. He cupped my breasts and pulled me to him, his breath warm upon my neck as he began to kiss me. My butterflies vanished, and became that oh, so familiar ball of warmth deep within my loins.

The Bey was very different now from the casual figure who had watched me strip off my veils that glorious night in his palace. This time, he undressed me with his own hands. I was made to stand perfectly still as he moved about me, undoing my buttons with surprisingly delicate fingers.

Slowly, he slipped my little jacket from my shoulders. He held me again, and kissed my ear and fondled my breasts, which felt the warmth of his hands even through the cotton of my blouse and my chemisette. The buttons at the waist of my skirt were undone next, and the heavy garment at once fell to the floor.

I had on only one petticoat over my drawers, and the Bey's hands slipped down over my hips, exploring me slowly. The warmth of his touch sent little shivers of electricity through my thighs and bottom as his hands moved over me, taking in every curve and crevice with such teasing slowness I was quite breathless by the time he moved up to unbutton my blouse.

With pretty well every other man I have ever been with, the aim has been to get a girl's clothes off as quickly as possible, to get to the naked and willing flesh underneath as fast as may be. With the Bey, the reverse seemed to be the case.

187

He stripped me with infinite slowness, such slowness, indeed, that as he paused to kiss and fondle me between each garment I had to hold myself back from begging him to go faster, to tear off my remaining clothes and throw me onto the bed.

As he undid the ties of my chemisette and slipped it down over my shoulders, goose flesh shivered over me as my breasts were bared to his eyes and touch. My nipples were standing like throbbing pegs. His wonderful mouth descended on one, the palm of his hand smoothed over the other. Oh, how I wished he had not enjoined me to remain still, for I longed to throw my arms about him, to crush myself against him.

It was a delicious agony to have to stand motionless as this skilful, insidious man teased and toyed with me, and I had to clamp my thighs together to prevent my legs buckling under me.

When I was down to just my stockings, he got me to stand with my feet apart and my hands behind my back. Every part of my naked body was now open to him. He stepped back and slowly looked me over. Never have I felt so available, so offered if you take my point. Never have I felt so eager, so pent up with desire.

Oh, what a cunning, devious man he was! He knew full well the state he had got me into, knew that by teasing and delaying thus he was driving me to such heights of excitement as were dizzying me.

He stepped close again, and I could feel myself actually shivering as his hands and lips explored every part of me. Oh, it was torture to have to remain still as he caressed and kissed and licked! The only time he allowed me to move was when he knelt at my feet, and then only to bend my legs and part my knees further.

I came near to crumbling as his hot tongue dipped into the oozing folds of my cunny. I know I gasped aloud, and stood panting with the effort of controlling myself despite the wild sensations that were surging through my body and bursting in my head.

He kept me in that state for a thousand years, on the very threshold of a come, but never quite there; trembling on the edge, yearning to dive over, but never being allowed. Such exquisite torture!

Then somehow – I was too far gone to register details – he, too, was naked and we were on the bed. So pent up was I, so longing for the culmination of a glorious fuck, that I was moving into a come even as he lay me on my back and parted my legs.

He would have tormented me further, I know, for he merely slid the bulb of his rampant cock along my sopping crease, only touched on my entrance, did not thrust. I prevented him teasing me more, avoided further torture, for of its own accord my body bucked, my pelvis thrust itself up, and I crammed myself upon him with a cry of grateful release.

He did not need to fuck me, for I fucked him. My legs clamped themselves about him. My hips jerked and bucked and writhed as I exploded into such a come that I was no more than an animal, a bitch on heat as my sheath squirmed about his beautiful cock, and my cunny-lips ground themselves against his root.

When he, too, burst into a come, flooding my depths with his fire, I collapsed. Exhausted, like an unstrung puppet, my limbs fell away from him. He did not pull out of me. Even though I felt him become smaller, he stayed inside me, rocking very gently, allowing me to rest but also ensuring that my sensations did not entirely die away.

My head was a red fog, my skin so sensitive that I could actually feel the impression of his nipple on my collarbone as he lay on me. Though he was heavy, and his hard body crushed my breasts, it felt so good I never wanted it to end.

And then, with a sense of awe, I felt him growing and stiffening again inside me. That second shag was even more wonderful than the first, though less wild. As he hardened he began to move more powerfully. It was not a thrusting and withdrawing, for he kept himself deep inside me. Instead, it was a circling, a pushing and relaxing, which kept me filled, and stirred and fulfilled.

After a while he grasped me in his arms and, still firmly embedded in my throbbing quim, rolled us both over so that I was now on top.

How did this wonderful man know me so well? It was as if his every thought, his every move was consciously designed to show me what the heights of lovemaking really were. The beguiling slowness with which he had stripped and caressed me; the forcefulness of that first delirious fuck; the way he remained inside me and gently rocked; and now!

That I was astride him: that I could kneel up, and brace my hands against his firm belly: that I could grind and circle my loins against his pelvis to my own time, to meet my own mounting needs, was glorious.

He reached up with his strong hands and grasped my breasts as I writhed upon his superb cock. He gripped my nipples between his forefingers and thumbs, and tugged and squeezed them. I did not care even though he caused me pain, for it was slight pain, and pain that made my other rapturous sensations even more piquant.

I do not to this day know whether we actually slept that night. I know that I was in a dream, in a daze of voluptuous enjoyment. I think we must have slept – common sense says we must have. But if we did it can only have been in brief snatches, for my memory is of constant writhing, of his unending, overwhelming pumping into my weeping quim, of coming and coming and coming, and disbelief that he could fuck me so well and for so long.

What I do know is that when a serving girl arrived to call us to breakfast she gasped with shock and conveyed her message staring at the ceiling because we were in that head-and-tail position adopted when lovers are pleasuring one another with their mouths.

I know too, though it was not a decision, more an inevitability, that I neglected to put on any clothes but merely draped a sheet about myself when, drooping on the Bey's arm with sated senses, I went to breakfast. I cared not for the servants who hovered about, cared not even for Felicity's gasp and giggle of shock at my *deshabille*. Nothing mattered except the wonderful night I had experienced and the sensations I was still only just descending from. Why, if my Bey had demanded to fuck me tied up naked to a post in the town square at noon for the delectation of his subjects, I would have dragged him there, so far gone was I!

It was almost the middle of the day when we got back to the palace, for neither of the men (and certainly not Felicity or I) was in a hurry to leave. There was a small bathroom in the house, and as Felicity and I bathed together, she waxed lyrical about her wonderful Tapak and how clever I had been to think of a way they could be together for ever without all the scandal and danger of an elopement.

I still could not for the life of me work out what it was about the man that had her so besotted, but besotted she certainly was. If she told me once that she loved him, she told me a dozen times. As I dressed myself in native clothes afterwards (my European garb I wrapped in a bundle and caried with me as being too hot to wear) I found myself becoming pensive.

Had I ever been in love, Felicity had asked. Had I? I could not be sure.

Could what I had felt for my wonderful Talesi be called love? He was the man who had first taught me the joys of my body, had opened me up as it were, and been my constant lover for all the months I had been a captive of his tribe. He certainly held a place deep in my heart, and the warmth of his smile and the gentleness of his glance came fresh to my mind now. But if what I had felt for Talesi was love, it was far from the over-riding emotion Felicity demonstrated for her Tapak.

Perhaps what Felicity thought of as love was actually a deep desire to surrender herself to the first person willing to accept that surrender? She had 'loved' Jonathan – my own Jonathan, for whom I still felt strong affections. She had even 'loved' me so recently, when she lay with me all those times in the harem and given me sweet, submissive kisses. And I am sure that had she been asked, when I witnessed her drying Solfina's body with her own hair and then kissing and nuzzling the magnificent Nubian woman to a climax, she would have insisted that she 'loved' Solfina.

If love, I thought, meant Felicity's kind of surrendering, than I had never loved. Surrendering to the raptures of physical sensation is one thing – and a delicious thing at that – but to become absorbed and enraptured one's every waking moment, as Felicity always professed to be, is quite another. I have not felt that, and do not wish to thank you very much, for to feel thus is to place oneself too much at another's mercy.

No. I would rather pass my time in pleasant company and enjoy the delights of sex for their own sakes than become besotted with anyone.

The delights of sex had caught up with me now, for my second night with the Bey (and indeed, half the morning) had fair drained me, and it was a very weary Lydia who gathered her *chadoor* about her and climbed into the closed litter to be carried back to the Bey's palace.

Tiliu and Samara were all agog to know where on earth we had been, and what was happening. There had been rumours flying about the seraglio, but nobody really knew anything, and they were desperate to discover all. My obvious tiredness and the veritable glow of contentment Felicity had about her only lent spurs to their curiosity.

They would have nagged me to a frazzle had not the wise Farah intervened. She had heard of our return and immediately hurried to my little sleeping chamber. Unlike Tiliu and Samara, though, her curiosity was well under control. Seeing at once how weary I was, she clapped her hands and ordered everyone out. I was to rest, and would tell my story at the evening meal.

Perhaps the gratitude I felt to Farah as I sank down among my cushions to sleep was something like the love Felicity goes on about.

Fourteen

Matters quieted about the harem after the banquet and its tempestuous aftermath, for which you may be sure I was very thankful. Farah and the others listened excitedly when, after my rest, I told them what had transpired with Felicity and Mr Nasseri, and Farah thoroughly approved of the plan I had come up with for them.

I had a beautiful night's sleep (alone) and felt refreshed and content when I ventured out for the normal morning walk with our ship's officers the next day. I was rather surprised to find that William alone awaited us. He at once asked where Felicity was. I could not possibly tell him that I had been unable to drag her away from her new love, and so I said she had a headache. Then William told me the reason he was alone. It both pleased me, and gave me a little pang of sadness.

It seemed that Sharpe and Donaldson had remained aboard the ship because the repairs to the engine had been completed, and everybody was now busy cleaning up and getting the ship 'Bristol fashion' (whatever that meant) and ready to set sail within the next couple of days.

The news delighted me, for it meant we would get home to England all the sooner. Yet I would be sad to leave this exotic place. When I worked it out, I was surprised that we had only been residing in the Bey's harem for a little under four weeks, yet so much seemed to have happened.

That morning's walk, with just William, Tiliu and I, was brief, for William was so excited about the prospect of setting to sea again that he was anxious to hurry back – so anxious, in fact, that he did not even suggest our usual little dalliance in the glen.

Our leave-taking, actually the very next afternoon, was as emotional as if we had been saying goodbye for ever to lifelong friends. I had a brief and poignant interview with the Bey, at which he kissed me and prayed Allah to watch over me, and I was hard put to hold back tears.

I could not hold them back when it came time to say goodbye to Farah, who had almost become the mother I never knew, and they came in floods when Samara, sweet, gentle Samara, threw her arms about me and we sobbed on each other's shoulders. All I wanted in the world at that moment was to carry the dear girl off with me. The last I saw of her she was clad in a *chadoor*, hurrying out to where I sat on the cart that was to haul us to the quayside. In her hands she clutched an ornate little chest which was surprisingly heavy when she handed it to me, along with two keys and an injunction to take great care of it. The last I saw of her was her little hand reaching out and squeezing mine in a final farewell.

I looked into the little chest when I got on board, thinking it to be a farewell present from Farah or Samara. You can imagine my astonishment when I saw that it contained the jewellery I had worn on my first night with the Bey. I had quite forgotten it, and was awed at its richness. This fresh reminder of the wonderful man brought renewed tears to my eyes.

I was in a very pensive mood that first evening back aboard ship, and was still lying awake in my bunk in the early hours when the ship's repaired engine rumbled into life and we began to churn our way towards England again.

It seemed to me at the time that my life was becoming filled with goodbyes. So recently, less than two months ago in fact, I had waved goodbye to Jonathan and father and Africa. Now, I was not waving, but lying on my bunk in the dark, the faces of Farah and the Bey, of Solfina and my dear Samara swimming before my tear-filled eyes.

* * *

My mood was lightened next morning at breakfast when I saw my beloved Alice Prendergast for the first time since I had gone to stay in the harem. She was all a-bubble with things to tell me and questions to ask. Clearly, much of what we had to say to each other could only be told in private, and after breakfast we repaired alone to a forepart of the deck, where we could sit alone under our parasols in the brilliant sunshine, and gossip to our hearts' content.

Alice wanted to know every single detail of my adventures, and I have to say that relating them to her brought them into perspective. Alice has a ribald sense of humour, and laughed heartily at the tale of Felicity and her 'Chamberlain', and at the way the Bey had tricked me into his bed.

She rather shocked me by revealing that she had guessed all along what kind of establishment we three girls had been taken to, and had been hard put to it to keep a straight face when her husband and the other officers spoke of 'the women's quarters', and congratulated themselves on our being safe from harm there.

Somehow or other, she seemed to know quite a lot about the eastern way with womenfolk. Perhaps she had read about it somewhere. However that may be, she was not at all surprised when I told her how the women consoled each other for the absence of men. It seems that the physical love of one woman for another is a well-known phenomenon, and even has a name. A woman who makes love to another woman is apparently called a 'lesbian', the name being derived from a Greek island where, in ancient times, only women lived.

Another surprise came when she asked me what I thought about 'eunuchs'. I became quite horrified when Alice responded to my professions of ignorance by telling me that it is common practice in this part of the world to have harems guarded by males who have had their manhood taken away. What an appalling idea!

I was aghast as she told me that these 'eunuchs' were highly regarded and often important people, and often actually *voluntarily* had themselves emasculated at a young age to gain a comfortable life. I could not conceive of such a barbarous thing. Thank heavens there had been no such creatures at our harem!

To change the subject, I hurried on to tell Alice about my night with the Bey, and about the banquet and its riotous aftermath, and about the beautiful maiden from Malagasy.

When I related the madness of Felicity and Tapak Nasseri, and my proposed solution, she found it vastly amusing, and wondered aloud how they would contrive their trysts. She described delicious images of Felicity scurrying along corridors late at night, and the Egyptian sneaking her off to secluded spots during the day, and we both laughed until our ribs ached.

As it transpired, no such sneaking about was necessary, for the atmosphere and arrangements on the ship became very different from what they had been before the engine failure.

The greatest difference was in Alice's husband, Captain Prendergast. Their marriage, though only some six weeks old, had wrought amazing changes in him. No longer the dour, puritanical man we had set out with from the port of East London, he had softened considerably, smiled readily, and treated everyone alike genially and with none of his old sharpness.

But the most important of the changes Alice had wrought in him, so far as the rest of us were concerned, was that he no longer watched everything that happened with a beady eye towards criticism. Of course, he was as alert as ever to the actual command of the vessel, but in so far as the off-duty doings of his officers and crew, and naturally we passengers, he was much more relaxed and forbearing.

This was especially lucky for Felicity and Tapak Nasseri, for at mealtimes they were so obviously wrapped up in each other, spooning together at the end of the table, that one would have needed to be blind and daft not to notice.

In former times, our captain would have frowned and probably berated them. Now, after the first occasion, when he did indeed frown but then whispered briefly with Alice and nodded, he proceeded to ignore them.

As for the rest of us, since we all knew what was going on we made no bones about it. For a day or two Donaldson was quite jealous, for after all he had been getting his shags off Felicity since the voyage began, and now he might have been invisible so far as the enraptured girl was concerned. He might actually have made some difficulties had he not been assuaged, as shall be related.

Thus it was that nobody remarked it when they saw the lovers wandering the decks hand in hand, or came upon them in hot embraces behind a pile of cargo. When Felicity deserted her own cabin to move into Nasseri's in open cohabitation, a few eyebrows were raised, but as much in arch humour as anything else.

Just as Felicity and her beau became an exclusive pair, so did Tiliu and Sharpe. They were not so openly besotted as the other two, and were much more circumspect in their public behaviour. Nevertheless, we all soon knew that they wished to cleave only to each other.

I could quite see why. Tiliu's delight when she had first seen and tasted Sharpe's splendid manhood had continued and grown throughout our time in the harem, and her almost daily shags on our morning walks. I myself had found him too substantial for comfort on the two or three occasions I had shagged him, but Tiliu obviously relished it.

As for Sharpe, it must have been a dream come true. When I first knew him he had been resigned to never having a woman because his cock was too large. Now, he had as partner a delicious and lusty girl who relished it, and would, I knew, fuck him to a finish at any time and in any place.

As for myself, dear William ensured that I did not become frustrated.

* * *

Thus it was that all four of we females were well sorted in so far as the pleasures of the bed were concerned. What did not occur to me, and certainly should have had I not been so contented with my lot, was that there were a considerable number of other men on board our vessel who were not so well sorted.

Inevitably, the situations of the lucky few became known, and irked the others, especially Donaldson.

Days aboard our vessel as we sailed through the Red Sea were a joy, for the weather was bright but not too hot, the seas around us were the most lovely blue, and all was calm and peace. I spent much time of a morning promenading with Alice, chatting about things past and what we would do when we reached England. Tiliu often found the opportunity to walk the decks with us, for though she was still officially a servant, and helped out in the officers' galley, she ofttimes escaped her duties to walk and talk with us.

Luncheon in the mess was a relaxed affair even when Captain Prendergast was present, and afterwards I would repair to my cabin for a nap until early evening. The afternoons were the hottest part of the day, and it was a delight to shuck off my clothes, rinse myself off at the washbasin with a flannel and a bowl of cold water, and lie naked on my bunk.

That William sometimes found it possible to visit me at those times was a very pleasant bonus, for a slow, gentle shag on a peaceful afternoon is a lovely thing. Mind you, I always had to give myself another cold-water wash after he had gone.

Thereafter, I would dress (as lightly as possible, for I found our European clothing even more irksome and sweaty after the light veils of the harem) and walk about the decks again to fill the time before dinner.

It was on just such an occasion that I began to notice the odd looks I would get from the various crew men I encountered, and more especially from Donaldson. He had tried it on with me before, and been put off. Now, though, there was a tension, a sort of coiled-spring feeling about the way he looked at me that gave me pause.

It was not that he seemed aggressive in any way. Indeed, quite the reverse, for he seemed anxious to approach me but nervous of doing so. Of course, I had rejected his advances weeks ago, and none too gently at that, and he probably suspected that I might do so again unless he approached me very diplomatically.

He was not unattractive to look upon, being tall and well built, and with rather nice eyes. When I had spurned him before it was not because of his looks; a man's looks are not, after all, the most important consideration. Rather, it had been because his approach had been rather arrogant, as though he only had to suggest and my drawers would fall off. Now, that arrogance had vanished.

I paused in my promenade about the deck, watching a pair of gulls wheeling and squawking in the ship's wake. As I had suspected, he drew near me.

'Miss Masters,' he said, his rather tentative tones confirming what I had suspected. 'I wonder whether you will allow me to walk with you. It is a lovely day, and a turn about the deck would be pleasant.'

It was indeed pleasant to stroll with him as the evening drew on. His conversation was polite and enjoyable, and he told me about the Suez Canal, which we would be sailing through quite soon. I had not seen this construction, which he called the eighth wonder of the world, for my journey out to southern Africa less than two years ago had been by way of the west coast.

I grew quite fascinated as he related how it had taken ten full years to build (does one *build* a canal, I wonder, or *dig* one?) and drew word-pictures of hordes of labourers shovelling and carting the desert soil under the direction of someone called Ferdinand de Lesseps.

What was more fascinating, though, was the undercurrent in the way he talked and the manner in which he comported himself. It was clear, though he tried to hide it, that his aim was to worm his way into my good books.

I defy any healthy girl to deny that she enjoys the efforts

of a man to please and flatter her. I certainly enjoyed myself now as Donaldson smoothed about me, all charm and gallantry. And what made it more delicious was his tentative manner, as though the slightest rebuff would send him into retreat.

I am a wicked girl in some ways. I knew full well that the main aim of his pleasantries was to get himself between my legs, and such a thing is flattering to a girl. I decided to play that lovely game of tease and parry; to let him believe he was winning his way with me, and at the same time to disappoint his hopes. In short, to tease and titillate, and enjoy watching a man wriggle.

I had done just that with Captain Mackay and the odious Dr Williams, and had thoroughly enjoyed both the game and the results.

Then, though, I had been able to play the innocent, for both those men thought me entirely naïve and inexperienced. Donaldson knew otherwise.

Even so, though he well knew that I was no wilting little virgin, the rules of our society forbade him from openly asking for a shag, or even from hinting at all directly. Thus, over the next few days we engaged in a happy flirting game – well, happy for me, though perhaps rather frustrating for him.

I got progressively softer towards him, allowed him to sit close at mealtimes, let him whisper in my ear, take my hand to help me over the many little steps and obstacles that lie about a ship, fluttered at him a little. Oh, it was a delight to watch his growing keenness – and to see the occasional stiffness within his trousers!

I had to be careful not to wind him up too far. Once, when I had behaved in such a way as he thought he had the chance to kiss me only for me to turn away at the last moment, and another time when I let him walk me to my cabin door but made it clear he would not get in, I had detected flashes of irritation, even anger, in his eyes. I did not for a moment think he would become violent, but had to be careful none the less.

I did not need to be careful about how William felt. He had long got over the possessive jealousy he'd felt when he discovered that I'd shagged Sharpe, and I had even told him about going to the Bey's bed (though not the details, of course). Besides, I rarely, if ever, turned him down when he wanted a fuck, so he had no grounds for complaint on that score.

We were actually into the Suez Canal when I at last rewarded Donaldson's persistence. It had been a beautiful day, and was now a soft, balmy evening. An enormous moon hung in a sky brilliant with more stars than I could ever have imagined. On either side of the ship, the land that is Egypt slipped silently by, dark and mysterious.

I was feeling mellow partly because Donaldson had been very pleasant, and partly because at dinner I had been moved by the tender, endearing way Felicity and Tapak looked into each other's eyes, and whispered, and helped each other to the various dishes. Now, as I stood at the ship's rail gazing at the stars, Donaldson appeared at my side.

I had not planned any change in our relations. For several minutes, he stood beside me without speaking, then remarked in a voice strangely soft, how beautiful the evening was. We talked quietly about how old and mysterious was the land of Egypt, and how huge the sky seemed in this part of the world, and how beautiful the stars.

Donaldson began to point out various clusters of stars and to tell me the names of some of the constellations. In doing so, he moved to stand behind me so he could point them out more clearly. I was suddenly aware of his closeness, of his breath soft on my ear, of the hand he rested so lightly on my shoulder.

In that single moment it became inevitable that Donaldson would achieve his goal, and that very evening.

He continued to tell me about the stars and to relate some of the ancient legends about how they came to be there. He moved to stand beside me, talking softly. I turned to face him. He saw something in my expression, for his voice tailed off. There was an age of silence.

Slowly, his eyes glowing, he raised a hand and oh, so softly, touched my cheek. I seemed to have been holding my breath, for when he leaned down and planted the softest, most chaste of kisses on my lips, I found myself breathing quickly.

It was most strange. From the way he had treated Felicity, and from the way I had teased him over the last few days, one would have expected him to leap upon me at the first sign of encouragement. He did not.

He kissed me again, a more protracted kiss, but no more forceful than the first. He took my hand and led me along the deck to where a pile of sacks covered with a tarpaulin lay in deep shadow. Not a word was exchanged. He took me in his arms. His kisses were more ardent now, but still gentle, more asking than demanding, if you take my point. I found myself melting into his embrace.

He undressed me very slowly, kissing my lips, my neck, my breasts. We were in a world divorced from reality. It did not occur to either of us that we might be discovered. The night breeze was delectable on my skin as he got me naked and lay me on the tarpaulin. He did not strip off his own clothes, but stood gazing down at me for long moments.

The night air and the excitement of the moment had turned my body into one tingling sensation, and when he reached down and with a single fingertip traced a line from my chin down between my breasts, and on to cup my quim in the palm of his hand, I veritably shuddered with pleasure.

He knelt between my welcoming thighs, fumbled with his buttons, lowered himself. My cunny was already hot for him, and I cried out with joy as he came into me with a single, commanding thrust.

Everything conspired to make it the most delicious of fucks. He was not frantic, but seemed to be taking care to ensure my pleasure. The cool of the air contrasting with the hotness of his body lent my sensations piquancy. The roof of stars gave it all an added exotic romance. Donaldson even showed unexpected sensitivity by holding back until I began my come before bursting into his. Oh, it was lovely!

Afterwards we lay side by side for a long time, drifting down from our rapture and drinking in the beauty of the night. I did not want to get dressed, but at last I had to. When Donaldson asked if he might come to my cabin later, I eagerly agreed.

Too eagerly as it transpired.

I was ready for his visit quite early. All through dinner I had been puzzling over what to wear – and getting quite warm at the knowledge that whatever it was would probably not stay on me for long.

I chose to wear the lovely black silk corset Alice had made for me. I knew he would like the way the little boned-cup affairs at the top pushed up my breasts. I also wore black stockings, with lacy white garters. Before donning my voluminous black chiffon nightgown, I examined myself in the long looking glass fixed to the wall.

I gave a little wriggle of pleasure. Donaldson would love what he saw, even though he had seen even more of me only a few hours ago. I knew that, for some reason, men seem to get more excited by a partially clad woman than a naked one. The black silk of my scanty garments made the paleness of my bare skin seem even more alluring.

My bush was still close-trimmed from my preparation for the banquet, and even I could hardly drag my eyes away from the pouting little lips at the join of my thighs. Donaldson would be entranced. When I donned my nightgown, the resulting shadow-show excited even me.

He arrived quite soon after I finished readying myself. As I had hoped, he gazed open-mouthed, his eye racing over me and his face flushing with excitement.

Once again, just as earlier out on the deck, he resisted the temptation to leap upon me. Instead, after a few minutes of hot kisses and fondlings of my breasts, he stepped back and began to unbutton his tunic.

I have watched any number of men get their clothes off, and it is not usually an enticing sight. Their one concern is to whip their garments off as fast as possible and get at the girl, and they pay no attention to the fact that their very undressing might serve as an excitement to the girl who is watching. Donaldson knew better.

He took off his tunic, folded it carefully, and placed it on my little settee. He turned to face me, smiling as he loosed his collar stud and cuffs. The torso he revealed as he slowly pulled his shirt off over his head made my mouth water. His skin was lightly tanned, as though he were often bare chested in the sun – though I had never seen him so. His shoulders were broad and his arms and chest well muscled. As he turned to fold his shirt and put it with his tunic, I found myself comparing his torso with Talesi's – and not unfavourably, for Donaldson's skin was just as smooth and his muscles just as lithe. Even the dusting of dark hairs on his chest did not detract from his handsomeness.

He knew the value of delay and teasing, for he was in no hurry. He sat down and slowly removed his boots and hose, rolling each sock neatly and placing one in each boot, before putting the boots neatly under the settee.

He stood and faced me again, a smile on his face as his eyes ran over me from head to toe. My nipples were stiff, and the way my breasts were pushed up by my corset caused them to stand out clearly through the chiffon of my nightgown. He reached out a hand and squeezed my left nipple between his thumb and forefinger, not hard, but firmly enough for a little shiver of pain to make my breath quicken. He smiled again at my little gasp, and stepped back.

Still smiling, he slowly unbuckled his belt. My eyes were fixed upon his hands as he undid the button at his waist, for I was by now very aroused, and eager to engage with the treasure inside his trousers. To tease me even more (and he was already teasing me very successfully, I can assure you) he actually turned away as he unbuttoned his fly, delaying my first glimpse of the organ I was now nearly panting for.

But I already knew better than him the game of tease and entice – what woman would not – and I affected indifference. I turned away, pretending to sort some things on my little dresser shelf. Naturally, that afforded me a clear view in the looking glass, and I got hotter at the sight as he bent to get his trousers off from around his feet.

His legs were long and shapely, the muscles tight and mobile as he moved. His backside was lean and firm. There was no trace of fat or softness anywhere about him. As he turned again towards me, while I was pretending to be busy, my tummy skipped at the sight of his long, firm thighs and flat, hard-looking belly – and at what I had been waiting for, there in the centre.

He might not have been so substantial as Talesi, but what gladdened my eyes was as delicious as one could wish for. I was perhaps a little piqued that it was still only half stiff, but was also delighted that the pale cock which hung out from his mat of dark curls was thick and gnarled and stirring.

He came and stood close behind me, his feet touching mine. His arms came around me, and he cupped my breasts and began to kiss and lick my neck and shoulder. Somehow, that part of me is especially sensitive, and I shivered with delight as his warm mouth explored me. At the same time, as he pressed himself against me I felt that lovely cock twitch and begin to harden against the cleft of my bottom.

As I have said before, the clothes made for me by my lovely Alice Prendergast, nee Barnet, are designed with fun in mind. Witness that enticing green dress she had made for me for my first grown up dinner party, and the corset she had made for my first ball. The chiffon nightgown I was wearing as Donaldson held me from behind, and squirmed his hardness against me, was voluminous, and could be removed either in the normal way, by grasping the hem and pulling it off over one's head, or by undoing the ribbons that tied the neckline and allowing it to slip down to the floor.

He found the ribbons. His hands flicked from my breasts to the ribbons and back. He pulled the little puffed sleeves from my shoulders. My nightgown slipped down my body.

You may be sure that I was by now very hot, but I was too deeply wrapped up in this luscious game to back off. My hands were still on my dresser shelf and I kept them there, preventing my nightgown falling below my waist. Donaldson's mouth was possessing my ear and neck, his hot breath dizzying, his tongue probing and exploring me. As his body crushed against mine, his hands were at my breasts, lifting and squeezing and kneading as though he were becoming desperate.

We were both panting. My tummy was crushed against the dresser as he pressed up behind me, his now steely cock up between my buttocks to my spine. He grabbed me by my hips and pulled me away from the dresser. My nightgown finally fell to the floor.

I let myself be pulled back several steps, then threw off his hands, stepped away from his eager body, and turned to face him. Clad now in only my black corset and stockings I paused, breathless. His neck and chest were reddened by his excitement. We caught each other's eye. We both knew that what had transpired so far was only a prelude.

Continuing the game, I turned away, knowing what would follow. In an instant he was upon me. I gasped with the joy of fulfilment as he grabbed me, his breath hissing, his hands everywhere. He was behind me. I bent forward, urged but not forced by his hand on the nape of my neck. He was in me with a power and an eagerness that made me groan.

He held me by my hipbones and filled me from behind as I bent over. He was rampant. He was taller than me, and my toes hardly reached the floor, my body jerking to his thrusts. Oh, it was a glorious fuck.

We had begun as players of a game. I had won the early rounds by prolonging our teasings. He now conquered in this bout by shagging me so hard and for so long that before he finished I was a rag doll, sobbing to be released I had been coming so long.

I took revenge as soon as he had finished his own come and we sank to the floor. I wriggled around, found him, and plumped my mouth onto his declining cock. I heard a groan of protest as from a distance. I ignored it. I sucked him as though my life depended upon it. No mere man is going to out-shag Lydia.

To give him credit, despite his groans and protests, he rose to the occasion. At least his cock did. As my mouth and fingers worked on him and he began to stir, I wriggled round and got myself astride him. His eyes widened with a combination of surprise and doubt as I rubbed him and aligned his plum with my swollen quim. He actually shook his head to tell me he could not, was not capable.

I knew better. Though he was still only half-hard, I rubbed his plum against myself, I located my entrance, I crammed him in, squatted upon him, circled my loins upon his. I could feel him stiffening inside me, pressing deeper into my greedy sheath, stretching me further. Ah, victory was sweet.

And then the proof that I had indeed been too eager in making this tryst with Donaldson crept through the door.

William's face, when I had enough composure to notice him, was a picture of shock and outrage. In my eagerness to engage with Donaldson, I had entirely forgotten that William was to join me after his watch, as usual.

Donaldson had not yet become conscious of William's entry, for my efforts had succeeded and he was eagerly bucking his hips between my splayed thighs. It would take a gunshot to distract a man whose cock is deeply and happily embedded in an oozing quim.

A gunshot, or laughter. The shock of William's appearance, the expression on his face, Donaldson's passionate gasps in contrast to William's shocked splutterings, all conspired to stab me in my funny bone. I started to giggle. My laughter grew. I howled.

Donaldson ceased his bucking under me. He saw William, still frozen inside the door. He tried to struggle up, as outraged as William had been. I was weakened by laughter, and easy to push off. I lay in a shuddering heap, tears streaming as my ribs began to ache. I struggled to control myself as I heard the men's angry tones behind me.

I turned, and the sight that met my eyes set me off again, howling worse than before. William was standing backed against the door. His face was an admixture of shock and fright as his superior officer loomed angrily before him. Men being angrily dignified in undignified circumstances always look silly. When they try to be dignified while stark naked, they become ridiculous.

I gasped and rolled on the floor clutching my aching ribs. I could not speak, could hardly see for the tears pouring from my eyes. The men froze into silence and stared down at me. Then William gave a little snort, gasped, tried to control himself, failed. Soon, his face reddened and his shoulders began to shake as he too burst into giggles.

Donaldson grew redder and more outraged, which set we other two off even more. Then, to give him credit, he too saw how ridiculous it all was. He sat down on my little settee and shook his head. Glancing from one to the other of us, he rested his elbows on his knees and rubbed the palms of his hands mock wearily over his face.

Our laughter was soon over, and when we had sobered up the situation became tense. For myself there was no difficulty. From the very beginning I had been used to playing with more than one man at a time. Among the Tukanna it had been quite common for two or more men to take me aside for a romp. Talesi and my other lovers among the tribe did not, though, have the conditioning imposed by our European society.

After his initial surprise, William too was able to accept

matters. After all, he well knew that I had shagged Sharpe, had lain with Tiliu and I at the same time, and had fucked me in the little glen in full sight of Sharpe fucking Tiliu.

Donaldson, though, was his superior officer. Consciousness of rank is of vast importance in our society, and especially so aboard ship. How could Donaldson maintain the dignity of his rank when he'd been caught stark naked writhing under a lusty girl, and by the most junior officer on the vessel.

I thought it best to shoo William from my cabin, whispering to him that he'd have his chance in the morning, and enjoining him aloud to keep silent. I turned to placate Donaldson to find him beginning to get dressed.

He was in quite a pet. William's intrusion had put him in a misery, and I was hard put to it to stop him leaving. It was so silly, because he had known about William and I. Indeed, I suspected that he had wanted to shag me as much just because he knew that William had.

Oh, I had to pet and persuade, kiss and coo, flatter and coax. At last, though, by means of charming him into another shag – up against the wall, just as he preferred with Felicity, and none too gentle I may say – I managed to assuage his mood and get him to be reasonable.

Fortunately, William behaved very sensibly, and treated Donaldson with even more respect than before – at least in public. When they were with me, of course, things were different, for it is impossible to maintain distinctions of rank when you are both rutting in an eager girl.

Fifteen

It was a very happy ship that steamed slowly through the Suez Canal towards a place called Port Said. William and Donaldson were entirely content to share my favours, and indeed took to visiting my cabin together at nights.

Since my bunk was far too small to accommodate all three of us, in fact was rather cramped for just two, Donaldson got some spare mattresses from somewhere. These we stowed under my bunk except when we spread them on the floor to make our romps more comfortable. And romps there were in plenty, for each of my lovers seemed to spark the other to greater excitement. Seldom did I crawl into my bunk, after they had stowed away the mattresses and left me, without having been very enthusiastically shagged into a state of contented exhaustion.

It seemed that Port Said was a rather exotic and notorious place. We were to dock there for several days, to take on coal and to tranship some cargo. Donaldson, who was by now relaxed enough with William and I to have become the source of some quite naughty ideas, suggested that he conduct us on an exploration of the town.

He had already regaled us with amazing descriptions of some of the inns and places of entertainment in the native quarters, and what went on there. He had me agog and disbelieving. Were there really establishments where women waited to accommodate any man who had the right money? And places where *exhibitions* were put on! And where *boys* served the function of women!

Donaldson laughed and said he would have proved it to

me if I had only been a man. Then he suddenly laughed even louder.

'We can always disguise you as a lad,' he said between guffaws.

He and William laughed heartily at the ridiculous notion. I began to think it less ridiculous. Why not? Why was the idea so ridiculous?

It was very difficult to persuade them that it could be done. It was too dangerous, they argued. Where would we get the clothes from? How would we disguise my long hair? How could we hide my figure? In the end, I had to get firm with them. They would get no more shags until they agreed. I would bar them from my cabin.

It is interesting how the threat of a little deprivation can change a man's mind. Soon, male garments appeared, and a cap, and preparations began.

Tiliu (sworn to secrecy lest Sharpe try to prevent our escapade) helped me alter the clothes to fit. We tore up an old sheet and bound it around my breasts to flatten them as much as we could without too much discomfort. The shirt, jacket and trousers were quite baggy, and when I had pinned up my hair and donned the cap Tiliu chuckled and said I looked quite the young lad, though a rather pretty one.

When I sneaked along to Donaldson's cabin, he fully agreed, and remarked with a wicked grin that, for the first time in his life, he found himself fancying a boy.

Only when William appeared and we prepared to sneak ourselves off the ship did I realise that we had forgotten something. My boots! I had quite forgotten my button boots which, with their little heels, were very obviously feminine.

We scrabbled about. I tried on a pair of Donaldson's, which were like boats on me. William's were smaller, though still too big. We stuffed the toes with handkerchiefs, and I put on several pairs of socks. They sufficed, though I had to take care lest I trip myself up, so clumsy did they make me.

At last all was ready and we sneaked off the ship, making sure nobody saw me. Our adventure had begun.

The moment we left the dockyard we were in the midst of narrow, crowded streets, with alleys running off, and people and dogs and donkeys all bustling about. There were open-fronted shops, vendors of all sorts of strange goods, sellers of foodstuffs, water carriers. Everyone seemed to be shouting his wares, and the noise was tremendous.

Our European garb and white faces made us stand out among the crowds, and children scurried about our feet apparently begging, while some of the vendors thrust their goods at us and shouted. I was lucky to be between Donaldson and William, else I am sure I would have been swept away in the throng.

Our first stop was at a coffee house. We entered through an arched portal draped with a curtain of wooden beads on strings. I gazed about me fascinated. It was a large, low-ceilinged room, crowded with all sorts of people sitting at round tables sipping from tiny cups. Donaldson led us, not without much pushing and squeezing between bodies, to an empty table in a corner. He waved his arm and shouted, and a waiter pushed his way towards us already bearing aloft a tray.

To my surprise, Donaldson spoke to the waiter in his own language as he deposited cups and a metal pot of steaming coffee on our table. He told me that he had ordered something called *el ful*, which was a sort of national dish and would serve as our introduction to Egypt.

While we waited for it to arrive I gazed about me at the motley crowd. Most of the men (I could see no women) appeared to be native Egyptians, but there were also some Africans and Arabs and a sprinkling of Europeans. Many were smoking, and all were talking nineteen to the dozen, and the noise and the exotic aromas made me nearly dizzy with excitement.

The waiter reappeared very quickly. The *el ful* turned

out to be a sort of brown mash made mostly of beans, with boiled eggs chopped up in it, and a topping of tomatoes mixed with pungent garlic. There were no spoons and no bowls except the one the *el ful* was in, and we ate by scooping it up on bits of bread exactly like the *pitta* I had known in the harem. Like the strong, sweet coffee, it was delicious.

If I had thought the coffee house strange and exciting, the next place Donaldson took us to was exotic indeed. Once again he led us through a maze of narrow streets, in some of which one had to be extremely careful of one's feet for they had what seemed, by the stench, to be open sewers running down their middles. Donaldson clearly knew this place well, for he never hesitated. I confess that I soon became totally lost as he turned from streets to alleys, and round corner after corner.

I had expected, from his earlier descriptions, to be taken to a large establishment, and was thus rather surprised when Donaldson led us to a small, rather mean looking portal that led to a narrow, dark passageway with several corners. I could hardly see a hand before me, and everywhere seemed deserted. I was just about to question him when he stopped and knocked on a heavy wooden door.

The establishment we then entered fulfilled all my expectations as to exotic, nay outlandish surroundings. We had not descended any steps, but even so the room we entered was for all the world like a great cellar. Its low ceiling was vaulted, with pierced brass lamps hanging from each apex and casting only a dim light. Thick pillars supported this ceiling, around which tables had been constructed.

The room was a haze of oddly sweet-smelling smoke, exhaled by the men sitting at the tables, who were alternately sucking on tubes which extended from odd, vase-like contraptions and blowing out clouds of smoke. Donaldson told me that these devices were called *hookahs* or water pipes, and the oddly perfumed substance the men were smoking was Indian hemp rather than tobacco.

We sat at a table which gave a good view of the room,

and were quickly served with coffee and a bowl of fruits. Almost as though they had been awaiting our arrival to begin (though they could not possibly have been, of course) a sort of band struck up.

A light drum began a complicated rhythm which was emphasised by small cymbals, and a piper began a high-pitched wailing tune. Suddenly, some drapes to the side of the room parted and a woman appeared. She was clad very scantily, just a sort of small bodice which hugged her large breasts, a pair of tight, and very abbreviated, drawers which hardly covered her loins, and a pair of diaphanous pantaloons. About her brow and her ankles were bands of jingling coins.

If her appearance was outlandish, the dance she performed to the strange music was more so. Though the music was quite quick, there were few movements of her arms or feet. Instead, everything was concentrated on rapid gyrations of her hips and belly. She was rather plump, and her body gleamed with oil, and what she was doing with her loins and tummy-button was amazing.

She circled around the narrow space left among the tables for her dance, now moving near to this man or that and wiggling herself close to his eager face, now dodging back if he reached out a greedy hand. I watched with growing fascination. This woman's dance had only one possible message, and that was to excite her audience to lustful sensations.

I thought back to my dance at the Prince's banquet, and to Tiliu's at her initiation. Both those dances had preceded what can only be termed orgies. How much wilder, more sensuous was this woman's performance. I grew nervous abut what the consequences of it would be.

I was surprised, therefore, when the woman ended her dance by falling to her knees and bowing her head to the floor, for all that happened was that the place burst into applause and loud calls and banging on tables. In my naïveté I had fully expected the woman to be dragged among the tables and shagged then and there.

217

Donaldson laughed when I whispered my queries to him. The woman was, he said, a professional dancer – he called her a belly dancer, which was certainly an accurate description – and not a prostitute, which is the name for women who sell sex for money. Those women were available in an annexe to this inn, as were boys for similar purposes, but he thought it best that we did not visit what he called the *bordello*. After all, I was a girl, and would have no use for them.

I was disappointed, for I would have enjoyed seeing such a place. How was it organised? Did customers simply go in, hand over money and take pot luck? If not, how did they choose their partner? Did they go off to separate rooms to complete their transaction? And what exactly did they do with boys?

The buzz of questions in my head was driven out by the appearance of another dancer. This one was very different. She was perhaps thirty years of age and buxom, with a mass of glossy black hair and heavily kohled eyes. Apart from a heavy *yashmak* and lots of bangles about her wrists and ankles, she was entirely naked.

She posed immobile as the music started, slower than the first woman's, then began to dance with surprising grace for such a large woman. Unnoticed by me, a large, lidded basket had been placed in the dancing space, and the woman moved around it, her body moving sinuously, her hands running over her hips and breasts, her eyes flashing at the now entirely silent audience.

It was as though she were addressing her dance to the basket, and indeed several times moved so that she was astride it, and made very suggestive movements with her bare loins.

I had not really believed the outlandish tales Donaldson had told us about Port Said, and now it was happening before my eyes. I caught a glimpse of William's face, and knew that mine must be showing the same amazement as his.

After several minutes of this very suggestive dance, the

woman dropped to her knees before the basket. Still moving her arms and shoulders sinuously, she pulled off the lid. She reached in. I could veritably feel the audience hold its breath. Slowly, she lifted something out of the basket. It was a huge snake.

I gasped aloud and drew back. What on earth could she be doing with such a deadly beast? I could not breathe from terror as the creature slithered up her arm and across her shoulders, its flat head waving from side to side, its black tongue flicking as though it was seeking the right place to bite her. It did not bite. Donaldson whispered to me that it was a python, which apparently do not bite.

Slowly, the woman rose to her feet and began to dance again, wrapping the great snake around her arms and shoulders and torso, even around her thighs. I was petrified and excited at the same time. I could almost feel the snake slithering over my own skin, and shuddered, yet the woman's eyes were bright and her movements confident.

How long the dance lasted I know not, for what happened next was so amazing everything save what my eyes were fixed on ceased to exist. With the snake writhing about her glistening body, the woman sank slowly to her knees. She parted them and leaned back. She grasped the snake's tail in her hand.

I could not believe what I was seeing. Slowly, she moved the snake's tail down between her parted thighs. She touched it to her belly. She rubbed it along the insides of her legs. She inserted it into her quim. More and more of it. She was shagging herself with a snake.

At the moment she slipped the first few inches into herself, the audience gave a collective gasp and began to shout and bang the tables. As she slid more in, moving her loins as though in a voluptuous fuck, the noise grew wild and deafening. Men began to stamp and cheer, and throw coins and banknotes onto the floor around her. When she began to pump as though she were having a come they almost went wild.

And then in the blink of an eye, the snake was back in

the basket, the woman was standing immobile, and a couple of small boys were scrabbling around the floor gathering the money that was still being thrown.

Never in a thousand lifetimes could I have imagined such a performance. I was actually trembling with the tension and excitement of it. With a bit of a gleam in his eyes, Donaldson suggested that perhaps we should begin to make our way back to the ship. I looked from him to William. To guess from Donaldson's grin and the brightness in William's eyes, I would have an energetic time of it when we got back on board.

And even before then, as it transpired.

It happened with terrifying suddenness. As we were weaving our way between the tables to depart there were shouts and screams, and we found ourselves in the midst of pandemonium. In an instant, men were fighting all over the place. Bodies rolled around. Chairs were thrown. Coffee pots and *hookahs* sailed through the air.

I was knocked to the floor, and found myself squirming between men's feet. Where were my companions? I was kicked. My hand was trampled on. I tried to scrabble away from these stamping feet and falling bodies. I began to panic. There seemed nowhere safe.

Suddenly, a hand grabbed my jacket and I was dragged under a table and out the other side. It was a big, Arabic-looking man. I thought he was going to attack me, and lashed out. He restrained my hands easily, for he was much stronger than I. He shook his head, threw an arm about my shoulders, and began to lug me towards a door. At once I stopped struggling. He was saving me.

He lugged and lifted me through the milling, struggling mob, and soon I was standing gasping in the darkness of an alley. Bodies spilled out of the door we had left by, and my rescuer grabbed my hand and hurried me away. In an instant, I knew I was lost.

At last he stopped our headlong retreat. I leaned against

220

the wall of yet another alley, too breathless yet to express my gratitude. At last I was able to gasp my thanks.

'Ah, you English boy,' the Arab said. 'I speak English good. Where you from?'

He did speak English, but certainly not 'good' – and his responses to me were most odd.

'From the docks,' I said. 'From a ship. Can you help me get back there?'

'You English boy,' he replied. 'Pretty. Soft. Me help, first fick-fick!'

I gazed at him in puzzlement. 'No, you don't understand,' I said. 'From the docks. Big ship. Which way?'

'Pretty English!' He grabbed my hand and began to tug me towards a dark doorway. 'Fick-fick, then docks.'

'No, not that way, you silly man! Docks. That doesn't lead to the docks.'

Still he tugged at my arm repeating this incomprehensible 'fick-fick' nonsense over and over.

'This is becoming ridiculous,' I thought. 'What on earth can the silly man be thinking of?'

Then I felt his hand grope at my bottom and I suddenly understood. I was dumbstruck. He wanted to – to ... A complete stranger, and thinking me a boy! I tried to pull away, but he was too strong for me. He turned and stared at me, still gripping my arm, then grinned.

'Ah,' his eyes lit. '*Baksheesh*, pretty boy want *baksheesh*.'

My head was spinning. I did not understand what he was saying, but knew what he wanted. Yet I was lost and helpless in this outlandish town. Without his help I would never find Donaldson or William or the docks again.

Suddenly, the grinning man was thrusting a bundle of banknotes at me, and tugging me towards the doorway again. I gave in. What else could I do? It seemed best not to struggle against such a strong and determined man, and I *did* need his help. He pulled me, no longer resisting, into the doorway, and smiled and stroked my cheek.

'Hm, pretty English boy,' he murmured, actually licking his lips. He thrust the bundle of money into my hand and

221

turned me around, bending me over and tugging at my trousers.

Since he thought me a boy, and was very eager, he used that part I have in common with a boy. He did not take long, but was rather enthusiastic, so that at one point I bumped my head against the wall, and he rather upset me by giving my bottom a hearty smack when he had finished. Afterwards, though, he kept his word, and led me back to the dock gates.

When we came into sight of them he stopped, and from the way he looked at me I thought he was going to demand another bout. Luckily, I heard a shout, and saw William running towards me.

They had been desperately worried when I got separated from them in the fight. They had searched about for a while, then William had rushed back to the docks to organise a search party, while Donaldson had stayed behind to look for me. He hugged me in relief that I was safe, oblivious for a moment of what a spectator might think at seeing one midshipman hugging another, then we quickly sneaked back on board.

William sent off one of the crew to fetch Donaldson and we repaired to my cabin, where I drank a little brandy to steady myself. William was all questions and concern, and I thought it better to just tell him that a native had aided me. The truth would have rather shocked him. Soon, Donaldson returned, and I repeated my bland story.

That turned out to be a little less than wise for, assured that everything was well, the men turned to discussing the exhibitions we had seen, and joking about what a pretty midshipman I made, and matters soon became as naughty as they usually did with these two.

I was not really in the mood, but they were both rather keen, and so I thought that we might as well get on with it. I took off my jacket and was just bending to remove my trousers, when Donaldson hissed 'What on earth – !'

I turned my head to see what was the matter. Two things

had gone wrong. First, when I had tossed the jacket onto the settee the money the Arab had given me fell out of the pocket. Second, there was a bright red mark on my bottom where he had smacked me. How on earth could I explain?

Donaldson did not really have to drag the truth out of me, for he ended up guessing it. He picked up the banknotes and looked from them to me. There was an odd, rather cunning expression on his face. He asked me again how I had come to be rescued.

'And was he an Arab, by any chance?' was all he said when I finished.

At my 'Well, yes,' he suddenly burst into howls of laughter. William looked as stunned as I, then more so as I slowly reddened into the deepest of blushes. Donaldson was spluttering.

'*Baksheesh*,' he snorted. 'An Arab. Oh, Glory!'

When at last he calmed enough to speak coherently, the whole story came out – or rather, Donaldson said what he thought had happened and I, blushing deeper and feeling more and more foolish, confessed. I have to admit that it did now seem comical, and what with Donaldson's suppressed laughter and William's increasingly shocked expression, I too soon began to giggle.

Our laughter became uproarious a few moments later.

'Well,' I said, with mock dignity. 'At least he paid me money. I can now call myself one of those what-do-you-call-'ems, a woman of the night.'

'No, my love,' Donaldson snorted. 'A boy of the night. And do you know how much is here?' He waved the bundle of notes at me. 'A little more than a shilling in English money. You, my wonderful Lydia, have sold your bum for just over a bob. And a damned fine bargain too, I may say.'

He collapsed to the floor, spluttering and clutching his ribs. For a moment I was frozen. A shilling! A shilling! The cost of a decent handkerchief. Then I too saw the funny side. After all, the man could have got it for nothing if he'd insisted. And after all, a shilling was more than an ordinary soldier was paid for a whole day's marching.

Perhaps a bit of quick fumbling in a darkened doorway was not so unprofitable after all.

And it did not turn out too badly, for when at last our laughter had calmed, both my lovers seemed more excited than usual, and I eventually crept into my little bunk a very well shagged and satisfied girl indeed.

We steamed out of Port Said on the afternoon of the next day, and were soon thumping steadily through the Mediterranean Sea. To my disappointment, we were not due to call in at any of the wonderful-sounding places I had read of in my schoolbooks – Alexandria, Athens, Venice, Rome, Syracuse. Oh, how I would have loved that!

The weather was glorious, and I spent much time walking about on deck with Tiliu. Her arrangement with Sharpe was now common knowledge among our group of conspirators in naughtiness, and she now clove to him pretty well exclusively. Their partnership meant that she no longer had to pretend to be the servant. She continued to assist the officers' steward in serving dinner so that Captain Prendergast would not be disturbed out of the illusions we still maintained for his benefit, but most of the rest of the time she was free to be with me.

It was a joy to stroll about with her, and chatter together, and stand gazing out over the ship's rail – although I confess there is little to see except water unless one happens to be close to the coast.

We spent a delightful day together in the company of Sharpe, exploring the Rock of Gibraltar. This is a British Colony, a sort of sea-girt mountain attached by a narrow neck of land to Spain. We went right to the top in a little donkey cart, and fed the Barbary apes, of which there were many, and quite impertinent to be fed they were too.

From the top of the Rock one can easily see the coast of north Africa. Looking out over the stone parapet, I suddenly felt a pang. Africa! Would I ever again see that strange and savagely beautiful land? What kind of unnecessary tensions were going on now between the Boers and the British in that huge and sweeping land, surely wide enough for all to live in peace? I think Tiliu felt a sense of loss too, for she was quite subdued as we rode back down the precipitous track behind a donkey which seemed to be more leaning back to stop the cart careering away than actually pulling it.

Still, we would soon be in England, and I would take my darling Tiliu to my aunt in Brighton, and watch her eyes grow huge when she saw our great cities.

The weather turned nasty almost as soon as our vessel ploughed through the Pillars of Hercules, a much more romantic name than the Straits of Gibraltar I think. For nearly a whole day and night I was not sure which way either up or down were. When waves were not crashing against the little porthole in my cabin, rain was sweeping over it. Neither floor nor walls would keep still. To move about was a test of skill gone mad, for the first step would be up a steeply sloping floor, and the next off a precipice. One needed both hands as well as very careful feet to walk without tumbling top over toes.

It seems that I am a good sailor for I did not become seasick (though I confess I felt peculiar more than once). Felicity was so unwell she looked like to die. She went from green to the whitest wax, and had been sick so much that, even though her poor body wracked and spasmed, she had nothing more to bring up. Even Sharpe looked a little trembly.

Then, as suddenly as it had hit us, the storm abated. The sun rose on a beautifully calm morning, and gave us all the chance to recover. The officers and crew had much to do, for there had been damage to various bits of rigging and such.

I, too, had much to be busy about, for Felicity was very weak and Tiliu was, quite frankly, exhausted. As you can guess, Alice, strong, solid to earth Alice, had come through entirely unmoved, and bustled about helping

225

Tapak Nasseri, who was also unscathed, in taking care of Felicity. Alice's practical cheeriness lifted me hugely.

I attended to Tiliu. She had been terrified; had been praying to her gods to save her from the monster the sea had become. She had never seen a storm – indeed had never seen the sea until we reached East London. She is a strong girl, though, tough and practical in her dealings with the world. And most of all, she had trust in me. When I assured her that all was now well, she accepted and re-laxed. When I told her that our ship was blessed by Queen Victoria and was thus stronger than any sea spirits, and in any case we were only a day or so away from England, she took my word. By midday we were out and walking about the deck in bright sunshine.

After luncheon, we took a much needed rest. Tiliu slept in her bunk, I slept on the floor beside her, having dragged in one of the spare mattresses William and Donaldson had stowed under the bunk in my cabin.

We awoke late and ate dinner in the mess alone, all the officers being busy about repairs and such, and Alice being still with Felicity and Nasseri. Perhaps it was simple relief, perhaps a sort of euphoria brought by the swing of the pendulum from stormy terror to quiet calm. I cannot say. Whatever it was, Tiliu and I, as we ate our dinner sitting side by side alone in the officers' mess, became giggly and confiding.

I told her something of my escapades with William and Donaldson. She nudged me in the ribs and giggled archly. I told her about the dancer with the snake, and she got serious and wide eyed. I told her about the fight and the Arab, and she near fell off her chair laughing, especially about the fee he had paid.

She told me about Sharpe. Not so much in words as in looks, and silences, and sentences begun but not finished. It was clear that Sharpe was catching up for lost time. I remembered his stories about his sad experiences in youth, and his resignation to the belief that he would never know a woman. I remembered my own amazement when I had

226

first laid eyes on his 'difficulty', and my voluptuous struggles to assuage it.

Now, it seemed, he had no 'difficulty' at all. Tiliu was the one who now had the difficulty, not because he was now well nigh constantly rampant for her, but because his size and his eagerness aroused her so much that, in her words, 'He make me come so much I shattered. I coming even before he up me. He don't know it; he very gentle, nice to me, but oh, Ridja, I coming before he touch me!'

Visualising Sharpe's astonishing 'difficulty' when he had first flopped out of his breeches, and remembering my own struggles to accommodate it the first time I shagged him, I did not wonder at Tiliu's reactions. What I did wonder at was her ability to take and survive it. Why, she must have possessed the fittest and most resilient cunny in the world.

The relief after the storm, our happy dinner alone together, had put us in a light mood – a mood perhaps aided by the wine we had drunk all unawares. However that may be, when we left the mess we decided to go for a stroll.

There was a brilliant moon, though strangely smaller than Africa's, and a million stars. There was also quite a chilly breeze. Since we were both in a high mood we decided to explore below decks rather than go back to our cabins.

Giggling and joking, we stumbled about along narrow passages and around corners and up and down ladderways, opening doors that gave only onto cupboards stuffed with boxes or drums or strange tools. We bumped our heads on overhead pipes, and tripped over door sills, and generally got more giggly and happy as we explored. By now we were opening doors at random, and stepping through without even looking.

I opened a door, tripped over the sill, and fell headlong. The room was brightly lit, which was unusual. Realising that I was perhaps a little tipsy, I shook my head and looked up. Tiliu stood above me, her hand to her mouth. Around her were gathered a number of crew men.

I struggled to my feet, all apologies for disturbing them, and all attempted dignity. Somehow, the door I had fallen through had disappeared, and we were in the midst of a circle of men. Tiliu, irrepressible Tiliu, dropped a hand onto my shoulder, glanced about her with wide eyes, and gave a giggle.

It sobered me a little. I too looked about me. There were perhaps half a dozen of them, all looking surprised and eager. It was just like that time we had explored at the harem.

A man stepped forward. Somehow, he looked not unfamiliar. He grinned. He reached out as if to touch me, but then drew his hand back.

''Lo Missy,' he said, grinning nervously. 'Me sentry.'

At once I recognised him. He was the guard I had 'distracted' from William's cabin. He was the one who had guided the 'sleepwalker' to that little storeroom.

The circle of men had drawn tighter. They were whispering tensely one with another. A couple were already rubbing their groins with very clear excitement. I gazed around the circle. It was odd, and in a way rather sweet, for though very eager, they did not seem at all threatening.

I looked at Tiliu. As our eyes met, her undefeatable sense of the absurd communicated itself to me, for she rolled her eyes and shrugged her shoulders.

We were here in the bowels of the ship late at night. We were surrounded by hopeful men with only one idea between them. At least one of them was well aware of what had happened that night we had tried to comfort William.

Tiliu looked at me. I looked at Tiliu. Ah, well, her eyes said, we may as well make the best of it.

As the circle of excited Lakars closed in Tiliu began to unbutton her frock. I followed suit. No point in getting one's clothes torn ...

NEXUS BACKLIST

All books are priced £4.99 unless another price is given. If a date is supplied, the book in question will not be available until that month in 1995.

CONTEMPORARY EROTICA

THE ACADEMY	Arabella Knight	
CONDUCT UNBECOMING	Arabella Knight	Jul
CONTOURS OF DARKNESS	Marco Vassi	
THE DEVIL'S ADVOCATE	Anonymous	
DIFFERENT STROKES	Sarah Veitch	Aug
THE DOMINO TATTOO	Cyrian Amberlake	
THE DOMINO ENIGMA	Cyrian Amberlake	
THE DOMINO QUEEN	Cyrian Amberlake	
ELAINE	Stephen Ferris	
EMMA'S SECRET WORLD	Hilary James	
EMMA ENSLAVED	Hilary James	
EMMA'S SECRET DIARIES	Hilary James	
FALLEN ANGELS	Kendal Grahame	
THE FANTASIES OF JOSEPHINE SCOTT	Josephine Scott	
THE GENTLE DEGENERATES	Marco Vassi	
HEART OF DESIRE	Maria del Rey	
HELEN – A MODERN ODALISQUE	Larry Stern	
HIS MISTRESS'S VOICE	G. C. Scott	
HOUSE OF ANGELS	Yvonne Strickland	May
THE HOUSE OF MALDONA	Yolanda Celbridge	
THE IMAGE	Jean de Berg	Jul
THE INSTITUTE	Maria del Rey	
SISTERHOOD OF THE INSTITUTE	Maria del Rey	

FANTASYWORLD	Larry Stern	
WANTON	Andrea Arven	

ANCIENT & FANTASY SETTINGS

CHAMPIONS OF LOVE	Anonymous	
CHAMPIONS OF PLEASURE	Anonymous	
CHAMPIONS OF DESIRE	Anonymous	
THE CLOAK OF APHRODITE	Kendal Grahame	
THE HANDMAIDENS	Aran Ashe	
THE SLAVE OF LIDIR	Aran Ashe	
THE DUNGEONS OF LIDIR	Aran Ashe	
THE FOREST OF BONDAGE	Aran Ashe	
PLEASURE ISLAND	Aran Ashe	
WITCH QUEEN OF VIXANIA	Morgana Baron	

EDWARDIAN, VICTORIAN & OLDER EROTICA

ANNIE	Evelyn Culber	
ANNIE AND THE SOCIETY	Evelyn Culber	
THE AWAKENING OF LYDIA	Philippa Masters	Apr
BEATRICE	Anonymous	
CHOOSING LOVERS FOR JUSTINE	Aran Ashe	
GARDENS OF DESIRE	Roger Rougiere	
THE LASCIVIOUS MONK	Anonymous	
LURE OF THE MANOR	Barbra Baron	
RETURN TO THE MANOR	Barbra Baron	Jun
MAN WITH A MAID 1	Anonymous	
MAN WITH A MAID 2	Anonymous	
MAN WITH A MAID 3	Anonymous	
MEMOIRS OF A CORNISH GOVERNESS	Yolanda Celbridge	
THE GOVERNESS AT ST AGATHA'S	Yolanda Celbridge	
TIME OF HER LIFE	Josephine Scott	
VIOLETTE	Anonymous	

THE JAZZ AGE

BLUE ANGEL NIGHTS	Margarete von Falkensee	
BLUE ANGEL DAYS	Margarete von Falkensee	

- - - - - - - - - - - - - - - - - - - -

Please send me the books I have ticked above.

Name ....

Address ....

....

....

.... Post code ....

Send to: **Cash Sales, Nexus Books, 332 Ladbroke Grove, London W10 5AH**.

Please enclose a cheque or postal order, made payable to **Nexus Books**, to the value of the books you have ordered plus postage and packing costs as follows:

UK and BFPO – £1.00 for the first book, 50p for each subsequent book.

Overseas (including Republic of Ireland) – £2.00 for the first book, £1.00 for the second book, and 50p for each subsequent book.

If you would prefer to pay by VISA or ACCESS/MASTERCARD, please write your card number and expiry date here:

....

Please allow up to 28 days for delivery.

Signature ....

- - - - - - - - - - - - - - - - - - - -

THE 1996 NEXUS CALENDAR

The 1996 Nexus calendar contains photographs of thirteen of the most delectable models who have graced the covers of Nexus books. And we've been able to select pictures that are just a bit more exciting than those we're allowed to use on book covers.

With its restrained design and beautifully reproduced duo-tone photographs, the Nexus calendar will appeal to lovers of sophisticated erotica.

And the Nexus calendar costs only £5.50 including postage and packing (in the traditional plain brown envelope!). Stocks are limited, so be sure of your copy by ordering today. The order form is overleaf.

Send your order to: Cash Sales Department
Nexus Books
332 Ladbroke Grove
London
W10 5AH

Please allow 28 days for delivery.

Please send me _____ copies of the 1996 Nexus calendar @ £5.50 (US$9.00) each including postage and packing.

Name: _____

Address: _____

_____

_____

_____

☐ I enclose a cheque or postal order made out to Nexus Books

☐ Please debit my Visa/Access/Mastercard account (delete as applicable)

My credit card number is:

_ _ _ _ _ _ _ _ _ _ _ _ _ _ _ _

Expiry date: _____

FILL OUT YOUR ORDER AND SEND IT TODAY!